whispering *in* shadows

whispering *in* shadows

A novel

jeannette armstrong

THEYTUS BOOKS LTD.
PENTICTON

Copyright © 2000 Jeannette Armstrong

Canadian Cataloguing in Publication Data

Armstrong, Jeannette C., 1948
  Whispering in shadows

  ISBN 0-919441-99-8

  I. Title.
PS8551.R7635W54 2000   C813'.54   C99-911230-9
PR9199.3.A546W54 2000

Content Readers: Richard Van Camp, Lally Grauer
Editorial: Greg Young-Ing, Florene Belmore
Design: Val Speidel
Special Thanks: Chick Gabriel, Hartmut Lutz, Anna Lizotte

Theytus Books Ltd
Lot 45 Green Mountain Rd.
RR#2, Site 50, Comp. 8
Penticton, BC
V2A 6J7

'frogs singing' and 'earth love' originally published in *Durable Breath: Contemporary Native American Poetry*, Salmon Run Press, 1994
'Moonset' originally published in *Flint and Feather*, The Musson Book Company Ltd., 1917

The publisher acknowledges the support of The Canada Council for the Arts, The Department of Canadian Heritage and The British Columbia Arts Council.

Moonset

Idles the night wind through the dreaming firs,
That waking murmur low,
As some lost melody returning stirs
The love of long ago;
And through the far, cool distance, zephyr fanned.
The moon is sinking into shadow-land.

The troubled night-bird, calling plaintively,
Wanders on restless wing;
The cedars, chanting vespers to the sea,
Awaits its answering,
That comes in wash of waves along the strand,
The while the moon slips into shadow-land.

O! soft responsive voices of the night
I join your minstrelsy
And call across the fading silver light
As something calls to me;
I may not all your meaning understand,
But I have touched your soul in shadow-land

PAULINE JOHNSON

frogs singing

my sister did not dream this
she found this out when she walked
outside and looked up and star
rhythms sang to her pointing their spines of light
down into her and filled her body with star song
and all around her
frogs joined
the star singing
they learned it
long ago

*T*his love that had come to her was a kind of madness. It owned her. It created a wreckage of her body. The way, after a long climb, there is no longer searing pain and the muscles give up and all that is left is a deep and silent quivering. All else is blurred and each breath is a sacrifice. The way when the body finally finds itself. This madness moved inside, not to the heart, but a place more hidden, yet more omnipresent. A place where one should never find it. It had found her; claimed her in the way it did to make her become what she must. This love. This is a map.

To her the snow looks yellow and silver grey in some places. Blue and mauve in others. It's definitely not white. Penny's hand, holding the rolled up, almost empty tube of white paint, stops. She picks up the brush again and dabs it into the yellow, smoothing it over into the thick off-white smear on the plastic board. The sun on snow. And the shadows. It's tricky.

How can I ever get it to look like that? The clean sparkle. It looks so buttery and warm, yet it sparkles. What do I want to get it like that for anyway? Why? It's talking to me that's why. It's singing. It sounds like an under-the-breath Indian song. Maybe, if I clean my brush again, I can make it crisper yellow. Oh, why does it just get muddier and muddier? I wish I knew. It wants to sing on my paperboard. It wants to move, from there on the snowbank, to my paperboard. Maybe I should try to get some canvas. Maybe I should tear up some of that old tent in the shed. This is the seventh one in the last two hours. I gotta stop. Oh, please, help me. Move. Move over the white. Satiny, smooth and glistening like that song. Oh! How did I do that? That little spot. That's it. That's what I want! Yes! Oh yes, yes, yes!

"Penny, aren't you ready yet? I thought we were gonna go downtown. You're still on the same sketch! You done a whole bunch the same already. It's just a snowbank. Why don't you put somebody in it or something? Maybe trees or the chicken house. Anyway, don't you ever get tired of it? You know, some pretty good looking guys are in for the hockey tournament. Come on. Get some town duds on. You're way too serious for a Saturday and I need somebody to hang out with. The guys always want to talk to you and you don't even make up your face. What do you got that I don't?"

"Oh, Roberta, you know you look great. And you know I don't try to get attention. Maybe it's because nobody takes me too seriously. Maybe I'm easy to talk to because I talk about crazy stuff to find out what others think. Anyway it's not just guys, I talk to everybody like that. Even old people, and they're the most interesting.

They like to have somebody paying attention to them. Yeah, but you're right, this is too, too serious. I was thinking that the colours were talking to me. Do you think they do? I read a thing about this artist from way back who went nuts. Maybe it was because the colours were screaming at him. His paintings sure looked like it."

"See what I mean! You're sooo weird. How do you think those things up! You don't make sense most of the time to me. Why don't you just think of normal stuff, like how that cool guy Michael has a new car. He's been hot on your tail, for God knows how long, and you don't even talk to him. I think he's a dream. You're seventeen only once in your life. Couldn't you, just for once, relax on that stuff and be a girl?"

"I am a girl. I just happen to . . . oh, never mind. I don't know if I really want to go anyway. Most of them guys just want to drink around and try to snag you for the night. They don't want to talk or listen or even look at you like a person. They . . . oh shit . . . we're arguing. Yeah, Roberta, I'll come and I'll be a goodtime girl for your sake. I know you don't get a chance to run around very much and have fun. You always have to be home cooking for your brothers and sisters. You wanna borrow my black pants? Your jeans look okay, but since you're trying them on already and they look great on you, you might as well keep them on."

"Oh, could I? Oh, I wish I had an older sister like Lena, who gave me presents like that. I never had a new pair of pants since last fall, from picking time. It's fading out, too. Could I borrow some of your earrings, too? Your mom always makes the best ones for you. What about those turquoise bead ones? Oh, lets have fun, fun, fun. I don't have to come back 'til tomorrow if I don't want to. My auntie Kate is around to watch the kids and she said I could stay with you if I want. If I get too carried away, you'll be there. Oh, Penn, I can't wait. Lets go! Watch out, guys! Get changed and wash that paint off your arms. War paint for the face is what we girls need.

I'll do your hair, okay Cuz?"

War paint? I never thought of it like that! What a way to put it! It is! Maybe my great-grampas understood it! Maybe colour only speaks power! Maybe it is power itself! That's why they painted up for wars or ceremony! And we still give colours at ceremonies. Holeee, even the way it's used by women, now, in the whose-conquering-who game! Power! Lipstick, eye-shadow, a red dress! An unseen force! It's not about beauty! It's about something else. Is that what becomes known as beauty? I better stop this. Stop. Stop please.

Penny looks down at her board. It's gone. Just like that it's gone. The electric feeling in the air. The way her hands and fingers feel disconnected to the rest of her. She feels heavy again. Not light and airy. Her hands feel itchy from all the dried paint, some of it now peeling in thin layers away from her fingertips. There is a strong smell of linseed and turpentine and the smell of the paint over that. She suddenly feels how tired her arms are and how empty her stomach is.

Yellowbells, on their thin single green stalks, necks bent over, scattered among the desert moss cover and last year's dry bunch grass stalks, were everywhere. They sat together on the still-cool and damp ground and carefully dug them down to their bulbs. Her and Tupa, gathering. Somewhere, a meadowlark was saying a half-remembered phrase over and over. The phrase was from some story Tupa had told her. A story about meadowlark telling chip-munk's grandmother how to hide her from mean old Owl Woman.

There is a crack that goes halfway along the ceiling. The cream coloured ceiling plaster is ripped away in patches showing the rich, dark chocolate of the old boards underneath. They are bronze toned in some places from the yellow light of the single bare bulb hanging in the middle. The gaps between the boards are velvety black ribbons. There are slices of a shiny foil paper showing here and there, like the silver lining in a cloud, sandwiched between the boards and the plaster around the edges of the crack. There is a brownish, warm-sienna stain spreading outward from the crack, slowly turning to a pale cream and matching the plaster. The sun rising casts a reddish tinge through a plastic curtain into the room, washing a flat rosy square across their legs.

I should try to remember those colours and the way it's put together. I wish I had my paints here. I could try to get the way the light makes that crack all the more harsh and even more ominous and yet look so perfectly nat-ural. What is it? Is it that the crack from this angle seems to be widening up and slowly spreading? What is it saying? Something about all cracks and how they just happen, a little at first and then wider and more raw until you can see the brown skeleton inside, behind the creamy white sur-face? How single drops of rain, one after the other, slowly invade until the whole roof caves in? Oh, damn. What is wrong with me? This warm body next to me, made me turn to pure jelly last night and all I want to do is sneak out to my house for my paints and get back here to start sketching before he wakes up. What would he say?

She moves her leg slowly toward the edge of the bed trying to roll with the move. She sits up feeling around for her panties, lost somewhere in the tangle of sheet and blanket. She looks up at the ceiling as she stands to pull them up over her, hips facing away from the bed toward the thin red plastic curtain. The rosy patch bathes her whole body and she stands there a moment looking up at the crack widening above, her head thrown back, her breasts bare.

She can hear the even breathing of Francis, face toward the wall. She turns and looks at him. His hair is tousled and he looks like a boy curled up like that. She can still smell him, his sweet musky smell. She can see part of his arm, it's muscle clearly outlined against the pale green wall.

His arms were so strong and his mouth so sweet.

She stands there as though caught in some invisible web.

I want to step back, away from the smell of him. To put on my shirt and my jeans. To pull on my runners and walk into the kitchenette to get a drink of water. I want to run to the car and drive home to pick up my paint box and come back. Why can't I move? I don't need this. I need to get that sketched. It's whispering to me. It's a promise. It's the light, the light moving and changing so quickly. It'll be gone to grey in an hour and a half. Wake up and pull me to your chest. Pull me away from this crazy crack opening up above me. I want to feel normal like I did last night, with nothing mattering except getting there.

She moves back toward the bed and climbs back in, turning toward his back, moving as close as she can to his neck. Spooning her body around his, she could feel his chest catch as he wakes up and she can feel his back muscle tighten as he begins to stretch. She holds unto him as he rolls unto his back, her arm caught under his neck, the other over his chest.

"Hey, girl. It's still early and you're wide awake. Why don't you make us some of that instant and I'll come around. We can get some chow later. Much later . . . hey?"

His eyes are half closed and he is dreamy and soft looking. He smiles at her and moves her hand to his stomach. She moves her fingers across and down the soft part and she hears his sharp intake of breath.

"Oh, sweet girl. I need a waker-upper. Lots of time for what you need. You sure know what makes me hum. Bring us both a cup in bed, okay."

Oh, if you only knew what I really need. But then again, maybe this is what it's all about. Keeping me here. Keeping me from hearing the voices whispering about things that scare me. Voices coming from cracks in the ceiling! Jeez! If all it takes is getting coffee to quieten it for awhile, then it's coffee you got. Anyway, you make me feel pretty, pretty nice.

"You got it. Want sugar or some of that powder stuff? Yes? Okay, just wait right there and I'll be back in a flash."

"That's my girl."

She notices the sun has already changed toward grey. And, some-how, when she looks up at the crack on the ceiling on her way back to the bed, it just looks dirty and cheap.

LETTER TO ROBERTA

Hi there, Cousin.

How are things? I thought I would drop a few lines to tell you first from people at home. Don't tell mom 'til I tell her okay, please? I'm gonna have a baby! Yeah. I don't really know what to think of that. If this is a girl I want a new kinda name for her. Not some same old name. We're living in a new generation now. I want her to be able to be free of the same old, same old. You know? I'm kinda looking forward to it.

Me and Francis are working for the winter in Keremeos. He likes to work in the orchards. It's not too hard I guess. I paint a lot but there isn't time for it in the day. He thinks I should just quit. It doesn't make me back the money I spend on it. I don't know, maybe he's right, but I don't care about money anyway, as long as I have paint. How many clothes do you need, anyhow? How much food can a person eat, anyhow? But he wants a newer car and he says we got to make a move to save up in case we want to move back to the rez and get our own place. He doesn't have his own place on his rez yet. I would rather be there and trying to get started but he says he likes to move around. New scenery. But I didn't get with him for that and I kinda like being with him. At least I don't have to feel like I gotta be out hunting around for some loving. He thinks I'm weird but he said that at least I don't boss him and whine about new this and new that.

I heard you and Mike split up and you're back home with both your kids. It's good your little brothers and sisters are older now and can help you some. I'm sorry it didn't work out. I never did think much of him for all his big talk about getting rich and own-ing everything on the rez. And getting a dream house and all. He just didn't appreciate you enough. You work so hard taking care of everybody around you. You never get time for yourself. You don't need somebody to get you that stuff anyway. You're a hard worker. You could put it together yourself. Is he even giving you money for the kids? He's such a tight-ass and all talk and a big drinker to boot, he probably doesn't. Well, I don't mean to tell you what to do. What am I doing that's so great anyway? I just care about you.

Anyway I'll be around sometime toward the end of the month after pruning time. There is always slow time in the orchard work until blossom time. I don't want him harping at me about paying my share of the groceries. I'll come home and help my mom with her beading and maybe get some painting done. I guess it's still hard on her about dad. It's probably why I kinda drifted away. I just can't think of home without him. And I know mom misses me.

But Francis hates it when I'm not there to do stuff for him. Jeez. Who decided that women are supposed to do the cooking and cleaning? I mean I work too, same as he does. Well, anyway, it's no big deal. There is just the two of us and we live in a two room cabin. I won't live off him though. So I will be home.

I bought some stuff for you and the kids. I always put aside my own money after I pay my share. I got a few winter things to wear and I'll bring them when I come. I'll be around in a month or two. We can visit then.

Penny.

The ground was still damp from the morning dew. Far down into the valley, the blue mist was rising from the ribbon of river. Dawn's shadow crept from the dusky patches and stretches of yellowing field toward the stands of cottonwood bush. Up on the mountain top, the first red haze was brushing the tree tops and the thin rock-strewn soil. The strong scent of balsam sap fused with the sharp sweet smell of the ripening huckleberries.

Susapeen sat waiting for the moment when the first rays would leap over the crisp, jagged edge of the glacier mountains to the east. The air was misty with the heavy dew of the early fall night. She could feel the chill through her cotton dress. Her thin legs and bony arms were folded close to her, to keep some warmth.

The camp is still and they all dream now. Their dreams flying even now toward the undershadows of the trees. The first light of the life-giver dances, red, even now, in their veins. It calls to them to wake, to see, to smell.

Susapeen pulled her old flowered shawl tighter around her. Her face tilted, chin pointing toward the fiery tinge spreading into the sky.

These old bones hurt and even now the flesh disappears. I am hardly here. I fade moment-by-moment, and I will soon fly into the shadows. The shadows even now whispering for me to come, to rest, to be free.

"Tupa! Tupaaaa?"

This one will find me even in the shadows.

"Tupa, you got up without me, to watch the sun come. Tupa, I want to sit down here, too, and listen to you talk to the world. I'm not too small."

Susapeen shifted and turned to look at her great grand-daughter.

She is like the sun, too. She speaks our language so easily instead of that borrowed tongue.

"Paen-aye, come sit close to me and share my shawl. You are small but you are way too smart. It's still time. Look! There! The red fires edge. It breaks over, now! It is a new day! I give thanks for letting me see one more day. I give thanks for being here on this huckle-berry mountain, to taste the sweet food of this place. I give thanks to sit here with my great grand-daughter. I give thanks for our safe night and ask for a safe day for the hunters and berry pickers. We come only to honour life. Paen-aye, the one whose real name is my mother's, sits with me, to greet the great sun, who gives us light and life. Give her its warmth to light a path ahead of her. I greet and honour this day."

Susapeen spoke into the morning air. Her thin, high voice drifting into the vast moment. Penny, too, sat absolutely still, looking down and across the valley toward the unbearable fire rising in the east above the white-tipped mountains in the distance.

I wonder, in the sun's risings to come, how this one, my mother's name, will look at this same sun rising over this valley when she is drifting into the shadows, as I do now. Will she come to greet the day, her family, a thick, warm quilt surrounding her? Will she reach this time of fading, under a sun which will then rise over many who do not greet the day?

Susapeen turned toward Penny and touched her hair with one feather-light stroke.

"The world is new. Today we are here, but the shadows follow us in the bright of day. Take care to wrap the light around you. To let it keep you warm. To greet it and give thanks each new day. Come, help me up, and we will chase the dreams of the others away into the last shadows of night creeping away down in the valley."

Susapeen spoke in the language, savouring the sounds, holding her great grand-daughter's small hand. Together they walked toward the thin patched canvas tents and the make-shift shelter of green fir-boughs and poles. The others still slept, tired from yesterday's hard work of picking the sweet purple huckleberries.

"Wake up. All the shadows are gone. There is daylight, even in the swamps. The bluejays are laughing, standing around the campfire. Laughing at the humans who don't know the sun is up and it's a new day. The huckleberries are watching the trails, waiting. Waiting to travel down to the lowlands in our baskets. Waiting to hear our singing to them. You are all turning yellow from too much sleep!"

Susapeen watched Penny as she tiptoed slowly toward the three bluejays hopping around the cold campfire, squawking importantly over the small crumbs from last night's late meal. They jumped away from her just out of her reach, making whistling sounds.

The greeting sounds from the tent overlapped like the bluejays voices. Susapeen listened for each voice.

Daughter of mine, she sounds tired, still. It is time for her to rest a little more in the day. She needn't wait until she is eldest, like me, to sleep in the warm sun, at noon. And grand-daughter, strong, strong mother of Paen-aye, always missing her man. Maybe he'll be home before snowfall, this time. Asking her sister if she is happy today that there is fresh meat in camp.

Susapeen greeted the boys piling out of the fir-bough shelter along with their uncles. Suddenly the camp was a busy bustling place, as the fire was lit and the tea pot and mush pots were filled to be heated.

The bluejays hopped from branch to branch above the camp, speaking in a variety of tones, comically sounding like Susapeen. Smiling up at them, she nodded.

They sound happy today. Not scolding and not worried.

"We can pick again today. The mountain is good to us. We are lucky. We will have plenty this winter."

The women and the men stopped a moment to look at each other and murmured their thank-you's out loud. Settling herself in close to the campfires red flicker, Susapeen closed her eyes to rest just a little longer.

The sun drives shafts of heat into her back and she can feel the sweat running down her neck but she keeps her muscles moving in time. One step up, to hold her balance, with her knee against the rung and the apple bag strapped over her shoulders to hold her weight forward. Her arms move in precise arcs up, to twist the apples off and bring them down gently into the bag. The sweet smell of apples and the pesticide spray mix together as fine bits of dust lift from the leaves. It coats her hands and sticks to her face, filling her nose and mouth with its bitter, bitter taste. There is no breeze today and even the birds are quiet. She can hear Francis in the next tree, ladder creaking and the snap, snap of apples being broken off their limbs. Only the sound of cars passing, on the road by the orchard, breaks the stillness.

It must be at least four o'clock. I hope Mom and the kids are okay. Only an hour or so and it'll cool down some. Maybe we'll get ten bins today.

Jesus, there must be a better way to make ends meet than this. What the hell am I doing up an apple tree? An apple knocker! That's what I am. Just what my dad always told me not to be. And what about this weekend? Payday. Him and all those ass-holes will be heading to town to drink. Ah, well, it's just for now, and I made my own bed and I'll sleep in it. Better not to worry. Just concentrate on another bin.

"Goddamn, Penny! Watch what you're doing! I can see bruises on these. Jesus, the foreman'll be giving me shit again. I told you to take it easy! These goldens are extra fancy. We're getting ten bucks a bin to pick them! It ain't like we're rich you know. This is the best orchard around here. You want us to end up picking those shit little reds, for him, for seven dollars a bin? Get down here!"

She can feel her chest tightening and her throat going dry. The bag is almost full and the straps are cutting into her thin shoulders. She can feel the places where the skin is raw under her shirt even though there are callus patches, now, in this fourth week of apple-picking season. She reaches high for the last few apples above her and gently puts them into the bag. She backs slowly down one step and swings the bag to the side so they won't bump into the ladder. The ladder creaks each step as she moves, one hand on the ladder for balance and one on the bag to keep it in place. The sweat mixed with dust drips down her face and burns her eyes. She blinks rapidly trying to clear her vision.

Crap. I'm going to tell him to frigging shove all the apples up his ass if he starts in again. I'm not bruising them, but I'd like to frigging bruise him in the face. I don't need this. What the hell am I doing here? What the hell good do I get out of this anyway? I can't stand this heat and this dust and this smell and I can't stand him yelling!

"What? I'm not bruising them. They're just getting too hot and you know it. It's too hot to be picking. We should have quit a couple of hours ago."

"Don't be smart assing me, damn it. Look here. What do you call these? I don't want to see any more of this shit."

He picks up three or four apples at once and flings them past her. They smash against her ladder. His eyes are mean looking and his face is streaked with dirt where he's been wiping the sweat. He stands there staring at her, breathing hard, and she can see the veins sticking out in his neck. He doesn't say anything. He just stares and breathes.

She stands with her feet wide apart. The heavy bag, hanging at her chest, drags at her shoulders and she can feel the dripping under her arms. She doesn't move. She doesn't even blink. She just stares back.

I didn't know God made honky tonk angels as they said in the words of the song.

Part of the Kitty Wells song repeats itself over and over in her head and she doesn't try to stop it. But she can feel her chest relaxing and her breathing slowing down. She shifts her weight and walks slowly to the bin and unhooks the ties holding the bottom. She lifts the bag over the waist high edge of the apple bin and lays the whole bag flat before easing it back to let the apples slide gently out of the open bottom. She can hear him walk back toward his ladder and she hears the steps creak as he climbs back up. She fumbles in her shirt pocket for her cigarettes and takes one out. She lights it walking back to her ladder.

I ndian Summer in the Okanagan. The sky, a clean blue, swept by the evening breezes, carried no hint of cloud. It was good for the apples. Extra Fancy Sweets, they were called by the boss. The sugar comes up with hot days and crisp fall nights. They shipped them all over the world and people paid grade A fancy prices to put them on their counters. The hills, slopes and benches on the sides of all the lakes, creeks and the river were a massive checkerboard of orchards bristling with sprinklers pulling water from the lakes and reservoirs. But in the hottest part of summer, when there is no wind and the mountains capture and hold the dust in the valley for weeks, the still air became hazy and heavy with the sharp smell of orchard spray.

The door to his office swings open and she can smell cigar tobacco even from where she sits on the slick vinyl chair. His thin balding hair is mostly grey and his face is chubby and red. His baggy suit coat is open and the frayed blue tie is loosened at the collar of a blue checkered shirt. His buttons strain over the bulge of his belly. His eyes go over her quickly. She suddenly wishes she had worn a longer skirt and a darker blouse. He doesn't smile as he picks up her application form. She stands up clutching her old black purse against her side. Her heart is beating hard and she can feel the nylon stockings, slick between her thighs.

Should I say something? Should I smile? No. He'll think I'm trying to butter him up or something.

"Miss Jackson? Have a seat. Hmmm. I don't see any work experience on this. How long have you been out of school?"

"Three years. I was mostly doing labour in the orchards. I want a more steady job. I have three kids now and . . ."

"Have you ever worked at anything for any length of time? I can't hire someone who jumps from one job to the next."

"I haven't had a chance. Unless you call packing apples steady. I packed apples steady every year, after harvest, 'til Christmas, since I left school. I'm separated now and I won't be doing seasonal work anymore. I would like a chance, that's all."

"Well, I do need a female on this here job. You look like you're Indian. Are you?"

"Yes."

"Yeah, well that helps, too. I get a better subsidy for hiring minority and women. I can kill two birds with one stone. But you get one chance. The first time you come in hungover, or late, you're ass is outa here. You get that? There's more where you came from. Everybody who works here, gets here on time and leaves on time."

What do I say? Should I tell him I don't drink? Shit you would think I was applying for some big high-paying job instead of a minimum-wage, half-ass, flunky job counting and stamping boxes and crates.

"Okay."

"You get paid twice a month. Your first check will be held back. Deductions for Unemployment, Workmen's Comp, CPP, taxes and union dues, will be done automatically. No overtime. Holiday pay when you leave or two weeks, with pay, if you make a year. No sick pay. One hour for lunch. Two fifteen minute breaks at the whistle. No smoking or drinking on the job and no hanky-panky with the men. There is no ladies' room, so the john at the far end with the lock is one you can use. Only during breaks. You keep up with the line and if there is slack time, then you clean up. Got that? Everybody works here. This ain't no easy breezy, women's packing shed. Wear jeans and sleeved shirts. No girlie clothes like that stuff you got on and tie your hair up. Lets take a walk around the line. I'll show you where your station is. Start Monday."

He turns on his heel and walks briskly away, not even waiting for a response. She follows him out into the long room past corridors of stacked boxes and crates. The noise is almost as overwhelming as the variety of smells. Clacking and humming and the steady grinding of belts and machinery. There is a strong smell of oil and paint and something else, like turpentine.

It's worse than my can of turpentine and linseed in my paint box.

Men stand by belt rollers moving cut pieces of wood which they fit into position before shooting staples or nails into them. Others are cutting exact lengths and doing various things with parts of boxes and crates. Some are in wheeled loaders lifting and moving short stacks of them around to higher stacks. Each of them nods but doesn't look up as they pass.

I feel sick and dizzy.

There aren't any windows except for a dim row of dirty skylight panels in the high ceiling. He suddenly stops and turns around.

"Okay, Missy, here is the dye stamper. Stand over here. All you have to do is take this lever in your right hand and pull down on it when the box comes to a stop, like Tom here is doing. Hold it and count to ten, then let the lever up and wait for the next one. If you hold it too long, the next box will crack up against this one and it'll jam the belt up. If you bring it down too soon, before it stops, it'll jam and mess up the line and the belt. If the dye runs out, there is a red button, to the left there, you push that and the dye will feed down into the stamper. You can see it get a lighter shade just before it runs out. Push the button when that happens or you'll have a dry run and those boxes will have to be fed in by hand. After every fifty boxes, you stick that little green sticker to the top right corner to let the stacker know. Don't miscount either. Each lot has to be exact for the shipment to fit the carrier. At the end of every day the other end of the tags are brought to my office. We stop and you mark the count. We start and you mark the count on that sheet there. Exact. Every mistake costs me. So don't make any."

She follows him back out to a small dingy office connected to the front office. On the wall there is a yellowed calendar with a blonde woman in a red bikini. Her breasts are huge and are barely covered by the tiny pieces of cloth. Her legs are spread wide apart and her smooth, white hips are arched upward. She is leaning on the hood of a long black car with lots of chrome. Her mouth is puckered into an O.

P enny sat at the top of a hill looking down into a deep, silent valley between two grandmothers. The sweet smell of pine sap and fresh green fir was like a blanket around them. One of the grandmothers was Tupa. They were making signs on the ground with little fir-boughs. The boughs were fanned in a semi-circle in front of them. Each little bough's tip was facing toward them and Tupa was speaking in the language saying, "That's how they are laid in the lodge. In a full circle, always pointing inward, but facing outward." And the other not looking down, but looking farther into the valley and saying, "And when this one is our age, will she remember which way they point?" Her voice was mixed with the moaning of the long swaying pines towering above them and the sorrowful trilling of robins calling for rain.

The circle painted on the green lino-floor, in the centre of the room, is black. The chairs are placed carefully, side-by-side, all the way around the circle. A second circle of chairs is spaced evenly around behind the first circle. Some people stand around the room a ways back from the double circle of chairs, chattering in small groups. The one row of ceiling lights turned on in the large room cast a warm glow instead of the usual harsh white glare. In the centre of the circle, a single candle in a glass is flickering, filling the room with a pine scent. Over the speakers, a Young Grey Horse Society tape is playing pow-wow music on low volume.

Donna looks at the people standing around. Most are in their twenties and thirties. Some of them are dressed in office-type clothes while others are wearing ribbon shirts, jeans and moccasins. She spots Wayne among them, talking animatedly to a young guy with braids and cowboy boots. Wayne looks up suddenly and flashes her a smile and waves her over. He has on a bone choker spaced with red-glass pony beads. She can see his turquoise and silver watch bracelet, briefly catch the light, as his hand moves to smooth his shoulder length hair.

"Donna, come over here and meet James. He just came into town and was checking out the centre. I told him we were going to have a circle and asked him to join in. He's from your neck of the woods. James, this is Donna, the program director here. She knows everybody. She might be able to help you. James is kinda stuck. He's here to go to school over at the college and is looking for somebody to share rent with. I was telling him that this time of year, quite a few Indian students drop in here looking for the same thing. Anyway, I gotta go get some stuff ready for later. Why don't you introduce him to few of the young people here? Hey, that dress sure looks good."

Wayne moves closer to her to drop his arm casually over her shoulder for a moment before he walks away toward the kitchen.

Donna watches him move with an assured stride. She notices several of the other women are watching him, too. She is suddenly happy she decided to wear her green wildflower-print dress with the handstitched ribbon front.

"Hi, James. Where from in Saskatchewan? I'm from out there myself, you know. I'm from around Prince Albert. But I've been out here for the last five years. Are you hungry? There's some sandwiches in the kitchen. I don't think anybody would mind if you had one now instead of after."

"I guess I'm from Red Pheasant. I never really lived there, though. We mostly lived in Regina. I can wait and eat later. What kinda circle are you having? I went to a few at the Friendship Centre over there but they were always sorta about the centre politics. I don't wanta horn in on anything like that. I was just resting up and looking to put up a note on the bulletin board for a roommate. I could come back later if you think."

"Oh no! This circle is always held on Thursday evenings. We just want people to be able to come here to share in their culture. This isn't that kind of circle. Those are during the day. Sometimes, in this circle, we have some singing and drums, sometimes we have stories, sometimes we just sit and talk about things. We always have a smudge and prayers. Tonight we have an Indian visitor from Bolivia. Wayne invited him to talk about the Indigenous people there. I think it'll be interesting. Anyway, the smudge and prayers are going to get started pretty quick. Why don't you find a seat over there next to those young ladies and I'll introduce you to them. Alright? Okay."

People are beginning to fill the chairs. James follows Donna over to the place she points to. There are three serene looking young women in their early twenties. Two of them have on blue jeans and tee-shirts with Indian words on them. The other has on a long blue-jean skirt and a print shirt. Her long brown hair is partly french braided on the sides. They have been openly watching James and Donna talk. The one with the skirt smiles at Donna.

"Hi, Donna. Do you want us to do anything?"

"No. Everything is in order. Thanks, Janey. This is James. He's a new student just in from Saskatchewan. He's looking for some-body to share rent with. You girls help him out, okay? He doesn't know anybody. Introduce yourselves. Later you can take him over to talk to Penny, who is now the Interim Referral person. You met her, Janey, she's sitting right over there. That one, with that wild patchwork vest. Penny might have more information on places to rent cheap. She's got all kinds of connections. Oh, and you can help pick up after, if you want. Nice to see you out for the circle again."

When Donna turns, there is only her chair, next to Wayne, left empty. As she hurries to take her seat, Wayne bends over in his chair lighting matches on a small pile of broken sweetgrass braid in an abalone shell on the floor in front of him. Somebody has turned off the pow-wow tape and the room is suddenly quiet and still. A smallish dark man, in jeans and a multicolored striped woven cotton shirt with a bamboo panpipe flute on a string around his neck and thick sandals on his feet, sits on his other side. The man watches Wayne, his hands together in his lap. It isn't until he has the sweet-grass glowing by fanning it slowly with a feather that Wayne speaks.

"Brothers and sisters. I welcome you to this circle of friendship. Tonight we have in this circle, Indian people from many different parts of Turtle Island, as well as our brother from South America. We all come here to this circle in appreciation of who we are as Indian people. We come here to renew ourselves in our traditions. We also come here to join our hearts for those of our people who are in need of prayer. Our brother has asked that he be allowed to add medicine to the smudge from his land so that he fully takes part in joining his heart to ours. Thank you all."

As the man from Bolivia stands and then kneels to place his medicine on the top to the glowing sweetgrass, everyone in the circle stands at once. The sweet scented smoke rising suddenly has another muskier quality to it. The man straightens and steps back. Wayne picks up the shell and slowly begins to move around the circle, stopping briefly to fan smoke on each person with the feather. A few bend over to inhale a little of the smoke or cup their hands over it. After fanning smoke on himself, Wayne begins the prayer in his language. His voice is hardly audible. Others around the room also murmur in their language or in English. The room smells sweet and heavy. Outside, an ambulance suddenly shrills the silence and horns blare insistently for a moment.

Donna nods and includes whoever it might be in the ambulance, thinking of that person's family, too.

Finally, Wayne ends by saying, "All my relations" in English and everyone sits down again.

Wayne looks around the room and then at the man sitting next to him and shakes hands with him.

"This is Manual Antonio Vitaro. He is Ayamara from Bolivia. He would like to share some words tonight, with you. He is travelling briefly in Canada, at a conference in Vancouver. I was lucky to be at the conference on Indigenous Peoples and I met him. I listened to him speak with our Indian brothers and sisters. We became friends and I asked him to visit here for a few days before I take him back to Vancouver. He is also going to play some Andean flute music for us later. I know you are all waiting to hear from him, so, I'll just say thank you again."

Manual stands up and walks around the room shaking hands with everyone. When he gets back to his seat he stays standing. He looks around the room and gestures to everyone with his hands held out, palms open and fingers spread. A familiar gesture of peace and offering. He stands there a moment, silently and then lowers his hands.

"*Si. Gracias*, thank you my brothers and sisters. I feel welcome and I try my best English. I give greeting to you. It's all good, no? We are here together on *Pache Mama*, our mother earth and we join as Indigenous People in the *espiritual* traditions."

Donna had to strain to separate his words out from each other. His English is surprisingly good but heavy with a Spanish accent and his voice is strong but sounds higher pitched than the throaty, burred tones of the Indian men from here.

"I do not speak on the political at this moment. I can discuss informally later with some of you. *Si?* However, I like, now, to talk about traditions. Today we meet as brothers and sisters under *El Sol* in the western hemisphere, our two islands joined like the mother's cord to her child. And we elevate ourselves with the medicine to talk as our ancestors. *Si?* I am gratified. I speak now on matters we discuss with Wayne."

Donna feels mesmerized by the way Manual is describing things. She looks around the room. All eyes are on him. Nobody looks bored or confused. Wayne sits with his arms folded across his chest, his face half turned toward Manual, his profile to her. The line of his jaw is strong and yet he looks gentle. The beaded choker at his neck sets off perfectly the even brown of his skin.

"Almost five hundred years, now, we are living under the calender of great turmoil. And our peoples await the close of that time. We mark a beginning, soon, of a new time of great *espiritual* unity.

When the sacred eagle of the North joins with the great sacred condor of the South, we see the beginning of a new five hundred years calender. New knowledge in the era of the *Indios*."

Manual turns and he seems to be looking directly at her. Her breath slows as their eyes meet. The air seems electric.

"And so Indigenous Peoples make change. To heal *Pache Mama*. This is happening now, over our lands. Brothers and sisters from the North and the South are greet each other and talk. Small groups like now and big *enquentros*, is same, no? We have one agenda, no? *Pache Mama*. We are hers like the flowers. We are only healthy if *Pache Mama* is. This is what our political and economic agendas strive for. It is *Pache Mama* yearning to see all her flowers bloom healthy."

Donna looks across the room at Penny, the new interim referral worker. The strange artist who talked last week about flower medicines and their spirits. Penny is nodding and there is a dreamy look on her face as she leans forward in Manual's direction. Penny's expression changes and she sits back in her chair. Then she closes her eyes and leans back, her face slightly pointing to the ceiling. Her whole body seems to shift gear and she suddenly looks absolutely still.

"Many things must end for that to happen. Perhaps the great turmoil will end in great destruction. Perhaps not. Perhaps it starts slow at first, like the small stream growing, drop by drop, in the rainy season. And only when the river reaches the houses do the people worry. No? We cannot know. But our Inca ancestors were great astrologers and scientists. And so our knowledge of order. Order, under the energy of *El Sol* and *Pache Mama*. It binds us all. The order which feeds us daily. And so it is the priority. No?"

There are nods and murmurs all around the circle. Donna shifts in her chair slightly, her thighs are damp. Somehow the temperature seemed to have risen and she is aware that others are slightly flushed.

"*Si*. These years are important to us. We speak our own sacred book and gather strength around it. And so the turnover. Our activity is convey this, no? To unite us in the school of Indigenous Peoples of the world. If we focus ourselves, just so, it becomes mystical. A power in the cosmic perfection. A strong force of order. The natural energy in all things. This we keep in mind at all times. And so, we seek to bind ourselves in solidarity and espiritually as brothers and sisters. To achieve courage to become serene and calm within and so to make good decisions. And so, now, I am happy Wayne to bring me here. I say *gracias*, now, and play the music for you."

Donna finds her eyes drawn back to Penny. Penny is sitting forward again but now she is looking at the candle flickering in its glass at the centre. As Manual lifts the flute and begins the fast trilling Andean music, Donna notices that the candle has now burned down below the rim of the bevelled glass and there is a perfect circle of flickering shadows on the floor pointing outward, dancing.

*T*hey never leave that mountain. It is always there in her dreams. A quiet tree filled valley filling her. A small green firbough there in her dreams, always. Over and over it is slowly being turned around. There is always something she doesn't remember. Something lost. All that lingers is the smell of pine sap and green fir.

The morning sun, outlined in magenta, is just creeping over the ridges, slanting red-gold shafts down into the valley. The mountain tops, still white with snow, shine in the strange light. It casts a warmth over the dark green of the trees before fading into deep blue and then into the softer teal and mauve tones of the distant peaks. On the rounded sides of the nearest mountains, swatches of white unmelted snow glow a brilliant pink in this light.

This place is known to her somewhere deep inside. A coming home. She feels each colour. They are inside her. The colours of warmth, of light. They are a soft voice whispering into the wind. A giving of thanks. Being held close.

How could I have stayed away for so long? There is nowhere more beautiful in the world than here. This moment, it stretches outward from me. How will I ever put this on canvas? Why do I want to? Who are you? Or what are you? I feel you.

"Penny, it's darn cold out here and I'm still half asleep. Couldn't we just look at the sun when it's way up, around ten or so? It's the same sun then. Anyway the guys are getting the fire going for coffee and brekkie. We've been sitting here for almost twenty minutes or so. The sun's pretty much up now anyway. I'm gonna head back to camp. You stay out here as long as you want. I'll call when the coffee's cooked. Anyway it's your only time alone before the kids wake up."

Donna stands up, her Pendleton shawl wrapped around her tightly. She stands a moment, looking across the deep valley at the magnificent fire ball rising over the mountains above the lake.

"I'm glad we decided to go camping and fishing. It feels so Indian. I want to help you pick some of those berries, too. They taste really good. I bet they'll taste like heaven in the pancakes. I'll help with the kids later, too, if you want to paint for awhile. It'll make a nice picture. It looks like a picture right now doesn't it? Holeee! Look at that sun! How come it looks like that? It's the first time I've really looked at sunrise from in the wild. Wow! No wonder you want to freeze your butt just to see this. It feels strange."

Donna slowly lets herself down again. She looks at Penny who doesn't even nod or make a sound to show that she heard. Her face is tilted upward, chin pointing toward the sun, her eyes half closed.

Finally. Quiet. I give thanks for the good night we had. For my three babies sleeping like little cubs in the tent. For my friends here with me. For the food of this place. Keep us safe today and give us your light. Give my friend Donna, who sits here with me, your warmth. She shares with all those who come to the centre. I give thanks for this new day.

Suddenly, Donna is aware, quiet tears are rolling down Penny's face. Donna doesn't know what to do.

"Pen? Pen, you okay? Do you want me here or not? I didn't know you were feeling bad. I can stay and talk if you need to. The guys'll get stuff cooked."

Penny shakes her head quickly, not looking at Donna or making a sound.

Hesitantly standing, Donna waits momentarily and then quietly and slowly leaves for camp.

What is this feeling? Like something I should say or do right now. Filling my chest. Making my head and my hands tingle. The same feeling the night Manual talked. Pache Mama. The earth mother. The same feeling when the paint moves and speaks. Calling to me. I know it's voice. I want to hear. Teach me. Show me.

Penny can hear a mourning dove far down in the valley cooing it's lonesome call and somewhere nearby a squirrel is chattering insistently. The slight whispering sound the pine needles make in the breeze and the first clicking of grasshoppers drying their wings are the only sounds she can hear for some time, next to her breathing and the steady beat of her heart. Then the faraway, sweet voices of her children drifts past. She closes her eyes and listens to the rhythm of her breath. The moment seems to expand and the sounds fade.

I can hear the mystery.

She knows she is changed in that glorious rising of the sun. She hears clearer that moment than in any other in her life.

LETTER TO LENA

Lena, Sis:

I just wanted to write you a short letter to let you know how things are going with me. I heard from cousin Roberta that you were back for a little while. I wish I were there, too. I miss you a lot, big sister. I heard you weren't doing too great. Maybe the big city lights are blinding you, huh? Anyway, I hope you can make up your mind to stick around for awhile. Mom gets pretty lonesome, now that all of us are gone. She worries about you. I tell her that you'll come home for good sometime. We all do. I guess you're something like me in a way. Maybe it's that you are the oldest sister and me the youngest. We should have been just like Josalie. She's so solid, like Mom and Grandma. Maybe it's because she's in the middle like our two brothers.

Anyway, I just wanted you to know that things are looking up for me. You must know that Francis is a thing of the past. The kids are great. Shanna always looks so much like you when she smiles. She's the oldest, too. I'm sorta working for awhile at the Friendship

Centre here. It's hard to get a good job because I don't have college, so I'm thinking I might try to get in, even though all I really want to do is paint. Maybe I could apply that somehow to a good job.

The Friendship Centre has some great programs here. There is a gathering circle once a week for people. They do Indian stuff. You know. Anyway, it feels good. But there sure is a lot of politics about the jobs. I don't think I'll last too long. What I really wanted to tell you about was that I had this thing happen. I know it's sounds hokey but I feel different, like what the Christians say about being born again. I can't explain it but it kinda started from that circle. Later when I went camping with some friends up at Fish Lake, is when something woke up inside of me. You know it's like it's always there but just out of reach when I'm painting, but all of a sudden it was different because it fell into place. I guess it's the same as falling in love. Only this ain't a person.

I wish you could come up here. Maybe you need something like that. You seem to be constantly looking for something, like me. The only difference, now, might be that I feel happy. You always seem so sad, so angry. Especially since Dad died. Did you ever think of trying something else besides the drugs? I don't want to be a pain-in-the-ass, Sis. But you mean a lot to us. Maybe what you're looking for isn't in the bright lights of the city or that silver cloud you shoot up. Maybe it's not in some place that we might think we have left behind forever, maybe it's in the rising sun of each new day.

Anyway enough already. I'm going to be back for the feast this fall. I picked some blackcaps up at Fish Lake and me and my friend Donna canned twenty-five jars for the feast. They are yummy. They taste just like long time ago. Please be there still. Love you lots.

Sis, Pen

There are no parking spaces. She circles around trying to find one between the rows and rows of cars. She finally spots one, way off to the end of the dirt parking lot. The rain is sleeting down and there are brown mud puddles all over. The mud feels soft and her heels sink into it halfway up to the tops her shoes as she starts across to the front of the building. She wraps her sweater tighter around her and tries to avoid the deepest puddles and the soft mud, now caking to the bottoms of her pumps.

Why does this always happen to me? I wish I could, just for once, make a good impression at the start. Maybe I should just get back in my car and leave. Damn anyway, I suppose they'll all stare at me like I'm a bug or something. No! I'm gonna go in there and ask for all the things I need to get me in. I'm never gonna pick apples, stamp boxes or clean motels again. I'm never going to stand in a work line again and have some fat fart fondle my ass just because he thinks I need the job so bad. I just need to look them right back in the eye and stand there as long as it takes. I wish I'd asked Donna to come with me. No, I gotta do this on my own like everything else. I can do it. What the hell does Mrs. Goddard from grade ten know? Telling me to be a damn secretary, that it's the best I can hope for, being Native, and me getting straight A's in everything. What the hell did she mean anyway! Damn it. Why am I thinking of her right now anyway? I want to go to college, and I'm going to. What if I can't make the grades though? Damn, everybody that's backing me, will be let down.

She stops at the bottom of the wide concrete steps leading up to the glass doors. She stands there for several minutes. The rain is now running down in little streams over her forehead and she can feel her sweater sticking to her back. She turns once and looks toward the car. It's raining harder and people are running past her into the building. Everyone has on a raincoat or jacket. A few are holding umbrellas. Only she is standing there, hair dripping, shoes caked with mud with nothing but a thin sweater on. A few look back at her, over their shoulders before going in. Only she is Native.

Oh, God, make me into a shadow. Make me invisible. Oh, God, why did I have to be born. Shit, I'm gonna turn and walk away. I'm gonna give up almost two years worth of planning and saving. I'm sooo dumb. I'm just an Indian. Who in the hell do I think I am anyway?

She can feel the tears start and she can't stop them. They are warm, running down her face and she can feel the tightness in her throat move down into her chest and she wants to start coughing. She automatically feels for her purse where her cigarettes are. She can feel her knees begin to shake ever so little.

All I want is to try. I hate most not knowing if my art is good, bad or ugly. I hate the way I think about all the things that are happening and want-ing to paint something about it. I hate reading and reading and feeling like I gotta say something too. Why couldn't I just be normal and resigned to things? I hate the world I'm stuck in. Oh please make me go in. Make me at least ask.

She makes her body turn toward the glass doors and moves her right foot up to scrape off some of the mud caked on it. She scrapes the other one trying to twist her foot sideways to scrape the mud off the sides. She opens her purse and takes out a used Kleenex and dabs her forehead and face. Her knees are still feeling weak and she is starting to shiver. It's only the end of August but there is already a brisk, fall cut to the wind. She walks to the doors and opens them and a gust of wind pushes it wide open, pulling her along with it. It takes all her strength to pull the door shut behind her. There are people standing all around, crowded against the long counter behind which several women are standing. Each is preoccupied with papers between them and the person they are helping. No one looks at her at all. Several are standing next to a machine taking turns feeding quarters into it and placing the styrofoam cup which drops down under a spout. Steaming coffee spills into the cup.

She sees a Restroom sign and heads for it. Inside, she takes paper towels and rubs her hair to get most of the water out. She takes off her sweater and stands close to the hand drier and pushes the knob. The warm air billows out her sweater and she feels the skin on her arms begin to dry. Her breathing is slowing as she bends down, using one hand to wipe her shoes with the paper towels, the other still holding her sweater up to the dryer.

Okay now. Okay now. Just don't think. Just smile in the mirror, then walk back out there and get a coffee inside you. You are in this far. Don't look back from here on. Do everything you need to do to get in. You are never going to pick apples ever again. Oh man, oh man, what am I getting into now? It's all unchartered from here. Oh help me with this. Stay with me just a little longer.

Out in the entrance hall again, she takes her time finding two quarters and feeds them into the slot. She punches 'black' and then 'start' and the styro cup drops and she places it under the spout, as the hot black liquid streams out into the cup. She turns slowly and lets her eyes move around the crowded room. Most of them are pretty young. The women's faces are fresh and carefree looking. A few older women with pastel pantsuits are among the roomful of casually dressed kids. She sips slowly, almost liking the bitter taste of the instant Nescafe. It allows her to focus. To relax her throat. One of the older women nods at her and she gives a half smile back.

"Ah, mmm. It sure isn't the best of days to try to register, is it? I'm a little nervous, I guess. I've decided to go back to school now that my kids are grown, but I wasn't prepared for everyone here, being so young. I feel a little out of place. I don't really know what one is supposed to do. It seems like everybody already knows which forms need to be filled and so on. I wonder how long this will take. I have someone waiting for me. Maybe I should just come back some other time."

She looks anxiously at her watch and pats her stiff perm. Her hands are shaking, just a tiny bit, but Penny sees it. Penny looks at her and nods.

"Me too. I say it's probably best just to get in line and find out. What are you taking?"

"Oh, I thought I would sign up for some general courses. Maybe take a psychology course. At least that's what I always dreamed about. I don't know how I'll do with that, though. What about you?"

"I'm going into Fine Arts. I know you can't make a living with that, but it's what I do best. I want to give it a go. I want to take political science, too, just because I'm interested, but I'm not sure what kind of career you could get with that."

They move together toward the nearest line and stand, not speaking anymore. Penny can feel that the woman is waiting for her to go first. She does. Her nervousness is gone.

The sun was almost overhead. All around, the tall sweet clover was waving and dancing, making shadows on the ground. Their soft yellow flowers sent tiny yellow dots down onto the sand. Here and there patches of pink and purple ground clover formed feathery flower balls in the sand surrounded by perfect four sectioned leaves. The sand was warm and golden brown, glittering with bits of mica. The sun was glinting off the lake's still surface. She could hear bees buzzing and far across the lake in the reeds, the *quack, quack* of ducks.

She was lying on her back looking up through her Tupa's silk shawl. Tupa had tied the corners to four sticks to make a shade for her. The colours were beautiful. The shawl was a deep, dark blue and the flowers were bright red, yellow and orange. She knew the colours but not their names. She had no need to know their names. The leaves twining the flowers of all sizes together made a square border all around the edge. The silk fringes hung down and waved all around her. They danced. The same dance the sweet clover and the lake's tiny waves danced.

She turned over on her stomach and the sand was suddenly magic. Blue, red, orange, yellow and gold splash over sand. She moved her hands up toward the thin silk and the colours covered her arms and hands. She was all colours and the sand was too. She reached her hands out and buried them in the sand, and moved the colour onto the sand. She moved the sand into mounds and gathered little pebbles in piles to capture the strange coloured light. She made tracks and pockets capturing red and orange and yellow in them. She crawled to the edge of the shade and pulled small twigs of driftwood and created faces in the sand with them, capturing gold, yellow, orange and red. Her heart was beating fast and she sang to the coloured faces in the sand.

Tupa's voice, by the water, sang along with her. The *splash, splash* of Tupa cleaning fish stopped suddenly.

"Paen-aye. Come over here my tupa. You're awake now. You can come take a look at the little fishes swimming along the edge. Maybe a turtle will come out. There was one over by that drift log a while ago."

Tupa's voice, talking in the language, sounded somehow like the ducks, the water, the bees buzzing and the song, all at the same time.

"Okay, Tupa. I just want to look at the coloured faces for a little while longer. Come see. I made them. They move."

She could hear her *tupa* crunch the sand as she stood and then the slow *swish, swish* of her footsteps coming toward her.

"Paen-aye! You made some painted faces out of the flowers on my shawl. And those white and grey pebbles they make pretty colours. You and the colours can talk, I see. They tell you things. Listen to them. They never lie. Come now, it's time to wash the sleep shadows away and drink some cold tea. Come, look! There is a turtle now, swimming toward the shore. It comes from the dark, down deep. It comes up into the light and the colours. It swims the song you were just singing. Lets sing the *Turtles Landing Song* before we go. Come, the lake was kind to us today."

Her and her *tupa* stood in front of the shining lake, with Turtle, bobbing in front of them just reaching shore and they sang *Turtles Landing Song*. Behind them the shawl tied onto four sticks in the sand brushed blue, gold, red and orange over the pebbles and the stick faces in the glittering sand and danced it's fringes along with the tall slender sweet clover.

Shmuuk! I should've just stayed home. What was I thinking? Oh well. Just go in. Don't sweat it. It can't be that much different than a rez party. A little music and laughs. Some booze. Smoke. Mostly snagging. It's research. You don't know a thing about this society. You gotta get a personal view of social customs. This must be how Margaret Mead felt.

From the street, Penny can hear the music. A couple of guys are outside standing on the lawn smoking up. They don't even look up at her as she walks by them to the front door and rings. When nobody answers, she rings again and a blonde woman, her hair in a huge afro, pulls the door open and yells.

"What? If you're here for the party just walk right in. I don't know where Florine is. If you're the Avon lady, fuck off. Ha, ha ha ha, I'm kidding."

She starts laughing hysterically and swings the door wide open before stepping back into the room. She doesn't even look at Penny or say anything else. She just starts dancing all by herself. Her pelvis jerking back and forth in time with the music. Her tight bell bottomed pants are cut low enough to see her belly button. Her eyes are closed. Her arms move in wide arcs around her, the long-sleeved stretch lace bodyshirt like a second skin.

She's flying high! I don't know if this is a good idea. I can smell the shit over the cigarette smoke. And it's only ten. I'll just stay for half-an-hour or so. Just so Florine knows I showed up.

Penny looks around her. Students crowd the living room floor, sitting or sprawled on the carpet munching chips, peanuts and other snacks. Beer, wine and soft drinks in their hands. Cigarette and marijuana smoke hangs thick in the dimly lit room. The music is so loud it vibrates inside her. People are shouting at one another.

Penny stands for a couple of minutes looking for Florine, or a place to sit. Nobody talks to her or even looks her way. In the corner of the room, a couple are twined together. The girl, back flat against the wall, pelvis thrust forward, is moving slowly back and forth with the music. The guy, his shirt loose over his pants, is pushing, pelvis to pelvis, against her, his back thigh muscles bulging at each thrust. Penny can see the sweat glistening on his forehead from where she stands. She looks away. Near the middle of the room, there is a space by the coffee table.

She sinks down onto the springy carpet. Beside her a small young woman with straight blonde hair, passes her the bowl of chips with one hand and tips her bottle of beer for a drink with the other. She looks at Penny over the butt of the bottle. The woman's eyes are slightly glazed, but she smiles at Penny when she lowers the bottle.

Man! Finally! Somebody actually can see me.

"Hi. I'm Julie. Want some chips? I hate these things. I don't know why I come. Free beer I guess. We're supposed to bring our own, but I never do. Somebody always splurges. You wanna drink or something? Florine said there was some in the kitchen, wherever that is. She's got a pretty nice place here. She must come from rich folk. You're in my political science class. You're new. First year always takes some getting used to. I'm almost a professional stu-dent. I'm a switched major. What're you taking?"

"Visual Arts."

"Oh. So how come political science? I thought fine art students spat on academia, if you can describe political science as such."

"I'm not really sure. I just liked the description of the course."

Julie is looking toward the kitchen doorway where Florine is now standing, looking worried. She looks around the room before mak-ing her way over to the stereo to turn down the volume and putting on a Credence Clearwater Revival album. As she turns back toward her guests, somebody pushes the door open.

"Hey everybody, this is a get-acquainted party. How're we supposed to do that if we can't hear each other? How about a little conversation?"

Nobody even looks at her. The couple in the corner stop, only to move together toward the dim hallway. There is some shifting around but nobody pays attention to Florine. The new guests are a couple of guys in sweat shirts and jeans and beers in their hands. Penny notices their square brush cuts, wide shoulders and bulging muscles. Julie has a slight sneer on her face.

"That's all we need. A couple of neanderthal jocks."

Penny looks around the room. The woman with the blonde afro at the door is still dancing, eyes closed. She hasn't stopped since Penny came in. A small group of young-looking female students are giggling and talking, their heads together. Several couples in the opposite corner are still talking loudly, discussing whether it would be better to keep renting or to scrape up a down payment for a house. A dozen others are scattered in groups of two or three sitting and drinking.

Opposite from her, she notices a dark frizzy head nodding. The head turns and his dark almond shaped eyes catch the flickering light for a moment. He smiles and his teeth sparkle white. Beside him, another guy with pale blonde hair hanging to his shoulders and a soft looking face with full pouty lips, is talking animatedly to him. His hand is resting on the other man's shoulder.

One of the guys in a grey sweat shirt with a big A in front staggers as he steps over legs and settles down near the group of giggling girls. He takes a long drink before leaning back drunkenly against one of the girls. She laughs but pushes him away and stands up. The others continue talking to each other but move away turning their backs. The guy at the door staggers and bumps into the girl with the afro. She mumbles something but Penny can't hear. He just stands looking around, swaying slightly. He looks at the two men opposite Penny and Julie.

"Hey Dean, what the hell kinda party we got here? Nothing but hippies, queers and immigrants. I told you we shoulda stayed over at the pub. What kinda fucking music is that? I wanna party, not go to sleep. Lets liven this thing up."

"Fuck you Brian."

He takes a couple of steps toward the stereo and deliberately kicks the blonde guy's leg out of his way.

"Move your faggot leg over. I'm gonna put some good music on."

The dark one with the friz half-stands as the blonde one's drink splashes over his shirt and neck.

"Shit! Watch it damn it! Goddamit!"

He stands, beer dripping from his front.

"What did you say? Watch it? You watch it, boy. You and your boyfriend, both watch it. We don't put up with your kind around here. You wanna fucking make something out of it?"

Julie is now standing up and Penny stands up, too. Everybody in the room is quiet.

"I said watch it."

Before he can add anything else, Brian pushes him back and he stumbles over the coffee table. He kicks out his foot and Brian grabs him by the ankle and drags him down and kicks him in the stomach. He grunts and rolls into a ball, flailing his arms. The blonde guy half-crawls away as Brian kicks him on the side. As he rolls onto his back, Brian is already kicking him again.

Florine shouts something. Julie beside her reaches over the coffee table, trying to push Brian from behind. Penny can hear somebody saying, "Kick him again, fucking faggot!" Brian reaches back and grabs Julie's blouse sleeve and jerks her forward and slams her on top of the blonde guy who is now puking.

"You, too, bitch and anybody that wants to butt in."

People shove and push and shout. Florine is screaming as she runs toward the hallway.

"Stop, stop. Please stop. I'm calling the cops."

The guy with the frizzy hair tries to get up as Brian pulls his leg back and kicks him in stomach, again. Julie crawls away toward the hallway, her blouse ripped open and half off her shoulder. Brian stands there laughing.

"Hey Dean look't the faggots crawl. Fucking A man. Can't fucking go to a decent party without them fucking crawling around. I'm gonna teach them a lesson."

He takes a step back and makes a move toward the blonde guy. Dean stands swaying drunkenly shouting.

"Kick him again. He's gonna get away."

Penny can see the blonde guy is hurt. Blood is dripping from his nose. She doesn't even hesitate. She moves quickly. She's around the coffee table in front of Brian before he can step back to kick again. She doesn't say a word.

He's big. His arms curled out, fists balled, his head back. She sees the surprise on his face as her hand lashes out and she whacks his adam's apple with the outer edge of her hand. She steps back as he gasps in pain and hunches forward, his arm moving up to his throat. She catches his wrist with both hands, stepping around him to wrench his arm backward over her shoulder. She can hear his grunt as his shoulder twists and she uses her hip to bump her full body weight into his back and side, throwing him off balance to the floor. She can hear him crash against the coffee table as she spins around. He rolls off hitting the floor, face down, with one arm up on the coffee table. She grabs his arm and twists it high up his back before he can roll over. Her foot, lodged square on his back gives her leverage against his arm. Every move he makes just pushes him forward away from the pain.

"I'm gonna break you're fucking arm if you even try to get up."

She's breathing hard, her adrenaline high.

"Get the cops, goddamn it! I'm gonna hold this sonofabitch till they get here."

She can hear scuffling and crashing behind her as the stereo tips over and bottles crash to the floor. She can hear Julie shouting.

"Jesus, keep that drunk back, push him back down. Christ, did you see that! She fucking judo flipped him! Break his arm Penny!"

It seems like only minutes and there is a siren and screeching tires in the street outside. By then, most of the students are either standing in the hallway, or outside. The girl with the afro is still by the door leaning against the coats by the door. She is smiling dreamily at Penny. Julie and the guy with the frizzy hair and the blonde are standing guard over Dean who is mumbling.

"I didn't do anything. I was just trying to get up to stop him. Let me up."

Florine rushes over to the door and opens it to the three cops who step into the room. One of them looks over at Penny still twisting Brian's arm. He's groaning and swearing.

"Okay, what's going on here? Is anybody hurt? Who's the owner of the house."

Florine shakes her head. "I am. I don't think anybody is. Not too bad anyway. Those two guys are drunk. We were having a social and those two guys crashed the party and are picking on my guests. Maybe they want to press charges. I just want them outa here."

The first cop calmly walks over and takes Brian's hand from Penny and cuffs it. He reaches around to pull his other arm and snaps the other cuff around it.

"Stand up. You're coming with me."

As he leads Brian out, one of the other cops is pushing Dean toward the door.

"Okay, you two. This is the second time this month. This time, you're gonna spend more than the night. We're gonna book you both for disturbing the peace and drunk and disorderly. Maybe you'll simmer down some. Let's go."

The third cop is talking to the blonde guy who is wiping blood from his nose and writing notes down. Finally he turns to Florine.

"I suggest you shut the party down. I don't want to have to take a look around. You get my meaning? I can smell more than beer in here. Go home everybody. Now! Bloody rich college students. No brains. No more parties here. You got that?"

With that he turns on his heel and walks out.

Penny's heart is still beating fast. Her face is still hot. She doesn't look at anybody. Nobody says anything for some minutes. Finally Florine clears her throat.

"I'm sorry people. I had no idea this would happen. I don't know what to say. Glen are you okay? And what about you Gerry? Oh Jesus, Julie, let me get you a sweater or something."

She suddenly covers her face with her hands and her shoulders start to shake. Julie walks over to her and puts her arm around her shoulder.

"Aw, It's not your fault. Those guys are always picking on some-body. That ass-hole Brian is a racist jerk. This is the best party I've ever been at. It was worth it, to see a woman flop him. Come on lets clean up a bit. Other than some sore guts, we're okay. You got any beer left? I sure could use one now."

As they pick up bottles and records, the guy with the frizzy hair touches Penny's shoulder.

"Thanks. I didn't see what you did, but I want to have you for a friend."

He grins at her.

"My names Glen. I could give you a lift if you don't have a ride. I got a motorbike. One of those Yamaha's. Not a Harley."

Penny looks at him. His eyes are sparkling again. His skin is olive and smooth. His mouth looks soft. His hand is still on her shoulder.

"Sure. I guess so. I came on the city bus. I'm Penny."

He is still looking at her.

"I'm impressed. I've never seen a woman handle a guy that way. Are you a black belt or something?"

Penny laughs. She doesn't move his hand from her shoulder. His hand is a warm weight. She can feel it's heat through her blouse.

"Naw. I grew up on a ranch. I could chuck fifty pound bales all day, by the time I was sixteen. I got two older brothers who don't have any mercy for girls when they wrestle. They taught me early how to handle guys for my protection, so watch out."

He laughs a clear ringing laugh.

"Believe me lady, I'm not about to make any move outa line with you. Lets go, okay?"

Outside, as he gets on his bike and kick starts it, he motions her to get on behind. She stands for a moment, hesitating. Finally, after she gives him directions to her place, she climbs on behind him. As he pulls away from the curb she has to put both arms around his waist to steady herself. The wind whips at her hair.

The ride is smooth. She can feel his muscles through his shirt. Each time he turns a corner she has to lean into his back pressing her face against his shirt. She can smell his skin. A clean soap smell. The narrow seat under her is smooth and hard. She can feel the steady rhythm of the engine between her legs. The inside of her thighs are squeezed tight to the outside of his. She can feel the heat rise in them, up into her groin.

This is crazy. This is research? First, flopping some guy and now riding a motorbike and getting a thrill. Jeez, settle down girl.

When he pulls up into her driveway and cuts the motor, he sits a minute not moving. She pulls hers arms away from around him and tries to climb off, almost falling as she steps down. Her knees are weak and shaky. He jumps off quickly and catches her around the waist with one arm, leaning to hold the bike up with the other. Suddenly his mouth is close to hers and she can feel his breath. She is breathing hard and can't step away. She feels her body move toward him and hears his quick intake of breath. He moves quickly and kicks the bike foot down to anchor it and turns full toward her.

I'm not gonna let him ride away. It's been way too long.

She makes the first move. Her body feels like it's on fire and she leans full against him. She can feel his muscles harden against her as his arms wrap around her and his breath turns ragged. His mouth finds hers and they kiss, mouths open, tongues touching. She can feel her heart hammering against his, her breasts pressed flat against his chest. They stand swaying against each other for some time. The night is soft around them. Above them, the leaves are making a fluttering sound. Neither of them speak as they stop to stare at each other. Her blood is racing as they turn and walk to the door.

LETTER TO DONNA

Hey Donna:

How are things at the Friendship Centre? Just as political as ever, I suppose. Do you think maybe it's because there aren't many chances for people to actually have a little control in anything? I was thinking that, the other day, when I was putting together an outline for my political science paper. I was trying to figure out how to work the Friendship Centre politics into a topic that could use the reading texts for reference, though, and it's a problem. The topic is to question the current political system and how it impacts the population it serves.

I guess I don't know much about how other people live. I was too busy living hand-to-mouth the last six years, trying to keep the kids in clothes and food, to observe anything else. I come from the reserve. That's all I know. And you know the reality there. There isn't anything anybody can get a job at. The few steady jobs are in the administration. That's it. And all those jobs are taken up for life, almost. Only a few jobs change hands in a decade, if there is an election turnover, or somebody dies. The reality is eighty percent welfare, except for the few bigger landholders, and they don't count. Some of them are on it, too, if they don't want to lease out their lands for industrial or trailer parks.

What I've come to understand is: if you don't have "capital" to start with or borrowing power or business education or a few generations of merchants in your background, you just can't start anything. I'm no different. But no welfare for me. My family always worked or made do with a little farming and trapping. I resist welfare like my mom does. She always makes things to sell for extra cash. And we grew what we ate. She still does, even after she lost my dad. But it's just too hard that way. Although I sure miss the good food. I hate Kraft Dinner.

I only know how hard it is to get a decent job if you are a woman or worse a NATIVE. Even the worst jobs are always filled. Did you know that the government gives money to companies willing to hire minorities, Natives or women? What does that mean? Is that an impact? Maybe I should look at the stats on unemployed women, Natives and minorities and compare what the government gives as employer incentives against the cost of education for them. Maybe I should do a comparison on all the freebies to business. It just irks me, that even when they pretend they're helping the poor, they're actually helping business.

I don't know. I just know you can't feed and clothe three kids properly with a single minimum wage and pay rent and pay taxes and UIC and CPP and Union Dues. Over a third of your check gets taken. The biggest part to income taxes. Income taxes!!! Think of it. Paying the government for the privilege to work!!! While the government gives out taxbreaks to business and hands out taxfree, raw resources to them. As if each person didn't already pay the government taxes every single time they buy anything. What further cut does that make it? Sales tax, Goods and Services Tax, Provincial Service Tax and municipal landowner's tax and so on. Does anybody know how much out of each dollar really goes to the government with all that? What about those hidden taxes? In gas and oil for cars and heating and in electricity and in alcohol and tobacco? Are those impacts of the current political system? You bet your ass.

No wonder it's easier to stay on welfare. Do you think that's part of the scheme? So a percent of the population stays on welfare. So there is always a reserve corps of the jobless, happy to pay for the privilege to work? Could it be that people have to be kept so busy surviving that they can't afford to question it? So that they keep paying and the companies keep profiting and the government stays fat on all the "service" jobs maintaining that system?

Anyway, I'm rambling on. I don't know what topic I could come up with that would make academic sense. The reserve population and the off-reserve Native population just isn't representative of THE population, if you know what I mean. I don't know much about the CANADIAN political system much less how it might impact the population it serves. I don't think it serves the population you and I represent. Come to think of it, it seems like it's the population that serves the political system.

If you have any thoughts on this, could you give me a shout. I was sitting up late typing on this old typewriter and thought it was about time I let you know I'm doing the college thing. I wanted to thank you for talking me into it. The painting and printmaking courses are just about the best thing I have ever done in my life. I sorta like my English teacher, too. And guess what? I took a statistics math instead of the business courses you recommended. I like the way anything can be connected and compared as patterns. It's revealing. And the political science, well, I'm indulging myself on that one.

Times are tough so I can't come home for Christmas. Send some care package stuff, instead of presents. Beans, rice and flour. The Indian education allowance doesn't get past the middle of the month after rent and the kids' other needs, never mind gas, books and art supplies. You gotta be an economist to stretch what I stretch. I wouldn't trade this for anything right now, though.

Oh! and I met this great guy. He sleeps over sometimes. He's an artist, too. He's a "minority" but doesn't know which one because he's a mix of a lot of things. He kinda looks like an Indian but with frizzy hair. I talk with him a lot. But no permanent thing for me. No. No. No. The kids are great. They like their school. Elementary school! All of them at last!

I miss the griping and hissing around the Friendship Centre. Stay on top.

Only, Pennies

Professor Larkin leans toward Bob, listening intently. The chairs are close together and some of the other students are pushing in to hear what Bob is saying. The pitcher of beer is almost empty and there are empty glasses crowding the centre of the table. *Strawberry Moon* is playing. The hot sweet saxophone voice of Grover Washington insistent above the chatter and laughter of other students crowding the lounge. Julie, sitting next to Penny, is twirling her finger in a wet spot on the slick table top.

Bob gestures with his hand, a chopping motion.

"What I meant is, there aren't enough management jobs right now, let alone for the surge coming out of business college. And what's the alternative? We know there are too many doctors, lawyers and teachers, so that's not an option. And semi-professional trades? Accountants, nurses and dental technicians galore! And the blue collar trades? Well! Nobody even cares if they strike anymore. They just find ways to lay them off legally and hire others lined up for the jobs. Even though they might be necessary, I don't support trade unions. They just drive up the cost of things."

Bob looks around checking to see if anyone will disagree. Nobody does. Professor Larkin leans back slowly removing his wire framed glasses. He takes a white and blue handkerchief out of his breast pocket and polishes the glasses. Bob watches his blue-veined knobby fingers and clears his throat before continuing.

"Who the hell determines what? Somebody sure got their statistics wrong. Business management is a mistake. We're at saturation point now. Oh sure, some of us'll fit into the picture, but what about the ones that don't. Move to South America? That's the trend all right, but who wants to do that? We know big development swallows up little companies. Management has to get smaller. And automation! It's cutting out jobs everywhere. What'll all of it mean to our complacent middle class? A future with just two classes? A high income class and the poor? And us, ending up edu-cated and jobless?"

Bob drains his beer and draws a long breath before running his fin-gers through his longish brown hair. Professor Larkin leans back and steeples his finger over his chest. He is about to make a com-ment. All the students look at him expectantly.

"You certainly have some strong points there, Bob. But you don't go quite far enough in your analysis on the trade unions. They should be dispensed with altogether. They're an archaic leftover of the past, but that's another discussion."

He clears his throat, his large, pointed adam's apple jumping up and down, before taking a long drink then licking the foam off his thin wet lips.

"I want to respond to your comment on management reduction. Bob, we're in an age of postwar building. Sure, it means strong competition. But it also means incentive tax breaks and bank rates going down. It attracts investment. Voila! More big companies! More big companies, more management, that's the formula."

Julie burps loudly. He peers through his wire framed glasses at Julie and frowns slightly. Julie is now lazily tracing the slick rim of her glass with her index finger before sticking the tip of her finger in her mouth and licking it with a slurpy smacking sound. The pro-fessor looks away quickly.

"Now, whether automation will impact lower management or not, is an interesting question. The biggest impact will be on labour, not on upper management. So you best shoot for those business degrees. More money in the system will boost the economy, not the other way around. As for the middle class shrinking? Actually, it all adds up to an expansion as labour gets smaller. That would be a good thing don't you agree?"

He smiles a thin triumphant smile. Bob, now scowling, scratches his head and looks around the table. But nobody offers to make any comment. George Thorogood's Bad to the Bone is now thumping hardrock bass over the speakers. Nobody except Julie looks at Bob. Julie takes a long drink of her beer and sets the glass down with a slight bang. She leans forward, her blouse slightly agape. There is a momentary flash of her rounded white breast. She opens her mouth and flicks her tongue over her lips before she speaks.

"And why the hell should labour getting smaller mean a bigger middle class? Actually it'll mean bigger unemployment. Bigger poverty. Bigger work subsidy spending. Bigger welfare. The first obvious thing is, if you project that picture over a twenty to thirty year period, say to our retirement age, you can see a big problem. The second thing is, only so much development can happen. You reach a point when it flattens and competition dissolves. Economic inertia."

Professor Larkin coughs slightly. He turns and half-nudges the skinny male student sitting next to him. The student nods at him and rolls his eyes. The professor turns back toward Bob and raises his eyebrows.

"Third, those of us baby boomers still around will bear the brunt of that bullshit. Costs would need to be cheaper. And stuff only the rich can now afford, will be cheap, cheap, cheap. You know why? Lower prices have to have steady sales. Things have to break sooner so more can be sold. Quantity over quality. Everything would have to be able to compete. Even education would suffer. More glorified job training. Bye, bye real university education. It couldn't do anything else."

Julie drums her index finger on the tables edge with the music as she stops briefly to look around the room.

"Finally, price drops mean less returns, yet wage scales increase. Companies would either cut wages, or cut jobs. Government would subsidize, of course, to prop up business. Then it would have to cut. Guess where? Basic social services, of course! Or, worse, it would steal from us! From security we buy, like the Canada Pension or the UIC. Our money. I think we could end up with a huge government deficit."

The students around the table stare at her. Professor Larkin closes his eyes and leans his head back. Bob smiles at her. She is still smiling but her foot is tapping on the floor under the table. Nobody says a word. They wait. Nobody even takes a drink. Finally Professor Larkin opens his eyes but he doesn't look at her. He speaks to the ceiling.

"And I thought the discussion was about whether business students should change career choices. If this is an economics debate, then perhaps one should at least have sound basics upon which to postulate. My dear, there are too many complex factors to make such simplistic assumptions. In any case, it is late, and I should take my leave. If some of you lads would like to take this further, I'll see you in class."

Professor Larkin doesn't even look at her as he rises and puts on his coat. He straightens his tie, drums his fingers on the table a moment then turns and walks quickly to the door.

The students around the table busy themselves looking elsewhere. They all suddenly start talking at once. The skinny student, almost tripping over his chair, quickly follows the professor. Several others also stand to leave. Only Bob is still looking at her. Julie's face has gone red.

"Damn, Julie, that made a lot of sense to me. I think he's a pompous ass and always wants to be right. So, okay, I grant that what you say could happen, but what does it mean for us? What? That's what started this whole discussion. I was thinking of going into computer science or something. It's a new field you know? If what you say is true, then maybe I shouldn't worry, should I?"

Julie has the attention again of the remaining students. She takes another drink and slowly sets her glass down.

"He's a frigging sexist is what he is! It doesn't take an economist to put two minus three together. And it would probably be a god-damn surprise to that starched shirt, that I was a third year economics major. I switched. There's no future in it for me. Too much male competition. Political science and social anthropology makes more sense to me, if I wanta help change things. One thing is certain, I won't be taking his business science class next term. He left because he didn't want a female making more sense than his lame-ass theories."

"No wonder you rattled that off like a lecture. You showed him up. He's a Mr. Know-it-all. He always has a rational response. He hangs around the students talking superior. He never leaves, even when the discussion gets stupid."

"Well, whatever. He also suffers from right-wing elitism. Dispense with the trade unions! Now that takes the cake! Job security would be out the door. And what would replace it? Short term contracting, that's what! Without benefits. The bottom would drop out of the bucket. Prices would spiral down. Of course, big companies would cash in for awhile. But that would end as the buying power dried up. One by one they would crumble. Big monopolies! That's what we'd end up with. Shoot! I think there's something scarier looming on the horizon."

Bob leans toward her and the other students do as well. They are staring at her again. Bob starts to say something but Julie shakes her head. She drains her glass and pours some more.

"I gotta think this through. I need a closer look at what's happening on a wider scale. No doubt, the government'll fuck-up big time, propping up it's economy. They would have to push our resources to outside developers to balance internal losses. That would trash Nationalism. We would just end up another labour pool, helping them to pack off our resources. Money would drain out. The economic gap would widen. It would mean a scramble for resources not yet extracted, here and everywhere else. It could mean countries warring over who controls what."

Bob fills his glass and takes a long drink. He looks at her over his glass for some moments. The other students look at each other and then back to Bob.

"Jesus, Julie. Stop already! That's too far out there. I just wanna know if I should stay in a business major in order to make it. Even if that happens, what does it mean to me? To us sitting here? What?"

Julie laughs and turns her glass around and around. She looks up at Bob and smiles a wide ultrabright smile.

"It looks like flipping burgers or South America for you, buddy, whichever of the three scenarios mentioned here tonight. But computers! Now there's a good bet. It's gonna take over business. Oh, I don't know, I'm just postulating, as that ass-hole, who huffed out of here, would fling at me."

She looks over at Penny, who has been sitting silently listening.

"What about you, Penny? You haven't said a word. What do you think?"

When Penny doesn't answer she pushes on.

"Come on, you're in my political science class. You said some things yesterday that sounded pretty radical. You always disagree with everything."

She is looking directly at Penny, challenging her to respond. Penny still doesn't.

"Hey you guys, did you know Penny's an Indian? I never met one before. She's the legend. The one last fall, who flopped Brian, that redneck ass-hole jock, who likes to pick on anybody with skin darker than Casper. She's absolutely irreverent to the status-quo. Are you an anarchist Penny?"

Julie's voice is slurring over some of her syllables. Her cheeks are pink and there is a wet spot on the front of her white blouse.

Penny eyes blaze as she looks at Julie steadily for several seconds. Finally she shrugs her shoulders and with one swift movement drains her ginger ale. Her voice is tight and angry sounding when she does speak.

"None of it makes a damn bit of difference anyway. The whole system is set up to suck everything from the powerless to serve the rich. Every one of you will just end up making more money for them. For their limousines and vacations and jewellery and facelifts, no matter which courses you take. Nobody even stops to think that those resources out there weren't made by the government. Why should only those who already have money profit from them? Maybe there's something wrong with the whole bloody system which drives it all. Maybe it's brainwashing at it's best and you're all sheep being herded around."

Her voice suddenly seems to echo in the room as the music stops momentarily. Julie is grinning at Penny and Bob is glaring at her. Nobody says a word and the whole room is quiet. Students all over the room are looking at them and listening. There are two red spots glowing on her cheeks and her hands are shaking but she continues.

"And by the way, I don't have a damn thing to be revenant about. And that goes a long way back to every extinct tribe and every missing buffalo. An anarchist? I don't have a clue. An Indian? You got that one right. And don't ever forget it. I'm gonna call it a night, too, before I say things none of you deserve."

As she stands and slowly puts her coat on, she deliberately looks around the table at each student. Every one of them, including Bob, looks down or away. Nobody responds. It's as though a big silent gulf has opened up between her and everyone else in the room. As she is walking toward the door she can hear Julie clapping.

"See what I mean? She hit the nail right on the head. It doesn't make a damn bit of difference unless we fucking change the system! Revolution! Revolution! It's the only solution!"

Julie knocks her half-empty glass over and beer spills onto the floor. She laughs, stands it upright and fills the glass again, sloshing the foam over the rim. Bob isn't smiling at her anymore. He's scowling again. The soft cajun rock sounds of Maria Maldaur's, *Midnight at the Oasis*, is playing and the chatter lulls momentarily. Students listen briefly and then continue, the buzz growing steadily in momentum.

She sat sideways, her legs hanging over the side of her Tupa's bony dark skirted lap. Tupa's thin gravelly voice was sing song talking. Naming her. "Paen-aye."

Saying her English name in the sounds of their language. Speaking it.

"My own Tupa, myyyyyy Tupaaaaa."

Claiming her.

The bright sun was slanting through the narrow window. The dust sparkling and swirling in it with her and Tupa's every breath. There was the smell of smoke and dried meat and leather. And the sharp smell of the long wolf hide hanging behind Tupa. A strong solid smell.

Her poppa, a tall shadowy figure with black black braids, was smiling, holding out his arms toward her. And standing beside him, her momma, thick brown braids down to her waist. Granma and Granpa sat at the long wooden table with her sisters, Lena and Josalie, and her brothers, Charlie and Andrew.

She could hardly say their names right. It was hard to make the right sounds. She knew her name was Penny but *Paen-aye* sounded right.

Tupa's voice carried on, rolling over sounds and words she could not keep up with. She wished her poppa to pick her up and swing her around and up. She wanted him to bounce her on his knee singing, "Wah cha kek, wah cha kek, wah chek, our pinto pony, wah cha kek, wah cha kek, wah chek."

Instead he picked her up, hugged her and sat her down on the floor. He took down the long gun hanging on the wall. The shiny blue of the metal glinted in the sun momentarily. She watched and thought of the scary sound it made. He walked away from her to the door. She wanted him to come back. To play with her. To not leave her.

She watched the door open as the wide shaft of warm yellow spilled across the brown wooden floor with the thin slits of dark cracks. Outside the trees and the sky and flowers were all colours. She wanted to go out there. To look at the colours. They were moving and dancing like the dust in the air. Her *tupa* was singing a sweet song about the dancing colours. She knew it was about the dancing colours. It moved the very same.

She could hear her poppa whistling as he walked down the trail. The yellow, yellow sunlight and the trees and the colours and the dust dancing, mingling by song breath and her poppa walking down the trail. That fleeting moment caught between darkness.

I can't do it. I'm, gonna crack. It's just too hard. How the hell did I ever think I could do this.

The door is open part way and she can see Glen sitting at the kitchen table sipping coffee. His dark mass of friz curls frames his face. His almond shaped eyes are on her latest painting, studying it intently. He takes a long drag on his cigarette and moves his head sideways puckering his full lips.

"Penny, honey. You know, I think your piece here is working out. I would say that this definitely has feeling. Some of your pieces seem so . . . oh I don't know . . . without passion lately. I like the way you used the lines, though, to move the eye around the composition. What's taking so long in there? We should get going. I wanted to get to the opening a little early, if you don't mind. You want some help dressing?"

What do I say? What? I want you, but I don't want you. I want to stop this. Stop what? This tug-of-war? But the tug-of-war is only me fighting with myself. I'm starting to feel too close. Too close to you? To what? I don't need something permanent, I only need . . . what? To use you? No, not that. But that's what it comes down to, unless I straighten it out. Oh, man, I'm shaking. I've got to talk. Things are getting way too comfortable.

"Glen . . . I was thinking . . . Do we need to go to that opening right now? I wanted to talk. Or maybe you should just go ahead without me."

"What's the matter, hon? You feeling okay? If you want us to just not go, that's okay too. You seemed a million miles away for little while in there. I must say, I wanted to see Ruth's work open, but we could always go to the gallery later to see it. You know I'd rather be with you. Talk about what?"

Why does he always have to be so nice? That's just it. Too damned nice. And pretty soon I'll give in. He'll move all his stuff over and that'll be it. And I'll have to live with the tug-a-war every day. I can't ! I can't! I need space to be. To be what? Lonely? To be a bonafide loony? No! An artist! What's that? I have to make a choice here. Why does it have to be a dilemma? Why is this stuff so damn hard on me? Why couldn't I just be normal. What's normal? Is full time mating normal? Isn't that what living together really is? What about companionship? Do we have to live together for that? Oh God, I'm selfish, selfish, selfish. That's the issue. And I can't help it.

"Glen, I'm sorting out some things. I guess. I'm kinda feeling like we're getting pretty serious together. Are we, or what?"

"I don't understand. Yeah, I'm serious about you. I want to be with you all the time. Do you want to talk about us moving in together?

It's about time! I've been hinting pretty broadly about that. We're good together. We could share expenses and stuff. Penny. I was even thinking of . . . you know . . . making the big leap. I even like your cooking!"

Oh no. What do I say now? This is just what I didn't want him to say right now! What do I say? I can't hurt him. My cooking! What's that got to do with it!

"Glen, I've been dreading this conversation. I guess. It's just that I'm not really cut out to be a live-in partner. I . . . I don't know . . . I can't really put it into words. I mean I have this feeling like I can't be myself. It's like I have to make myself be normal or something. I know. We have a really nice thing. We have a great time. It's not you. It's me. My art dominates everything. Even me. I mean being a mom and with other family too."

"But, I'm an artist, too. I can live with that. I'm pretty weird about it, too. We could work around that together."

"Oh, I know. It seems to make sense, but it's really not the painting, I guess, either. It's something else, like an obsession or a quest for something. I don't know what. It owns me. I do my best with the kids. I have to. And I'd die for them, but even there, a part of me resents the burden. It's like having two heads. One is trying to think and do everyday stuff and the other is off on another plane, whispering or yelling stuff at me. Always."

"It sounds to me like you've been working too hard again. You just drive yourself. You wouldn't have to if I could take on some of the everyday stuff, as you put it. You know people go stark raving mad, if they get too stressed."

Cripes, now he'll say I should get some mental counselling. Maybe I do need it! Maybe I am crazy! They say people don't know when they are.

"I don't know. It's not stress. I was like that since I can remember. I just learned how to act normal around people. Oh shit. I don't want to analyze me. I just wanted to sorta make sure you have a clear understanding about what we're doing. I don't want to mis-lead you."

"Mislead me? What exactly are you saying? That you just been pre-tending to be in love with me? That you don't want me around? Are we breaking up? Penny, I can't stand this!"

Glen is now standing, his hands are pressed to the top of the table and his eyes are burning at her. He's shaking ever so slightly. She can see the muscles in his jaw quiver.

No! Yes! Oh, what to do? What to say? He's not getting what I'm trying to explain.

"Glen. Don't. I'm just trying to tell you that I don't want things to get farther than they are. I feel like shit right now. I enjoy being with you but not to live together. I can't get to that. "

"You can't or you won't? Either way it sounds like a cooling off to me. Look, I'm not pressuring you to make a move on it. But we've been a thing now, going on two years. I want something stable. I'm alone. I don't want to be. Maybe I should just go. What's so hard? Don't answer. I'll just be on my way. I'll call you later."

She watches as Glen walks stiffly to the door.

Don't stop him. No! Let him walk away! Oh, why does it hurt so much? We can be friends. Don't even move.

The door opens letting in a gust of icy wind. Fine bits of powder snow swirl lightly in the air for a few seconds after the door shut gently behind him. She can still smell his scent on her. She can still feel his breath warm on her neck, from earlier, listening to Koko Taylor, in her warm bed. There is a deep silence, settling in the house as she sits, finally, on the kitchen chair and lays her head on the table's red formica top. Saturday night is coming down.

*I*t was night and she and her sisters slept in a double bed and she whispered to herself as someone snored loud. She whispered and there were lights, tiny ones floating by in the dark. She whispered to them. Then the snoring stopped and someone coughed and the lights vanished. The colours were spectacular.

Sometime, after midnight, Julie awoke. The room is dark and she can hear someone rustling in the next room.

"Penny? Is that you?"

"Yeah, Julie it's me. You feeling okay?"

"Not really. How'd I get here?"

Penny stands at the door. A dark shadow framed against the light behind her.

"Oh, I brought you after we left the student lounge. You looked like you needed to sleep awhile. At least I wasn't gonna let you get on the bus alone. You can stay the night here. The kids are next door for the night with Mrs. Beamer. It's Saturday tomorrow any-way. I'm about to make a cup of coffee. You want some?"

"Yeah. I guess. That'll settle things down."

"Julie . . . I'm gonna work on my paper for awhile, I think. I got some ideas after that discussion earlier. Before things went down-hill. You know I was thinking about what you said about competi-tion and free enterprise."

"Oh yeah. I sorta remember. Most of it. Oh God! I remember leav-ing now. Shit, I guess I told that bugger from engineering off. Riffraff my ass. He's the riffraff. What the hell do they do to those guys anyway? Do they all hate minorities, women and the poor? I guess I didn't have to call him Spock either. Not that that's really an insult, from his view. He probably thinks I paid him a compli-ment. He probably thinks having absolutely no feelings is a bloody virtue! Imagine that. I'll have to think about that whole episode and it's message to the devoted fans. What's it really saying? What morals we should be embracing? Huh? Well what's your take?"

Julie sits up looking animated again. Penny stands a minute looking at her and laughs.

"Julie, you amaze me. You were passed out cold ten minutes ago. Anyway, I'm gonna get that coffee pot going. I have some Indian corn stew. I'm gonna have some. Join me. I think you're right about Spock and the Enterprise, though. I mean how obvious. The only other Spock anybody ever heard of was Dr. Spock, and I think his advice may just create the worst future disaster of the century. But actually I get a kick out of science fiction. Maybe it's the continuous search that's the main metaphor of Star Trek. The holy grail, maybe?"

"Oh, you artists. Metaphor, smetaphor! The search is always for the treasure. It's about enterprise. You know, ENTER and PRIZE. The prize is money or power, which equate to each other. No matter how cute the rules work. There is always a boss in command."

"But that's what a metaphor is!"

Penny laughs and pads away into the little kitchen.

As Julie slowly stands and takes a few steps toward the door, she can hear the water running. She straightens and smooths her hair.

"Penny, mind if I take a shower? I feel like I have cobwebs stuck to me. I'll join you in a flash. Yeah, the stew sounds like a good idea, too. I can't really handle booze that good. It's just that I always feel so stiff in a crowd, you know? And then I just get carried away . . ."

"You don't have to explain anything. I stick to ginger ale because I like to stay crystal clear. I might miss something. I just go to listen. I'm getting my education at the drinking hole. Go get under the shower. There's towels under the sink."

Penny is just dishing herself some thick corn and dried deermeat stew when Julie comes out, towelling her hair. She has on Penny's checkered robe.

"I was thinking about competition in there. About free enterprise. I wonder when that idea got started? Did people compete for the aristocracy's business in Europe? Didn't it used to be, that trade guilds were like big families who specialized and who shared the work, from the gophers and apprentices up to the masters? Wasn't quality the main idea of a guild?"

Penny points in the direction of the cupboard.

"There are some bowls right up there and I already poured you some coffee. I only have sandwich bread if you want some. It's right over there on the counter."

"Yeah, thanks, but I had a thought. Maybe it's just behavioural. An old psychology that isn't necessary anymore. Psychology can be changed."

Penny chuckles and motions Julie in the direction of the comfortable looking champagne lounge chair with bright satin pillows.

"You just don't stop, do you? Eat. Drink coffee. I have the time to listen and I really am interested. It's more than just a discussion topic for me."

"Penny, this chair is heaven. I would never have thought of putting it in the kitchen. All your chairs in here are great. That's the trouble with us displaced Europeans. We think of kitchen chairs for the kitchen and sitting room chairs for the living room. To you a chair is to sit on. Period. Comfortably if possible. You're always so radical. I like it."

Penny looks up, stops chewing momentarily, and blushes.

"Maybe not knowing stuff like that is radical. I'm not sure. But I think it's just common sense. Anyway going back to your points about when competition for the right to make money all started. Maybe guilds were undercut by outsiders. Maybe outsiders undercut because there was more being produced than was actually needed. Maybe they offered things cheaper because their quality wasn't as high and they didn't live there so they could get away with it. I don't know. That's why I wanted to hear your thinking on it."

"Yeah, the thing is, competition has to lower quality. Things have to be made cheaper and cheaper. Mass production! That's it! That's what upset the applecart. That would've knocked the guilds right off line. Manufacturing versus individual pride in your handiwork. Everything from shoes to bread. Even clothing. Could you imagine making a shirt and decorating it with hand embroidery and so on? Competition is driven by affordability. How many shirts do you own?"

Penny looks toward her closet.

"I don't know for sure. Why?"

"Lets count them. Come on, Pen. And you're probably poor, like most students, in comparison to somebody with a real job."

Julie stands up. Her bowl is already empty. Penny smiles.

"Holee, I didn't even see you take a bite! Come on, Julie, you don't mean that!"

"Yeah, I do! Let's do it just for fun, okay?"

Penny follows Julie to her closet.

"Julie . . . "

"Wheeee! Look! One, two, three, four, five blouses on hangers. Got any casual cotton shirts in your dresser? Lets see . . . okay! One, two, three, four . . . what about teeshirts and pullovers. No sweaters though, to be fair. Oh here we are . . . bonanza! One, two, three, four, teeshirts. One, two, three short sleeve pullovers and two turtle neck pullovers. What does that make it? Seventeen? You got one on and how many in the laundry? No hold outs!"

"Jeez, you're embarrassing me! I like a clean shirt every day. I have about three or four dirty ones in the laundry."

"Penny, that's over twenty! Twenty shirts! Of various styles and textures and colours. Now tell me, Penny. Do you need twenty? How many do you really need? Huh? See my point? You would have had to have been upper-class rich, in the days before mass production, to own twenty shirts. Then, you probably owned one good embroidered one for company. A plain everyday one and one sturdy one for work. Yes?"

"Julie . . . That's an absolutely great way to illustrate it. And those shirts were all cheap-o. It's all I can afford. A person with an income might have forty or so! Holy cow! That's ridiculous! Stop now. I get the point. Lets go back to the kitchen. I want another cup of coffee."

Julie doesn't stop talking on the way to the kitchen.

"It's like that with everything. Everything! I remember mom having only one pair of good shoes and one pair for everyday. She used to wash the dishes so carefully not to chip them. Now sets are replaced almost yearly. Like everything else."

"Anyway, going back to the idea of enterprise and exploitation, where do you think that idea came from? I mean, the fantasy. Like Cinderella. The idea of somehow finding the treasure and turning into a princess, with jewels, servants and so on. Isn't that what it is? The whole idea of free enterprise is that anybody could get rich."

"I think that's what drives it alright. Like I said, psychology. Everybody believes in that dream. They work all their lives toward it. It's what creates big business. Big bucks for somebody. And most of us can't look at what it's doing. We just dream of making it and try to keep a foothold on the ladder. Shit, is what is happening, that's what. The resources are getting plundered and everything polluted. Do you know the extent of damage that free enterprise has caused? Never mind the fact that there is a rigid class system, as a result, keeping the rich powerful and the poor powerless. The same class system which got the whole thing going, keeps it going. But the horrible condition it's causing! That's what I'm getting at. It's not just a human philosophical issue. It's effecting the environment and it's getting worse. It's got to effect people in the end."

Penny takes a sip of coffee and lights a cigarette. She watches the smoke curl up in the air above her.

"I never thought of those connections, I guess. I've really just been trying to get a handle on the economics thing and poverty."

"Well, there are lots of ways to look at poverty. North America is wealthy with resources, so why is there so much poverty? Anyway the poverty is in what we have become. I'm going to a festival rally next weekend on the environment. There'll be several good speakers talking about this stuff. You wanna come? You could bring the kids. It's more or less a campout. You could paint some outdoor scenes. You might meet some great guys, too. That weirdo you sometimes hang out with might like it, too."

Penny laughs.

"He's not a weirdo! He's an artist. Anyway, we're just friends, really. I'm not serious about him. I'll see. Maybe I will go. Let's get some sleep. I'm bushed."

Outside the wind is blowing. The moon is shining in through the window into the dim living room. The shadows of the trees move across the floor. Her easel, with a new painting, using squares and hard edge lines, is glowing with moonlight and dappled over with moving treelimb shadows. From outside, she can hear blues music drifting by, from a party nearby. She sits on a silver-green brocade covered chair with satin pillows. The moon-washed light and the shadow-leaves over the grid of blues and greys whisper urgently to her.

LETTER TO JULIE

Julie:

I wanted to let you know that things are pretty crazy here at UVIC. But I love it. I'm glad I decided to come here in the end to finish off. That year at UBC was too weird for me. I know. I know. It's been too long since I last wrote. How are you doing, my friend? I wish you could be here. There are lots of good discussion groups. You know, I always wanted to tell you how much I admired your views. I guess I never really said it, but you are the one who inspired me in this direction. I made my first real painting break-through after that time we went to that environmental campout. Remember that tall tree that they were lighting up with strobes to make it look like it was dancing with the hundreds of people surrounding it, that night at the concert? That image is a theme that I have been exploring for the past few years in all kinds of media. I have had several pretty good shows at smaller galleries. And I get to talk about technology and it's effects on the natural world.

After living in Victoria, and before this, in Vancouver, I see exactly what you mean. You should see the miles and miles of cut logs moored along the Fraser. And the sludge from every kind of industrial operation is something else. It stinks. Them salmon must be choking! And you know, I took the kids to Beacon Hill park over here, to the beach. Cripes, the garbage that washes up! You'd think the ocean is too big to pollute! It's dangerous. It makes me so outraged! How could it be allowed? It's like one huge bloody rape scene. No wonder you got so fanatical. You are right to be so full of rage! How could any sane person not be?

I wish things had gone better for you. I'm still here to listen, my friend. You know I heard from some of the old college crowd back in the Okanagan, that you went away for awhile. It's good to know that you've given up the juice. Did you ever try to figure out what addiction really is? Don't say it's just psychology either. I've been thinking about us, the human, as "natural environment", too. Aren't we? I don't mean as individuals. I mean the body human. How is the human organism, as one whole unit, faring in what it has wrought? The pinnacle of evolvement? After eons of other life forms perfect-ing the cosmos for us to be able to exist? I attended several really interesting workshops on Healing the Wounds, Healing the Earth. There seem to be a lot of addiction's "Healing" workshops spring-ing up everywhere. In one of them an American woman spoke about being wounded by technology. She has a book out on it. I thought about you and thought you might be interested. Let me know if you want to come out here and rest awhile, again.

Anyway, as I said, it was truly not an accident, from my view, that you appeared, like a warm lantern on a moonless night. I do appreciate you and thank you for your rage. I hope we can visit next time I'm home. It's always so hectic, when I get back. Everybody in the big, big family I come from, wants a chance to visit. And the kids! You wouldn't recognize Shanna. She's a teenager now! My God how time flies. Like the bird of paradise. Most times up your nose, too! The other two are fine.

Pen-sive too (at times).

Cars are parked for as far as she can see. People in halters and sarongs, shorts and teeshirts, hippie dresses and sandals and beads and blue jeans are streaming up ahead on the narrow rutted and dusty road. There is dust everywhere and it makes her throat and eyes itch. The striped tops of the big tents are just visible ahead, behind some trees.

I'm going to keep going and not stop until I get to a spot that looks like we could camp next to our car. If not, I'm going to back all the way outa here and go home!

"Mom, can't we just go back to Vancouver? It's so dusty and hot here. And look at all the cars. We'll never get to find a spot to camp. Why do we have to be here all weekend anyway? You only got half an hour tomorrow, for your talk. Look at all those old timers with beards and beads! My hair is going to look like shit with all this dirt!"

Not now! Pleaseee. I can't take it.

"Shanna! Don't you use words like that! You hear? And don't start that again. You'll enjoy the concert tonight. And everybody's hair will be the same. There's a great lake further past the festival site, where you could wash it. I went swimming there when I was up here to help set up. Old timers or not, there are a lot of young people that I can see. Anyway, they're not old timers, they're the same as me. Let's have a good time, okay?"

"Well, I don't mean you. It just seems like we always have to go to these things. It's boring. I'd rather be in Vancouver. There's more stuff happening there. Anyway the music is always stupid."

Oh, man. This is just great! It's so packed! I hope we can at least park within walking distance of the car.

"Shanna, you brought your ghetto blaster, with a suitcase full of tapes. Dustin, did you remember to put your fishing stuff in the back? It was still out on the steps when I was loading the sleeping bags."

"Ahh . . . ya . . . I think so, mom. But I didn't bring my flippers. I forgot. Shanna, you always say that about everything. Then you meet some friends and you want to stay forever."

"Shut up, you Bean Sprout! Just because you don't have a clue, doesn't mean I have to listen."

"All right, that's enough. You'll just be fine once we get settled. We can all cool off. It sure is dusty. I hope the campsite isn't. I was hoping to hear that guy from Greenpeace this afternoon. What about you Merrilee, you haven't said a word for over an hour. Are you feeling okay?"

"Merrilee?"

"Ummmm . . . huh?"

"Are you okay?"

"Sure, Mom. I was just kinda wondering if I shoulda left my flute home. I don't wanna ruin it. With this dust and everything. But I wanted to practise some more. I'm just about getting this really hard part . . . It goes something like this . . . laaaa liiiiiii llliiiii-iii . . . it's sweet."

"Sweet! Oh great! And we have to listen to you squeak around all day and night, too, I suppose! Sure it'll be a great weekend . . . And I suppose I have to babysit you all the time, too!"

"Shanna, don't be mean to your sister! You bet you got to watch out for her. And no, I don't think dust will get inside. It's pretty sturdy. You can practise as much as you want. There'll be lots of time. You're really getting to sound good."

Dustin and Shanna are both make farting sounds. Merrilee just looks out the window.

"Look Mom! A sign for the camps. Lets see . . . the sign says camp A, festival registration. Camp B, security. Camp C, speakers. Camp D, visitors. Does that mean us?"

"No, Dustin, we get to camp in style with the speakers. We'll have to get pass badges at the registration. Here we are, lets get signed in and get our meal tickets and passes. Whew . . . am I glad to see that sign."

Outside, over the sounds of cars and people talking and laughing, a South American group's trilling pan pipes greet them. Someone is speaking on the main stage but it's too far away to follow what he is saying, though the tone is unmistakable. It's anger.

Oh Rats! That's probably the guy from Greenpeace. I was hoping to hear his talk on disconnection to the land. But the reconnecting to earth panel, later should be good. Oh well, at least I'll get to hear David Suzuki. I hope I get to meet him.

Dustin stands outside the car looking around at the people walking around in hordes. He stands for a long moment quietly.

"Mom, are there going to be any Indians besides you speaking?"

"I'm pretty sure, there is. Why?"

"Well, I was kinda hoping there would be some of my cousins from home. How come the Indians don't have environment gatherings?"

"This is an Indian environment gathering! It's to save a sacred wilderness area for the people from this area."

"Oh. Where are the Indians then?"

"I'm sure they're around here. They probably have camps set up with everybody else. It's not a pow-wow."

"It's not the same, fishing by myself or with town kids."

"Why not? Anyway, we got to get a move on and get the tent and stuff set up. Let's get this registration out of the way. I'm sure some of the boys from the local reserves will be around."

"Yeah. Anyway, couldn't we go home to camp out up in the hills? We never went since last year. It's just not the same."

"Dustin, I'm working. It's hard to get away. It takes us a whole day just to get home. And then we'd have to come right back. I'll try to get a week before summer ends. Okay."

The registration doesn't take very long. As they wait for their passes, Penny looks at the speaker's lists. She notices there is only one Chief listed to speak for ten minutes, and that is to do a welcome and make a comment on the importance of this area. All the other speakers are names she is familiar with from various environment and activist groups. Big names. There seems to be a lot more entertainment groups.

Setting the camp up is fast. The new tent she bought is a snap to put together. Their sleeping bags and other stuff have all been readied for a fast set-up.

"Mom, what do we do now? Sit out in these old lawn chairs and do nothing? It's so boring here. I wish you didn't have to drag us over here. I just want to do normal stuff. I hate all this activist stuff. How come you have to do this stuff?"

Shanna is standing with her hands on her hips. Her mouth is covered in a slick, wet looking lipstick. Hardly any colour but her mouth looks slippery. Her cheeks bones are glossed over the same way and she has the worst shade of mauve on her lids. Her stiffly curled eyelashes are tinged with a darker purple. The lime green mini-dress with a wide white plastic belt looks rumpled now. She had spent hours ironing it. And her hair. The permed shag, sprayed to stay, has attracted a thin film of grey dust. She stares defiantly at Penny.

"Shan, I already told you. It's part of what I do. My artwork is about the environment. This is an important talk for me. I'll get to make some good connections here. I think you should give it a chance, before you judge it."

"You don't care about us! You just don't want me to have any fun. I don't want to be here! Dustin doesn't either. Of course, Merrilee, the big baby, she'll do anything as long as she can blow her stupid flute. I hate you!"

"Shanna! Don't ever say that! I do the best I can for you and you know it! Who said you had to have fun! You just want to run around with that bad mouthed Dodi. She doesn't like anything. And another thing. I don't want her coming around to our place and bringing her boyfriends there to fool around with. She can do that somewhere else. You got that! She's just getting to be too much of an influence on you. Now you better settle down and quit pouting. You just make yourself miserable."

"You make me miserable! I'm gonna leave home as soon as I get old enough. And then you'll have nothing to say to me! I won't have to go to these stupid pissy-ant things for nobody!"

Shanna's voice is raising and she looks scared but she is pushing it as far as she can.

Damn. She drives me mad. What's wrong with her? Why is she acting like she hates me? She wants me to fight with her! I can't lose my temper. Stay calm. Don't argue. Lower your voice. Look her straight in the eyes.

"Shanna. I'm sorry you feel so miserable. I have to do this talk. I won't leave you back in the city without supervision. You know that. I can't make you like it, but you don't need to carry on and on. Make the best of it. That's what growing up is. At least there aren't any dishes or chores here. Relax. Put some of your tapes on and get into something more comfortable and let's all walk over to the lake for a dip."

Shanna lets her eyes drop. A tear slides down one cheek leaving a wet trail and she sniffles a little and kicks at a rock with one foot.

Well there goes my hope to listen to some of that Greenpeace panel and their views on rampant technology.

"I'm gonna get some shorts on and get the lemonade I packed in the carry cooler. Come on Dustin. Merrilee. Get your swimming gear on. Shan?"

"Yeah, I guess . . . Mom . . . uhhh . . . sorry."

"Okay."

As they walk to the lake, the breeze picks up and suddenly whips a small dust devil across their path. It flings leaves and dust up into the air, twirling it's way toward the lake ahead of them. The lake is shining and still. Far out in the lake a drift log is floating, a great dead limb sticking clawlike up into the air. The lakes smoothness is momentarily ruffled by the whirling funnel. Like a small mouth, it sucks a fine spray of rainbow before sinking quietly back down into the sun speckled surface.

NOTE FOUND IN HER DRESSER DRAWER

I take the things in the world and reduce them into symbols revealing what they actually are. Television as teacher. Replacing storyteller. As custodian of brain. Of free-will. Computer as guardian of information. Coyote how will you transform these monsters? Pretending to be real and sucking kids and adults alike deeper and deeper into the trap.

Penny looks around as she climbs at last out of the van. A few of the students are picking up their packs. The others are crammed together, already disappearing into the trees, following a shaded opening in the dense green. The trees are the tallest Penny has ever seen in her life. She follows the group, looking up at the trees towering in a great bank in front of her.

The narrow dirt trail stretches ahead and away into the trees. Salmon berry, salal and ferns in dense clumps, fill the spaces between the trees. Their rough trunks, wider than can be believed, surround them, changing distance and space.

It seems solid. It's so familiar.

She stops still, caught by a brilliant misty glow of sunlight shafting down through the trees from the canopy overhead.

Golden light touching green.

The drooping branches, festooned with pale lichen, pick up the light as they move silently in the aftermath of the passing walkers.

Even the air seems close and thick.

The smell of cedar and something musky fills the air overriding the sharp clean smell of earth.

It feels like it's humming a dark green song. Like someone familiar.

All around, shadows appear and fade in the soft, almost unseen, movement of fern and lichen. The small clearing where they had parked off the logging road, is now out of sight behind them as they round a corner in the short trail. A faint blue smoke drifts in the air along with the smell of fresh coffee.

Penny can feel the mist covering her, clinging to her clothes. Her hair is damp, the pores on her face open to the mist and the damp coolness. Overhead, two helicopters, one distant and one somewhere above the canopy, beat a rhythm drum-like in their movement of air percussion against the ears. Around her the camp spreads away into the trees.

The camp between.

The image is there in her mind. An image from when they were arriving. Framed in colour. An image of the camp, first visible only as brilliant bits of colour at the road's end, between the hulking machinery and the dark green line of the trees. A small line of parked cars and tents pitched between the miles of stark clearcut stumps they had passed on their way in and the thick shadowed old growth forest stretching away into the mist.

Between plunder and sanity. Between the jagged edge of the saw and delicate lichen.

Somewhere far in the distance Penny can hear the rise and fall of sound from some big machine. It's angry buzz seems to hang in the air as they near the main part of the camp. Freida, the woman who had escorted Penny's group in, walks quickly up ahead, chattering in an excited voice about the court development earlier that day and it's ramifications on the "peace" camp.

Here I am. The famous five valley coast of Vancouver Island. Home to the Nitnat and others. People of the mist.

Freida stops near the main meeting tent, curly reddish-blonde hair escaping the blue cotton bandanna she wore to keep it in check. Penny notices she has freckles sprinkled profusely across her nose and cheeks. Some are clearly visible on the backs of her hands and arms even from where Penny stands. The floral cotton blouse tied at the waist and khaki army pants gives her a soft, yet tough look, as she hoists one booted foot up on a block of wood.

"Hi folks. I want to take a few minutes to welcome you and to let you know some basics. This is wilderness. There are other unfriendly animals around besides the loggers, so be careful."

People look at each other laughing nervously. Freida holds her hand up momentarily grinning before continuing.

"As you probably all have heard, things aren't going our way in the courts. The injunction was denied. You know what that means. It could get ugly tomorrow. We'll get back together before dark to touch base, here in the meeting tent. Get yourselves settled in. Get some food over there at the food tent."

As soon as she finishes, people begin heading toward a small clearing with their backpacks. All of them seem familiar with the routine. Picking up her pack and roll, Penny looks for a place to pitch it. Walking to a small cleared area by the trunk of a large cedar, she kneels down and begins to stake her tiny nylon tent. She can hear footsteps approaching from behind.

"Hey Penny. Can I pitch my tent next to you. We seem to be the only singles in this bunch. Where are your kids?"

Penny turns around to find one of the women from her sculpture class.

Clairisse. Carves and inlays rock, shell and glass worn smooth from the beach. Always asking questions.

"Sure, go ahead. The kids bussed it home a couple of weeks ahead of me. They're finished for the summer. I just have the final intercession project to do and I'll join them. I'm glad. My teenager, Shanna woulda hated this place."

"I didn't know you were an actual activist. Do you do this stuff often? This is my first time at something like this."

"Oh. I'm not really. It seemed like a good opportunity to work on some sketches."

Clairisse smiles and nods.

"I know what you mean. I work in wood. Mostly drift wood. I feel like I have a connection with trees. So here I am. I'm not really involved but I don't support clearcutting any forest, let alone old growth like this. Also, it was one reason to get away from the city."

"Me too. I never thought university could get so depressing. So much reading. So many lectures. So many projects. I can't even think straight anymore. I think it's the tension of the city, too. Always having to be afraid. Always worried for the safety of the kids. Always feeling the hostility. I don't know why I'm here, really. I don't know much about the situation, either. It's just that it made sense to come. It gives me a chance to see the land here. I was hoping to meet some people from the reserve near here. I want to know what they're saying."

Clairisse looks toward the cook tent. The smell of food drifts in the slight breeze toward them.

"I'm totally famished. I think I'll set my stuff up later. I'm gonna head over to the cook tent. Coming?"

"Later. I'm gonna catch my breath first. I hope I have some time to sketch before the sun sets. The light's so strange here."

Once her tent is up, Penny throws her small pack in. Her sketch board and pastel kit with her pack of sketch paper goes in last with her waist pouch. She stands for a several minutes looking around.

A few people are busy setting up their tents, most are already at the cook tent, lined up, hungry from the long van ride up the winding roads from Victoria.

I'm so glad I came. It feels like homeland even though it looks so different.

She slowly lets herself down next to the tent, closes her eyes and draws in a deep breath. For the first time in long months, she can feel her whole body relax as a familiar lethargy takes over.

It feels like deja vu, or like someone watching me. What is it?

She opens her eyes again. Just then the breeze stirs, just slightly, and the light green wispy lichen hanging from the branches of the tree nearest her swings and sways around her. The ground is suddenly speckled with splotches of sun and shadow which move over the small orange flowers and large bluish mushrooms at the edge of fern spreading out over a rotting log disappearing into the soft cover of moss, leaves and pale green plants. The ferns and salal bushes move, too, and she can hear the great tree move high up above her. She hears it's whispering of needles and the barely perceptible creak reverberating down to the ground she sits on.

Look up! It's the tree moving!

She leans so far backward, looking up at the swaying tops of the trees above her, she almost falls backward. She watches them nod toward each other, whispering.

They're talking! → in trees, forest [handwritten: Native spirituality all around]

An overwhelming emotion washes over her. She can feel her throat tighten and her chest hurt. She reaches into her tent and pulls out her belt pouch and unzips it. She straightens up with her loose tobacco pouch in one hand and a couple of pennies in the other.

It's the trees! It's them watching!

As she gets up and walks to the base of the cedar tree nearest her tent, she can feel her legs shaking. She sinks down facing the tree, knees and legs folded under her.

Up close, the trunk of the great cedar is rich with life. It is shedding thin strips of bark, reddish brown undersides turned away from the darker brown of new bark. Mosses, tree fungus and tiny plants sprout from every possible crevice. She can see ants, spiders and insects she has never seen before moving on fast legs up and down the trunk and among the limbs. Up above, high in the branches she can hear birds warbling soft whistling tunes to each other. Two black ravens are sitting on a lower limb watching her, too. They're *talking, talking, talking.* They spread their wing's every so often and fan their tails out, preening. They make grating noises at her.

She feels her eyes filling with tears as she lifts the furry moss near the thick root and places the pennies and a pinch of tobacco under and pats it down.

She leans close to the tree, her cheek pressed sideways against the trunk and closes her eyes. Her words are barely audible in the still air. The sounds of her language mixing with the soft movement of ferns, the whispering of branches and the sound of birds overhead.

Ancient one. Thank you for your welcome. I offer copper and sweet tobacco. I seek your comfort and ask for my spirit to be filled with your beauty.

She can feel the tremble and vibration of the trees movement under her cheek as she presses her ear closer to the damp bark.

It sounds like a long sigh. Like a breath drawn in and slowly let out.

She sits still, face against the tree, the tree's each sigh matching her own. A calm moves over her.

It feels the same as a relative holding me. Soothing me.

When she finally moves away from the tree, it is because she hears footsteps behind her.

Clairisse. Coming back from the cook shack already.

"Penny? Are you okay? Are you not feeling well?"

"I'm okay. Just relaxing. Drinking in mother nature. It's so peaceful out here. I forgot how good it was. I just wanted to touch the tree."

"That's what I told the others, but you were sitting there against the tree without moving for so long some of us got worried. Are you doing some kind of Indian meditation or something?"

Penny glances up at her. She has that I'm-curious-but-I'm-sincere look. Her grey eyes are steady and clear.

"Something like that."

Clairisse just continues looking at her, waiting.

What does she want?

After a moment, Penny continues, her voice quiet and husky sounding.

"The tree. It's alive. Aware. I touched it. It touched me. I don't know. That sounds kind of hokey."

"It doesn't. Tell me." Clairisse is still looking at her in the same way.

"I can't. I don't know what it is. Oh, I could say what I just said but it doesn't tell you what I really mean. It's kinda like art. The way only another artist ever really gets close to your meaning. Maybe if you could speak my language, I could tell you better."

Clairisse moves next to her and sits down looking up into the tree.

outside view of non-Indian artist

"I feel something, too. Inside. It's very small and quiet, though. Like a whisper, really. Sometimes heard and sometimes not. Something wanting a voice. It makes me sad and shake. It's there when my sculptures begin to come alive. I feel it now. Here. A presence of something. Is it like that?"

"Sort of."

They sit together, their backs to the ancient tree, quiet for some time as shadows lengthen under the canopy. The two ravens above them are quiet now, too, eyes closed to the late afternoon sun, drowsing or simply letting the tree hold them up in the world.

Finally Clairisse stands up, facing her.

"Maybe I can't get close to what you mean. But I do feel a calmness here, like nowhere else. I wish I did feel it the way you do. I can see it in your face. You look transformed. Like a glow coming from inside. It's pure. I want that. Lots of us want it. It's what all that new age-ism is about, I think. You know? Why can't we find it?"

Penny looks up at her.

Clairisse. Thirty-some. Gaining weight. Divorced with a good settlement. Faded blonde hair. Childless. Third generation Canadian. No real roots anywhere. Retired father and stepmother in Oshawa. Mother in Florida. A half sister, in Texas. Dispossessed without knowing of what.

"Find what? What has been lost and why? Maybe that's the place to start. What do you think people are searching for?"

To feel that the tree is alive? Aware? Speaking a language your body knows? Has known for the thousands of years of your various ancestors? That it's as simple as those raven's up there talking about it?

She can see Clairisse's face change. The look of sadness deepening.

"I don't really know. Something better. Something more meaningful."

"More meaningful than what?"

"It's not clear. Maybe Christianity. Maybe todays atheism or agnosticism. Maybe we need mysticism like Joseph Campbell says. Maybe it would give us more meaning than what society offers now. But how do we accept it with the way modern science is?"

It's right here all around you!

At that moment a couple of guys, both with long hair tied into pony tails, came up to them.

"Hey, Clairisse, your friend must be hungry. We saved a plate of food for her."

The one with brown hair and a red checkered jacket looks down at her, concern showing clearly on his face.

"Not feeling too well? The med tent is over behind the cook tent."

Clairisse, smiles at the blonde one, with a plate of stewed vege-tables and a chunk of bread in his hand.

"Oh Dan, that was sweet of you. This is Penny. She's an artist, too. We were talking. She was meditating. Penny, this is Dan and this is Jim, his friend. We met during the rally at the legislature last week. He's one of the organizers of this protest action."

Penny can see the way Clairisse looks at Dan.

Oh, oh. One of Clairisse's reasons.

Penny gets up and dusts her now damp bottom. She takes the food being handed to her by Dan.

"Thanks. I'm fine. This looks good."

Jim is still looking at her. His eyes are a soft brown.

"It's time to go over to the meeting. The others are starting to gather. There are some blocks you can sit on over there, to eat."

Dan looks over at Clairisse.

"You should get that tent set up. It'll be dark by the time the meeting's over. Here, I'll give you a hand."

Clairisse and Dan are already laughing and chatting as Penny turns to walk with Jim to the meeting tent. They settle down on blocks outside the tent. A few of the students look curiously her way and continue talking. She looks around. She can see inside the meeting tent's open front. There are lots of people sitting or standing inside the tent. Quite a few more are standing outside where they are sitting.

"There are more people here than I thought."

"Yeah, it's a good thing, too. We're gonna need all the bodies we can muster tomorrow to stop them moving into this block."

Voices from inside the tent suddenly carry out to the people sitting around waiting for the meeting. Penny can hear Freida, her voice hard.

"I don't give a damn! I have to insist! Those students were recruited to a peace camp! To demonstrate in solidarity with our actions. If there's violence expected, they need to be told!"

A louder male voice drowns her out.

"Just a minute, before we get all hysterical, lets get some things straight. We don't know what'll happen tomorrow, but if they decide to go ahead and try to move past us, we'll try to stop them no matter what! I'll goddamn chain myself to a tree if I have to. They're either here to defend the trees or they should go!"

Jim sighs and stands up. He hesitates a second, shrugs and walks into the tent. She hears him talking in low tones to the group inside who have gone quiet. She can't make out what he is saying. Finally she hears a shuffling and they all come out of the tent.

One of the men, with wire framed glasses, a floppy canvas hat and what looks to Penny like a safari jacket comes out with a sheaf of papers in his hand. He looks at all the people, silently surveying the whole group. Penny looks around, too. There are about a hundred and fifty people standing around. Some, dressed in various types of "outdoor" sportswear, are obviously students. Others, dressed in faded bluejeans, cotton and army type khaki, are just as obviously not. The man finally looks down at his watch and clears his throat.

"Folks. Just to get the meeting started. I'm Scott. I do logistics. We have confirmation that our legal action against the logging company didn't go well in the courts today. It might mean that the company will try to start up again tomorrow in this new block.

Maybe not. It's always hard to predict. But in any case, for us, it means we have to take a different tactic from this point on."

He looks around. Freida is standing with her hands on her hips. He looks directly at her.

"Right now, what we need most, is to increase the media attention. The public needs to see this kind of destruction. Let me just say that I'm happy so many of you came up here. But let me be clear. The members of our organization are prepared to do whatever we can to delay or stop the massacre of those trees. Now let me turn it over to Freida who is in charge of rallying support and the media."

Freida nods at him and moves her foot up on the block next to her.

"Over half of you are students. The rest are either members or long time supporters of our actions against logging in this area. For those students who came up today, I just want to mention that we believe that there will be an attempt to move into this block tomor-row. I've alerted our friends in the press to cover things. I hope you will all join us in holding the line. It could get ugly. Remember civil disobedience can be effective if we keep our heads. We don't need any accidents or fatalities."

At that point, one of the students behind her, laughs nervously and Freida swings around to look directly at her.

"I'm serious. Have you been following the coverage lately? The dri-vers of those machines are angry. The tree fallers are angry. If they can push their way in to cut, they will. Well, we're angry, too. Look at that moonscape back there and look around you. It was like this a few months ago. We're going to do what we can to stop them. We have no idea how they will react or whether there will be law enforcement or not. If there is, there could be arrests.

Basically you'll be on your own. We'll want you all to put your names and phone numbers on the list so we have a register of everybody here. I'm gonna turn it over to Jim now. He's gonna go over some practical stuff."

As Jim stood, Penny sees his slight smile disappear.

"First things first. As one of the organizers of this protest, let me add my appreciation to those of you who came up to add your sup-port. I just want to mention that our organization has a huge amount of support here and internationally. We are not alone. We are committed to halt the irresponsible and rampant violation to our earth. Join us."

Jim is looking directly at Penny as he says those words. His eyes are on her for several seconds before he continues.

"Now, as for tomorrow, first camp call will be at daybreak. We want everybody up by 5:00 am. No exceptions. Any new devel-opments will be announced then. Otherwise, get coffee and food and come back here. The main support members already know what they are to do. The students who are here to show solidarity with us, have two choices. You can stand with us or you can choose to add to our number but not engage. You'll be asked to indicate that choice once we take our various positions. Nobody makes any decisions for action other than has already been dis-cussed in our tactical meeting. Any student press members should identify themselves to Freida. Any questions?"

One of the female students across from Penny stuck her hand up, her face going a bright pink.

"I was wondering if you could tell us exactly what tactics you've decided on. Seems to me, it would help us make a choice."

Jim is quiet for a few seconds. Penny can see Freida's I-told-you expression.

"All we can say, at this time, is that we'll be doing several things at once, depending on how things look on their part. The main thrust will be to foil the movement of equipment into this block to cut in the logging roads. We won't discuss how we plan to approach that. You'll just have to decide to engage with us or stand back to witness. Either way you'll be helping. Now everybody check out the location of the med tent and so on. Have a good rest. We'll see you all, bright and early, in the morning."

As Penny is getting up to go to her tent, she is suddenly aware that Jim is standing directly in front of her.

"Penny. I was hoping I could spend a few more minutes talking with you. Would you mind?"

Watch out girl.

"Sure, I guess so. Do you want to talk here?"

"Maybe over by your camp? I just wanted to ask you something."

As they walk toward her and Clairisse's blue domed tent, now up, the last light is fading fast in the west. The trees suddenly seem huge and dark. She shivers.

"Are you cold? I have an extra heavy shirt if you'd like. Here we are. The ground is pretty damp. Why don't you sit on the tent door flap."

As he folds her zip-flap down and motions her to sit, he squats down on his heels next to her. She moves to the edge and motions for him to sit on the remaining part of the flap. He nods matter-of-factly and sits.

"I wanted to ask what tribe you are? You're Native aren't you?"

"I'm from the interior. The Okanagan. Why?"

He looks at her steadily.

He doesn't drop his eyes the way a lot of non-Native men do, once you look them square in the eye. What's he getting at?

"I think it's extremely important that Native people be a part of this. We've been meeting with the local bands in this area, and they're opposed to the clearcutting, but there just aren't the numbers we'd like. We've alerted them about tomorrow and some of them will be here in the morning. I was hoping that you might have some ideas on this. What brought you here, if you're not from this area?"

Penny looks up and she can hardly see the tops of the trees. A mist is settling in, shrouding the camp. Finally she turns back to face Jim.

"I'm just finishing some final projects before I head home. I'm a student at UVIC. I'm opposed to clearcutting. I wanted to do some sketches. I've never been out in the wilderness area of the island. I don't have any ideas. I don't have any connections to Native activists. I read that the local tribal council has their own legal action going, I was hoping to meet some of them."

Jim leans slightly toward her. He is still searching her eyes.

He's making me nervous. Is he gonna make a move on me, or what?

"Penny, we have some difficulty communicating with them. I'm not sure they trust us. We're just not sure how to approach them. We've been trying to get them fully on side but usually only the Chief and a few others come out. I'm not sure why. I was hoping you could help us out in some way with that."

Penny let her body ease slightly away.

"I'm not sure how I could help. I think of my own people back home and maybe the reason's are the same. People are shy and quiet. I don't know. But I know that the communities here are pretty small. Maybe, like non-natives, they're forced to take jobs where they can get it. But this is their homeland. I don't know anything about their culture. But I think of the way I feel here and know that even if some of them work at logging they must feel, in a much deeper way, that the forest is sacred. That it's wrong to kill it's life. There must be thousands of living things here that get wiped out. It's not just the trees, though they are the base of it all. Also, they have their own way of doing things."

Jim nods. It is now dark and Penny can't see his face clearly.

"You know, they have the strongest position, because of their land claims, to help stop what's going on here. If they took a really strong stand, we would be a lot stronger in our whole action."

Penny hesitates a moment before answering.

"That may be true, but what it comes down to, it seems to me, is that nobody is willing to back them all the way on that one. Nobody is willing to return local control of their homeland to them. They live here. They'll be here forever. Like everywhere else in this country, the resources are controlled by governments who licence out their extraction. It's never decided by people at the local level. Decisions are made by people in offices in some city. People who see maps and read reports. Not people who live here and walk in these trees and love them. The land claims fight may not seem to be an answer but better decisions would be made if people who lived here were in control."

Penny can feel Jim shift slightly. His shoulder is now touching hers.

She can feel the warmth from him. He scratches his head and coughs before answering.

"But then, like you said, jobs are a priority. There is a lot of poverty here. Why wouldn't the same thing happen? If the bands here had full control why wouldn't they do the same?"

"It seems to me what you just said is the real problem. They haven't devastated any of their lands in the thousands of years of living here. Why would they do it now? I don't think there's enough research on the fact that Native people understand real sustainability and practise it even on the small reserves left of their homelands. Maybe backing Native people in their fight is the only real way of protecting these and other forests. I would rather put my trust in people who love their homeland than those who care about profits somewhere else. I think they would make better decisions over-all because other things important to them, like berries, medicines, hunting and fishing, would come into it, as well as their strong spiritual connection to these forests."

Jim is now very close to her. She can feel his breath on her cheek.

"It makes sense to me, but that's a bigger question than what our action here, in the immediate sense, can wait for. Tomorrow the machines will come in here and trees will fall. If we don't stand in their way now, there won't be any old growth forest left to protect, whether or not there is any resolution to the land claims question. I just wish a lot more of the Native people would get in the immediate struggle. I would like to see hundreds of them here. I wonder why they don't?"

"Maybe it's just not the way they do things. Maybe they don't know that they could make an impact. Maybe like in my community, the Chief and council are the ones that go out and deal with things outside their community. Maybe it has something to do with the way Native people get treated every time they do make a stand. Here and everywhere else. There's a lot of racism that surfaces. Maybe they know in the end that nobody really wants them to be a part of the forest. That people want the trees saved but not with them in it. What they really want is a park managed for tourist dollars. I don't know. I think I'm gonna turn in. I'm getting cold. It's damp out here."

Jim's cheek is now brushing hers. He draws in his breath and lets it out slowly.

"Penny. I wanted to ask if you wanted my company tonight. I hope you don't mind me asking. I think you are the most beautiful person I've seen in a long time. I'm alone a lot. It's gets lonely on this road. Don't be offended. I saw you when you first got here and I watched you and I can see how you feel about the trees here. I feel the same."

His voice is low and husky. Penny turns in the dark toward him and puts her hand on his shoulder. His head is down and he sits quietly waiting for her to answer.

"I'm not offended, but I would rather not, though it sounds tempting. I don't want to offend you either. I like you and it would be nice to get to know you more, but I'm gonna be leaving for home after the weekend. Let's just be friends. Okay?"

She can feel him straighten up in the dark. He sits for a moment more and sighs.

"Okay. I'll be pretty busy but lets try to spend more time tomorrow talking, if that's okay with you. I want to introduce you to some of the local band members and the Chief if he comes out. I'll see you in the morning. Have a good rest."

He leans over briefly and brushes her cheek with his lips lightly before he stands. She looks up at him, a tall dark shadow framed in the flickering light from the cook tent's fire behind him. She smiles at him in the dark.

"See you in the morning. I'll look for you. Rest well."

The camp is quiet as he makes his way toward the fire near the cook tent. Penny sits quietly for awhile before crawling into her tent and rolling out her sleeping bag.

It woulda been a lot warmer with another body. Oh well, best not to get tangled into anything on the spur of the moment.

As Penny crawls into her tent she can hear an owl hooting and somewhere in the distance a coyote yipping an answer back. Her sleeping bag feels damp and the air is cool on her face. The image of stumps, stretching away into the mist, is there in her mind and the image of the magnificent old cedar next to her tent. It fills her with a deep, dark sadness. She lies there listening to the night sounds of frogs singing and insects whirring nearby. She whispers in her language into the shadows.

Beautiful land, keep us safe for the night. Give them your strength in tomorrow's struggle. Move in the hearts of all those who come here as I have been moved.

It seems like she has just closed her eyes after going over all the images in her mind, trying to remember them for her sketches, before she hears a loud clanging and voices. She quickly unzips her bag and struggles out of her tent. It is still half dark out but she can see people running around and yelling to get up. She can hear machinery starting up in the distance. She looks over at Clairisse's tent just as she pokes her head out looking tired and messy-haired.

I didn't even hear her get back. I wonder if she stayed up most of the night.

Clairisse is looking wildly around her as she crawls out of her tent.

"What's happening? It's just getting daylight."

"I don't know. But sounds like something is up."

Penny just has time to stand up and straighten up her clothes, which she had slept in, before Jim comes toward their tents, walk-ing fast.

"There are some police cars and a couple of paddy wagons pulling up and there's a bunch of company officials gathering out there. They're gonna make a move. Get out to the parking area as soon as you can. It's coming down. We'll get people into groups in front of any machines moving toward this area. We got the one nearest padlocked with chains but it sounds like they're moving several more at once toward us. Let's go."

Before he even turns and begins running toward the trail out to the road, she can hear shouting coming from that direction.

Penny straps on her belt pouch and throws on her jacket about the same time Clairisse finishes lacing up her boots. They move together, without speaking, toward the trail. People are streaming from their tents hidden in the trees. Everyone is running. The sound of machinery is getting louder and she can hear more people shouting. The sound of a helicopter approaching overhead adds to the commotion. Penny's heart is beating fast as they round the bend in the trail opening out to the clearing where the cars are parked. It isn't as dark now, but there is a foggy mist shrouding everything. She can see the police car's red lights turning the mist pink and the orange glowing lights of the machinery moving toward them from the clearcut area across the road.

People are gathering in groups lined up in front of the police cars shouting and chanting. People with T.V. camera's and loggers with hard hats and other gear are knotted together near the police cars. She sees Scott, Bob, Freida and Jim along with several Native men standing in front of them talking to the police. One of the police-men has papers in his hands. He begins speaking in a loud voice.

"We are here to inform you that you are obstructing the legal rights of this company to proceed with work in this area. You are breaking the law by creating an interference. Please disperse now. Move out of their way. You must also remove your tents and vehi-cles from this area. We will arrest those of you who don't comply. Now, please remove yourselves."

His words are met with jeers and more chanting. The machines are now directly across the road. She can see at least three of them. They look like huge alien insects, crawling steadily along with huge pinchers in front. The sound coming from them almost drowns out the voices of the people chanting and shouting. The machines keep moving forward and people begin to group themselves into three larger groups linking their arms, directly in front of them.

They look so tiny next to the machines.

"Stop. Stop. Stop the slaughter. Stop the monsters. Stop the killing of trees. Stop. Stop. Stop the slaughter. Stop the killing of trees."

The chanting grows louder but so does the angry sound of the machines.

Penny can see some of the students are standing back but some of them are also in the front row. She looks over at Clairisse next to her. Clairisse has a look of fear and anger on her face. She looks at Penny and shouts.

"What do you wanna do?"

"I'm gonna go over next to Jim and them. I wanna hear what they're saying."

She starts walking fast toward the middle of the group with Clairisse right behind her.

"Penny! Stop! We could get arrested!"

Penny doesn't answer. She just keeps walking toward Jim leaving Clairisse trailing behind. As she gets closer she can hear the obviously older of the Native men talking in a calm but loud voice to one of the company officials.

"This is our hereditary territory. The Supreme Court of B.C. is still in session on this matter and you know it. You do not have the permission of my people to move your machines into this area. You are breaking the law of our lands. You are violating the laws of the Creator. I am ordering you to stop your machines."

The company official jerks his head toward the Native man, his face red and angry looking.

"Ordering me! We have a licence to log this area. That's the law. I don't give a hoot what claims you think you have in this area. That's the government's problem, not mine. We're losing thousands of dollars every day those machines and their operators sit. Enough is enough. We're gonna get to work. Now get the hell outa the way. Why don't you order those idiots around you to get decent jobs. Or go back to your welfare line. Move! These machines aren't stopping. Those fallers are gonna go in today."

"This is a sacred area."

Jim, Scott and Bob move to stand next to him and the two younger Native men. Others join the front line. The first machine is now only about twenty feet away and inching slowly forward. The lines behind them suddenly separate and people begin streaming forward half-circling the machine. Around her, Penny can see the same thing happening with the other two machines. The loggers move forward spreading out next to the machines, as well, three or four around each. The police begin fanning out advancing on the lines, trying to push people back with their sticks waving in front of them, but there are more people than police.

The policeman holding the papers waves them around shouting into a horn one of the others has handed him.

"Disperse now! Back to your camp! Take it down, now, and there will be no consequences. Disperse, now! I order you!"

Nobody stops. The machine nearest is still slowly inching forward and one of the loggers standing directly in front moves a few more feet toward the front of the line directly in front of the Native man who spoke. His face is red, his lips pulled back into a snarl. Penny notices he's glaring directly at the Native man, his hands curled into fists at his side.

"Fucking Indians and tree huggers! Go home!"

The older Native man answers calmly.

"I am home. This is my home. It always has been and it always will be, regardless of what you do to it. I'm here for the duration. Get used to it."

The logger turned an even darker red. Penny can see his neck muscles bulging even from where she stands. Around her the chanting grows in pitch. She can feel the tension in the air.

Something's gonna snap any minute, Get ready, girl.

At that minute the logger lurches forward toward the Native man and one of the two younger Native men steps in front of him, shielding him with his body. At the same moment someone from behind her pushes past her and with one leap jumps up on the great machine standing up on the front using the pincher arm to hoist himself up. He scrabbles crablike up toward the cab holding something in his hand. The machine stops abruptly and moments later the others do as well.

The logger swings around, toward the man on the machine, shouting something Penny can't make out. As he reaches for the man's leg, grabbing hold of his ankle to pull him down, the mans hand swings out and up, and a huge splatter of red paint blossoms across the windshield of the machine. As the logger drags the man off the machine, Penny can hear shouting around her. The logger has the man down on the ground and they are rolling around as others from the line jump forward trying to pull them apart. Two police move in with clubs and begin hitting the men who are trying to stop the two men on the ground.

Suddenly everything goes crazy as people press close around them. She can't see what's happening as people push and shove her forward from behind. The police are suddenly in the middle of the crowd along with the loggers and company officials. People are getting knocked down and there is screaming and swearing and fists and clubs smashing into flesh all around her. Someone slams into her from the back and she pitches forward, face down, just breaking her fall with one hand. She feels the crunch as her shoulder wrenches under her. She is just scrambling to her fours when she feels someone's hand grip her arm.

"Come on. Get up. I'll watch your back."

Before she even looks up, she knows it's one of the Native men. His voice is calm.

By the time she gets up, some of the people are lying on the ground with cuffs on. The police are working, two together, pulling people down and cuffing them. Several of the loggers are still fighting with some of the men. Several women are lying on the ground scream-ing. The Native man is moving her away from the worst of it toward the other two Native men. She can hear the policeman with the bull horn shouting.

"Desist your actions! Now! We're here to maintain order! Anyone refusing to obey this order will be arrested. Desist!"

The Native man urges her forward.

"No use getting your head cracked open. If you wanna get arrested just go up and put your hands out. We can't stop them today."

Just as they near the two other Native men, the logger who started the fighting jostles his way toward them, as well. The guy holding her arm lets her go and tries to push his way back toward the other two. Before he can reach them, the logger reaches out and slams his fist into the older mans cheek, and he reels backward onto the ground. Even from where she stands, she can hear the crunch of bone on bone. The other younger Native moves quickly and wrestles the logger down as the one helping her reaches them. He moves to help his partner trying to keep the man down. The logger flops around growling and frothing and they roll around trying to pin him down.

She reaches the older man's side as he sits up, blood spurting from his nose. She pulls her handkerchief from around her neck and hands it to him, kneeling beside him. He's looking behind her at the struggling three. She hears a shout and turns in time to see two police jerking one of the Native men off the logger and cuffing him. They grab the one who was helping her and are already pulling up his arm to cuff him as the logger is getting to his feet.

"Fucking Indians! Somebody should shoot you all!"

The older man is now getting to his feet.

"Just a minute, there. All those two did was try to keep that bugger off me."

The policeman nearest turns and looks at him for barely a second.

"Tell it to the courts, Chief. They're coming with us."

"I need somebody to drive me back. I don't drive. They're here guarding me."

The policeman looks over at the other one and Penny sees his barely perceptible nod. He lets the arm of the one who was helping her go. The one who nods, looks over at the older Native man. Something like shame is on his face.

"We're gonna take this one in. You better get on outa here, Chief. Unless you want us to arrest you, too."

"No. But that bugger just walked up to us and hit me. How come you don't jail him?"

"I'd like to but it's not about that. This is about obstruction. Loggers aren't causing the obstruction here."

He slowly turns and looks squarely at the logger and spits on the ground before speaking.

"However, I could change my mind pretty quick. You got that ass-hole? No more shit from you. Now get back behind those machines where the others are. We'll get things in order here shortly. We might have to do this job but we don't need shits like you."

They turn and walk away, leading the Native man to where the others are being loaded into the paddy wagons. By now they are almost full and the struggle is down to the police dragging protes-tors, one by one, to the waiting vans. She notices that a helicopter has landed sometime during the pandemonium. A group of reporters, with camera's rolling, follow the police dragging the pro-testors. Their cameras are rolling, panning all the protestors stand-ing around.

Why weren't they shooting when the worst of the struggle was going on?

She sees that most of the students are in a group by their vans, Clairisse is among them.

The older man touches her arm.

"Do you want your handkerchief back? It's all bloody. Are you hurt?"

He's looking at the scrape she can now feel stinging on her cheek. Her arm is aching as well.

"No, keep it. I'm okay, nothing serious. I'm Penny."

The older man nods, wiping a few dribbles of blood from his nose.

"I'm Henry. This here is Mark. Where are you from?"

"The Okanagan. I'm a student at the University."

He nods again rubbing his cheek which is now swelling and turning purple.

"Well, I guess we should get moving, Mark. I don't want to see them moving into those trees. I'll do something stupid if I do. I can't do anything from inside a jail cell. I didn't come to get arrested. It's a good thing we made the rest stay outa this too. They wouldn't stop at protesting if they saw this. Then they'd have to get the army out. We gotta keep moving on our case. One day we'll have the upper hand."

He's studying her face as he speaks.

"Dammit. You know, it's enough to make a person like me get stark crazy mad. Let alone the whole works of us. But, we gotta move slow on things like this or a lot of our people could really get hurt or killed. But it doesn't mean we don't feel like kicking ass, full out. It's so bloody hard to keep things from getting to that point. If they only knew. Give your people a fair rundown on what's happening here, eh?"

She nods. Feeling his rage. His grief for what lies ahead. His frus-tration. Something moves inside her. The anger wells up inside her. She wants to smash something. She can't even speak. She just looks at him. She knows he can read it in her face. He nods and pats her on the back.

"Go on, girl. They're waiting for you over there. Don't let up, either. Maybe sometime you come out to our community. We'll treat you right."

She nods at both of them, not saying anything, and turns toward the students waiting at the van. As she approaches she sees Clairisse has her tent pack and roll on the ground by the van. Clairisse just hugs her and they pick up their packs and climb into the van for the long ride back into the city.

She turns once to look back as the van is bouncing along the road behind a paddy wagon full of protestors. The machines are already starting their crawling advance on the trees. The magnificent old cedar, which sheltered her for the night and soothed her, is just visible above the other trees, swaying and nodding.

It has seen maybe a thousand years and today will be it's last.

A great and aching pain fills her chest and she weeps openly with others around her.

PENNY'S NOTES FROM HER DIARY

AWARENESS	------------	CONSCIOUSNESS
:		:
:		:
:		:
AS A PROCESS		AS A PROCESS
:		:
:		:
:		:
as a witness		as a participant

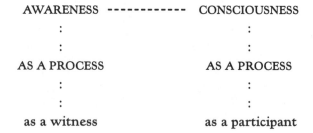

Can we overcome dualism can we over-come living in disassociation the inner being yearning for connection the physical being disconnected from the sun the ground the grass the living waters the flat long shadow stretched in front slanting against the fall wind drinking in the clean clean sweet rain black berry juice running down the chin the fire of ice forming in the nostril and the sky spitting streaks of brilliance overhead

QUESTIONS:

WHEN DID BEING HUMAN
BECOME AN INTERNAL PROCESS?

IF WE ARE HEALING
WHY DOES THE EARTH KEEP GETTING WORSE?

IF WE HAVE SHARED PERCEPTIONS OF
WHAT IS WRONG, WHY DO WE NOT HAVE SHARED
PERCEPTIONS OF WHAT IS RIGHT?

The last guest of the show is still standing looking at her *Moist Moon and Twisted Steel Grid* painting. The room feels suddenly quiet and still. Earlier the room was full of animated people. Now there are only her works and one last guest. The centre of focus is her large eight by twelve painting of Cracked Earth and Crystal. She stands facing it.

I wish I could have spent more time talking to that woman from the environmental network. I wonder what she meant? I never thought of my works as the current dichotomy of world-view. Could she have been referring to the dualism we experience as a result of technology? I wonder if she was making a reference to my being Indian? Whose world-views?

"I stayed behind to talk with you, if I may. You were so busy there, surrounded by people wanting to talk with you. I wanted to discuss a couple of your works? I'm an agent for a gallery in Portland, Oregon."

The guest stands right next to her.

I didn't even hear her walk across the floor.

"Hello. I'm happy to speak with you. I was just thinking about some comments I heard tonight. It's really always amazing to me how people read your works. Anyway, I'm intrigued. What does an agent discuss about the paintings? I usually leave the discussion about purchase to the curator."

The woman grins at her, nodding.

"Oh, I wasn't going to discuss that. I've already decided we need several of your works. And perhaps a show this coming year. I think your artist talk was wonderful. What does an agent want to discuss about paintings? Actually it wasn't the agent asking, it was the artist cum philosopher. I am so taken by the painting which is the focus of your show as well as the Moist Moon. The titles are so poetic. Are you a writer as well? Can you indulge one more fan?'"

Penny studies her for a minute.

Oh well, at least I don't have to be here tomorrow night to meet the inter-
ested buyers. I'm glad I begged my way outa that. I hope Shan's doing okay.
I'll just head home right after this. I wonder why she didn't answer the
phone earlier. I'll just call again before I take off. Two hours on the road
to go yet and it's raining as usual. Oh well. Smile. She really might have
an interesting view.

"No. I don't think so, but I'm beginning to see the force in that art form. I was just thinking of a comment one of the other guests made. She used the term 'a dichotomy of current world-views.' I didn't get to question where her comment was coming from. In any case, I'm sure you have your own comments."

"Actually, I was interested in your comments on the Cracked Earth piece. I was thinking of the images being not only symbolic but almost messianic. My question was mostly around the juxtaposi-tioning of the images of crystal. Why crystal? Beyond the posi-tioning of a hard edge oppositional force to the soft natural and organic forms present in all your works."

Penny turns back to the *Cracked Earth and Crystal* painting.

My God! Messianic! What the hell do I say to that! Messianic?

"It's true. The hard edge force. It is oppositional to everything nat-ural. Things in nature flow around each other establishing a coex-istence rather than dominance. Why crystal? It's a challenge first of all. Perhaps the play is on the word crack. I was thinking of my sister when I did this work. It is a force to be reckoned with. I think too of other meanings regarding class."

"It's exciting. I particularly like the presence of such organic form overlaid with hard edge to create the illusion of gashes in the earth and skin. There is indeed a foreboding message on many levels."

Penny lifts her arm to look at her watch. The woman's eyes move up to her face.

"I hope you don't mind me asking this question. But I wanted to know why you decided to work in a purely contemporary format."

"As opposed to what?"

"Well, you are Native American aren't you?"

"Native American? Oh yeah, that's the term used in the US. Is there a Native American format?"

"Oh no. But it seems that most Native American artists incorporate or reconstruct symbolism from their heritage in their works."

Now what do I say to that? What the heck is she asking?

"Really? I hadn't thought of it that way. It's my subject, I suppose. My concern has been in the way colour moves. It speaks. It's not something I choose. The imagery is a way to explore meaning within that. But the imagery is secondary. Although at some level the preoccupation I have with the positioning of warm nature against hard science comes from my Indigenous world-view, I suppose. I'm sorry, but I do have a bit of a drive tonight. It's been very nice speaking with you."

Penny is already turning to move away when the lady touches her arm.

"I just wanted to add that your work is about the most exciting I have come across in awhile. The depth you present could only have come from a deeply ecological view. It is very Native American, free of cliche. I hope my question didn't offend. It wasn't meant to."

"I strive to become accomplished enough to even approach the use of symbolic imagery from my heritage. Perhaps in the future I will have the courage. For now I will let my paintings dictate to me. I must be on my way. Good night."

Why do I feel anger when she's trying to compliment me? But she just lumped me in, without realizing. Twice. Talk about cliche!! I'm gonna damn well paint arrows ploughing into spandex!

The woman still wore an I-want-to-continue-this look but Penny waits a moment and then smiles.

"I really must go. Thank you for your comments and for coming."

There is a pay phone near the door of the gallery. She dials and lets it ring about ten times before hanging it up.

She could have that darn headbanger music on full blast again. Or maybe her and Dodi decided to go to the movies after all. I hate this. But she's almost seventeen. I can't get a sitter for her. I should have made her go home for the long weekend to Ma with Dustin and Merrilee. Now I'm really glad I'm going home a day early.

The drive home is one long blur of lights through the silhouettes of trees and big buildings looming against the navy sky. The drizzle is steady and fine. It makes slanting lines in the street lamps glow across her vision. The road in front stretches away into the shadowy wet night, the white line stark against the black wet pavement.

As she pulls into the driveway, she notices all the lights are on in the house and there is a strange car in front.

As soon as she flings open the kitchen door, a distinct layer of smoke swirls out. The windows are open and the curtains are flapping damply in the slight breeze. Remnants of sandwiches, juice glasses, potato chip bags and a can of opened sardines litters the table. Music is drifting from the living room but there are no sounds other than the cat munching on something under the table. The distinct, sweet smell of marijuana comes from the living room.

Oh, please let her be okay!

"Shanna! Where are you? What's going on here?"

She walks into the living room and stops. There are three boys looking dazed sitting on the floor, propped up by couch cushions. One is holding a small clay pipe. Two girls are sitting together, their backs against the cushionless couch, ashtray in front of them. One looks up and smiles a wide smile and then starts laughing uncontrollably. She looks like she is trying to cry. All five start laughing and laughing. One of the boys holds his stomach, gasping and laughing at the same time pointing at her. Shanna isn't there.

Oh God! I knew I shouldn't have trusted her. Where is she?

She spins around and heads down the hall toward the bedroom.

Steady, steady girl. Don't panic. She's probably with a guy! What to do? Don't lose your temper. Breathe slower.

She glances in Shanna's room only to find the room empty and messy as usual. She whirls around and jerks open Dustin's door.

Where is she! Oh God. Oh God.

She suddenly hears somebody mumbling and mumbling from the bathroom. In one step she is across the hall and throws the door open.

"Shanna! Oh baby, you scared me!"

Shanna is sitting on the floor of the bathroom with Dodi. Their backs are leaned against the pink tub, legs sprawled across the floor in front of them. An ashtray is sitting on the tub's edge. They are just sitting there, talking at the same time. The mumbling stops and it takes several long seconds before Shanna turns her head and movs her eyes up. They are dreamy and wide. A confusion wrinkle crosses her smooth forehead.

"Mom I'm a good girl, I'm a good girl. Dodi is. I'm a good girl, you know what? There was some music we were listening to and now we're in here in the bathroom and where did you come from and anyway, I don't know why you have to be a speaker and I wish you and me and Dustin and Merrilee were home with Nanna and what are you doing back now Mom? I'm a good girl . . . Mommmmm."

Shanna looked away and started mumbling to Dodi again. Dodi isn't even looking at her. She is looking at her fingernails painted a bright turquoise blue. Behind them against the sea green wall, Penny's own image stares back at her, from the mirror. She stares at her image. A plain looking Indian woman. She is wearing her good print dress with tiny bright blue flowers scattered on a field of deep green. Her long hair is parted and held with two beaded barrettes. The moment stretches back, back a long way, as the hall mirror behind her is caught reflecting a receding corridor of her, standing framed in the doorway. Framed over the sprawled legs of her daughter, deep in a sweet smoke dream.

LETTER TO JOSALIE

Josalie:

I'm writing to let you know that I'm moving home. I'm tired of the kind of life out here. Actually it's that maybe I made a mistake. I seem to have become entrenched in the very way of life I am opposing and it's having an effect. I've alienated my children along with myself from something valuable and I'm afraid. I'm having some problems with my daughter, Shanna. She started to hang out with other teens who are turned off and angry at the world. She doesn't even pretend to try at school. Her only interest seems to be in how outrageous she can dress to copy what they call punk. Also she's started getting into the drug scene. I can't even talk to her. She's threatening to run away. I'm worried. I can't handle this alone anymore.

And now that Dustin is getting to his teens, I don't want the same thing for him. I have to admit, life is shallow in this culture. It's really that there isn't anything with meaning, I guess, just things. And somewhere in my rejection of all that, I guess I left out something. Maybe they need the family. No, maybe not so much family but what our family has. Maybe it has something to do with being surrounded by something powerful rather than being absorbed in fighting what surrounds you daily. That would turn anybody off. I've spent so much time on resistance, I've risked the things that give purpose.

Now that I have my degree and I have some teaching credits, I think I could make a sensible living teaching art at home. My paintings are still doing fine and I do a lot of talks, so there is no reason I couldn't. Anyway, I miss the people on the rez. I miss the big gatherings and the giveaways and the ceremonies. I miss going out to pick berries and canning fruit and planting. I miss the land. Sometimes it seems overwhelming. How could I have stayed away so long? How could I have deprived my children of all that has so much worth? I should have been more like you. You are so solid.

In any case, I've only got this month to finish out and we'll be there. Let Mom know. Have you heard from Lena lately? I guess Charlie and Andrew and their families are okay or I would have heard. Say some prayers for Shanna.

Love, Penny

There were flowers everywhere as far as she could see. The thick sprays of yellow sunflowers and their pointed long leaves reached all the way up to her thighs. Scattered here and there, reaching higher than her, were the spindly red saskatoon bushes loaded with white blossoms. A few silky purple lupine stalks, shooting up over sprays of thread-fine, brilliant green, bunch grass. Here and there clumps of grey sage take over, their top silvery spikes crested with soft gold flowers as small as seed beads. A few mauve sage-brush lilies and honey red-bells waved on slender stalks. The sandy ground between was covered with bitterroot roses lying flat to the ground. Bright pink centres in small wheels of green, spokes point-ing outward. Even the fat little prickly pear cactus, in patches by the rock outcroppings, had big feathery canary yellow blossoms with impossible peach pink tinges.

She could see Penny far across the digging field with her *tupa*. Her own mother stood with her watching the two tiny figures move slowly.

"It's good Gramma is with us, Mom. Penny really misses her, now that she doesn't go anywhere very much. You know how Penny just watches the window for the wagon to come from your house. She asks if she can stay with you and Gramma."

"I would like her to come, but I think she's already too spoiled by her *tupa*. Pretty soon her *tupa* will get even more weak and she won't get around at all. Your gramma is old, Juliana. She will rest soon. It's good for Penny to know her *tupa* the way she does but it will make it hard for her. Let's get busy digging these roots. It'll get too hot before you know it."

Juliana watched her mother bend over, pushing her digging steel down into the damp sand. She watched her mother for a moment as she turned over the clod and shook the small clustered root free.

Beyond her she could see her Gramma Susapeen and Penny bent over in the same way.

"I wonder how many years our people have gathered right here and dug roots. Thousands? Look at Gramma, she's almost ninety and look at you. You're over sixty. Every year, she has come here and so has her mother and grandmother and so have you, and now me and I'm almost forty. But what about Penny, my last baby? Just look at how much of this digging field is turned into alfalfa field."

"Juliana, you can't spend too much time trying to predict the future. Maybe Penny is to be your last baby, now that the one you carried is lost. And sure, things are changing. Your gramma says she is worried that the people are changing the world. She's right. But what can be done? We are just to go on doing the best we can. We still have to pick the berries and dig the roots. They will leave us if we don't. So let's get busy. No more talk. The roots are waiting to be dug. Waiting to go home with us to the feast house. Shush now, daughter, it is your loss which speaks. Let's speak only of good things on this day of first roots."

Juliana could feel the heat of the sun on her back as she bent down to push her digging steel into the sand. She could feel the great weight of the past years sadness wrap around her, pushing her down. The roots were waiting. Waiting for her hands.

Across the field, two small dots against the blazing red rising of the sun, had cast long pointed shadows across the land.

The ground is covered with a large tarp. Mounds of folded blankets, print fabrics, bath towels, tea towels and other giveaway
items, from packaged cutlery to toys, are spread around. Rows of
jars of home canned fruit and salmon are lined up at one end of the
tarp. Ribbon shirts and dresses and fringed shawls are laid out, dis-
playing the fancy colours. All around, folded lawn chairs are filled
with people of all ages. The large drum, encircled with a group of
singers, beats a slow honouring song.

"Penny, come on, you and the kids have to lead the dance.
Everything is ready."

"I feel so funny, Mom. Why don't you and Josalie and her bunch
come with us. Maybe Charlie and Millie and their kids. And
where's Andrew and Mabel? I thought they said they could get
here even if they had to work all night to finish the hay."

"No, Penny. This here's for you and Shanna and Dustin and
Merrilee coming home. We'll all dance with you once you go all
the way around. Okay now? Andrew phoned and said to go ahead.
The tractor had a breakdown yesterday and they got to get the hay
off the field. It's clouding up. They'll get here later to eat."

Shanna stands looking around at the people gathered. Her face
looks drawn.

*She changed into blue jeans! I'm just glad she didn't throw one of her
tantrums about this whole thing.*

"Shanna, you stand over here by your mom. Dustin and Merrilee
you can follow. Shanna, the shirt I got just fits you. It looks good."

Her grandmother reaches out and lightly brushes Shanna's hair and
hugs her briefly and winks at Dustin and Merrilee.

The drum starts the round dance song and Penny and her daughter begin the steps inside the circle of people, around the giveaway tarp on the grass. The people stand to shake their hands and to hug them one by one. The sage pot sends out its musky sweet scent and covers them with its cleansing power. The smiling faces of her people, all around, greet her and her children. Her eyes fill and she feels like her tears will fall. She glances at Shanna beside her, awkwardly letting herself be hugged and kissed by some of the women.

I forgot how this feels. It's like we're being embraced by something so strong yet so gentle. Oh, my people. You are my medicine. Heal this small family of it's wounds. Help us to become whole again as part of you. I give thanks that you are still here. I pray that you will always be here. I pray for each of you and I give myself back to you. I give you my children to be part of you again. I commit myself to honour you and to do all that I can, that there will always be community, in this way, here and wherever such community thrives. I give myself back to this land, our home.

In the second round, her mother and Josalie lead the rest of the family into the dance. Finally, everyone joins and the drum beat picks up as people move around the things gathered by her family, to give as celebration and thanks.

During the giveaway, Penny watches Shanna handing out ribbon dresses and shirts to the younger people. She seems more relaxed.

That must be Jimbo's son, smiling at her.

Dustin and Merrilee run back and forth handing out things.

They're so at home and happy. Why didn't I come home a long time ago? I feel like I've been in prison and suddenly I'm free. It was so simple. Everything was always right here, waiting for them. Right here at home. Nobody belongs out there, where everything has a price. I wish Lena were here. I wonder why she just can't seem to find her way back.

"Penny, let's go and get the food onto the tables. I think Andrew and Mabel and the boys are just pulling in. Good. The rain can't hold off all day. I made up some elderberry pies. Wait'll you taste them. I found out if you use a little flour to thicken them, instead of cornstarch, they taste better. We're gonna have more than enough deer meat. Those uncles of yours. They want any excuse to go out in the mountains."

Josalie hurries her off to the warm kitchen where all the food waits. Tables are set up on the back veranda and in the living room and even in the car port.

Penny stops on the veranda and looks out at the people still standing in groups talking. A new group of youngsters is sitting at the drum singing forty-nine songs. Dustin and Merrilee stand close to them, spellbound. She quickly searches the crowd for Shanna.

There she is, talking to that boy again. She gave him the green shirt with the yellow and white ribbon work that her and her grandma worked on together. Ah huh.

She watches Andrew and Mabel walk from their pickup. They walk slow and Andrew has his hand lightly on Mabel's shoulder.

I wonder how two people can stay together for so long. I envy them. I wish I could be that way. It's so lonely for me sometimes. Oh well, I guess I'll just have to get used to it.

"Okay, everybody. The food is on. We're gonna make a little offering and we asked my mom to say a few words of thanks for the food. If you could all gather up here, we can get to the best part. Here's Mom."

Her mother moves to stand in front of everyone. She holds up a paper plate of tiny bits of all the food. Her face is serene and happy.

She speaks quietly in Okanagan.

"This day is good. We thank the food which comes to us, to feed our bodies and we thank the land which provides this for us. We thank the Creator who made it so. With this food we give medicine to this gathering. We celebrate the homecoming of my daughter and her family. I'm happy to see my granddaughters and grandson here among us. Bless them and everyone here with this medicine and now we give this offering today to ask for this to be so."

The people begin to move toward the tables. There is laughter and joking and the sounds of small children having fun.

Above them the sky is turning darker. Thunder clouds hang on the western horizon. In the distant hills the first flashes of lightening and a distant rolling of thunder can be heard over the drum's rhythm.

The rain will come later. For now, the air is fresh and the day warm.

enny was sitting by the door step watching the wagon coming toward the house. The sound of the harness buckles *clink, clink, clinked* and the soft muffled throat greeting of the lead mare, Pindaho, made her heart leap suddenly. The creaking of the wagon and the steady crunch of the heavy wheels were singing a song she knew. She felt it more than heard it. Somewhere deep inside her, it had flowed like an ache, but sweet, sweet. Tupa's flowered shawl was flying as she sat beside Uncle Alex, pulling back on the reins. Tupa, a slight, dark figure in her long black skirt and silk bandanna, seemed to her to be the tallest person in the world. A smell of apples and leather came from the wagon and the sound of bees buzzing. The others crowded onto the porch behind her to shout greetings to Tupa.

I try to look anywhere else, but my mind concentrates only on what is obvious. Most of the stragglers in the audience have left and he is standing there waiting to talk to me. He takes my breath away. His eyes flash toward me and he arches an eyebrow. I can't move my eyes away from his, I can only breathe. My heart is *thump, thumping* inside my chest so loud, I hope he can't hear it. I feel lightheaded and stuck to the floor. The light, striking his face, casts a satiny bronze to the even brown of his skin. A fly is buzzing somewhere nearby and time seems to stand still. I notice he has a small mole high up on his cheekbone. I think crazily about Liz Taylor and her beauty mark. My stomach feels funny.

"Hello. I thought I would wait until everyone else left to ask you something."

The laugh lines at the corner of his mouth get deeper and his eyes become darker, if that is possible.

"Ah, yeah. I mean, sure, if I know the answer."

I notice that the two top buttons of his sea-green shirt are open and I can see his pulse at his throat. I see a bit of silver chain and I wonder what he has hanging from it.

"I just wanted to ask how you think this issue could be explained to ordinary people. Do you think there is a way? Because, I think for the most part, they're too busy trying to survive from day-to-day. I'm talking about working people. You know?"

His voice is deep, but soft, and he has a slight accent.

He must be from up north. Maybe the Peace River area.

"That's exactly the problem, I guess. Sometimes, I think it's impossible. I guess so far it has been, but there has to be a way to get to

ordinary people on an everyday level. I mean, if somehow adver-
tisers can turn them into puppets, then there has got to be a key in
that."

He laughs. A clear easy laugh.

Oh shoot, why did I say puppets! I should have said consumers.

"I liked your talk, especially the points around value currency. It's
the first time I've heard it put the way you put it. I agree culture
doesn't have a lot to do with it and non-culture does. Puppets don't
have culture they just keep jumping. It's something I've been trying
to put into words, I guess."

He is looking serious now. Almost hesitant.

"Yeah, that's it. But if we go with that analogy then it's not as
simple as learning to pull their strings. Somehow they have to come
alive, to awaken and be real, instead of being wooden dolls."

I'm suddenly shy. I want to talk to him some more. Not necessarily
about non-culture and the state of the world. I want to know
everything he thinks. I am looking at his lips and their fullness and
I breathe in his clean soap scent and I forget what I just said.

"By the way, I'm David. I already know your name. Do you want
to go for a coffee or something?"

"Yeah, that sounds good. Just wait a minute while I gather my stuff
and talk to the hosting prof."

I'm shaking inside.

*Now what? I'm supposed to have coffee with the professor and friends.
Should I lie and tell him I have an emergency? Or what!*

Professor Jim Doyle and several colleagues smile as I approach their tight little knot, their faces unreadable.

"Penny, that was such an interesting perspective. I'm sure everyone enjoyed it as much as I did. Are you ready to go? I thought we could all go in my car. There are just us four and you."

Oh shoot! How do I get out of this?

"Thanks, Jim. I actually was thinking of begging off. Is that a possibility or would that create an inconvenience?"

"Oh . . . well . . . we always have coffee with our guest speakers. We sort of make a tradition of it. We reserved a table at one of the nicer restaurants. We thought you might enjoy a drink and a nice dessert and or even something light. But of course if you really don't care to come, we could cancel. The faculty pays for it, so it's a little treat for us as well."

Shit! I'll have to ask them if he can come. I can't just cancel out.

"I have a friend here. I would like him to join us, if that's okay with everyone. We could take a cab and meet you at the restaurant."

Professor Jim hesitates momentarily, and for a minute I think he is actually going to say no. I feel like backing up, turning and running. I feel like telling him and those other smug-faced, know-it-all strangers to go to hell, that I don't want to chit chat, drink wine, and smile. I'm about to add something to the effect that I didn't want to abandon a friend, when the professor nods.

"I'll call the restaurant and let them know, in case they have to change tables. I'm sure a cab won't be necessary. We'll have one of the others bring their car so we'll manage."

What if he doesn't want to go with this bunch? I'll be so embarrassed. I've really presumed a lot. Oh darn.

I turn and there he is, watching me and I don't care if I inconve-nience the world just now.

NOTE IN HER SKETCH BOOK

R aven told Coyote a story. He told a story about the star sisters and how they called to Coyote. How they made the invisible strings he used to climb to the stars on. Raven talked about Coyote's desire for them, being the main reason. And how they cut the strings. And how he fell and his bones were ground up by his only relative. An old grandmother. And how all the coyotes come from that one coyote's bone dust. And Coyote said, "Bullshit! I never fell. That must'a been you! Probably how you learned to fly. Besides, my grandmother would've just called Fox. Fox would fix things."

David walks up the long wide concrete steps with Penny. Indian people are walking up the steps ahead of them and some are standing at the top mezzanine floor's landing. Even from here, he can see the information table is stacked with papers. He glances at Penny. She is looking around at the people. There is a small group of brothers from Ecuador at the top of the steps talking with a couple of Maori men. They turn as one of the men from Ecuador waves at him. He smiles and waves back. Beside him, Penny stops suddenly and places her hand on his arm.

"David, I was thinking about what you said earlier. I haven't actually been trying to avoid conferences and things. I've been spending a lot of time with the girls showing them stuff I should have made sure I did earlier. I think I've missed the boat on Shanna. But she seems to be settling down quite a bit, now that she's with this guy from home, but I still worry for Merrilee. She's so quiet and shy. I don't want to make any more mistakes with them. It's been good having you stay with us. Dustin's really taken a liking to you. Probably because you like fishing. And the big surprise is that he really likes planting the gardens with his uncles. I would like to be with you a lot more, too, I guess. I just don't do too well with relationships. My art work makes me selfish."

He stops, as well, and turns toward her. There is something of a serious look on her face.

"Penny. It's just that there is so much to be done on these issues and I know you understand the political aspects. I've heard you talk, remember? The thing about Indigenous Peoples rights, is that it takes people who are Indigenous and who have a traditional worldview, to talk about how it's connected to environment issues. I just wanted you to come with me and share some of this with me. This is my life. It's really not just theory. People are suffering worldwide. Indigenous Peoples are suffering the worst because of some of the very things you see. You can't just talk about it. You have to do things about it. I'm an activist because I do things. I'm glad you decided to come. And I know you need to paint."

"I was just thinking about something coming in here and seeing all these Indian people and the other Indigenous people. It's like I've seen it in a dream before or something. Maybe it has to do with my coming home. I don't know. You know, I spent quite a few years away from my community. And when I did come home, I realized that there was nothing like it anywhere I lived. I mean, our community and how we are on our land. It's really a lived experience, not just in the head. I've never really thought about other Indigenous communities. I'm glad I'm here, too."

David turns and looks up at the registration table. The line was thinning out. The opening would be starting soon.

"Lets get up there and get signed in. We can talk some more about this after. Okay?"

The registration takes only minutes. David registers as a speaker and he registers Penny as his guest.

As they enter the large room, the emcee is calling for everyone to be seated. A long table, covered with Pendleton blankets, is at the head of the room. Various items from various Indigenous groups are laid out on the table. On the table an abalone bowl with sage and sweet grass sends thick curls of smoke toward the fans whirling overhead. On the low stage beyond, seated at a long table, are the speakers for the opening. Indigenous delegates from Central America and South America are seated alongside Native people from Canada, the USA and Mexico.

David guides Penny toward the front row which has been left open for speakers. As they take their seat, the emcee calls on an Elder to come forward to give the blessing for the opening.

David listens to the familiar words of greeting and giving of thanks. And then the Elder recites Black Elk's last prayer in a soft voice. As his words fill the room, David closes his eyes and thinks of his own people on the extinction list, and follows the prayer, murmuring its familiar words.

"The tree does not flower. Its roots wither. Oh, let my people live."

He can hear Penny beside him, murmuring as well.

To David, the morning is long, filled with speaker after speaker giving a summary of their situation in their homeland. But Penny hasn't moved from her seat during the entire morning. He has gone out to the foyer to look at the material being handed out in print form, and returned. David can see her write notes from time to time and once he watched in amazement as she took out a small sketch book and pencilled in with deft strokes the scene before her. She is utterly absorbed. Finally, they break for the morning.

As they get up to walk to the foyer for a standup lunch and coffee, he smiles at her. Her eyes are bright and her cheeks are flushed.

"That was intense. When it's all put together like that, it gives you a different perspective. Then you realize that millions of Indigenous people are being violated and displaced and forced into total poverty! You can see how things are so awful on such a wide scale. I mean you see stuff on TV, but it's always isolated events and it's always being portrayed as small groups of guerilla fighting against some government. You never hear the real story about why they rise up. It's like the same thing that our peoples went through here, when we were being colonized."

"Our peoples are still going through it. Think about it. Every road block and militant action is about stopping a dam, a clearcut, a pipeline, a mine, and so on. We're still confronted with the same thing. We find out quick enough what happens when we try to protect our environment and our way of life. We get beat up and criminalized. They use the military. Granted it's not as desperate and as violent. But the results are similar. Just look at the conditions and statistics on any reserve. They find ways to get access. Indigenous Peoples in this western hemisphere have all been dispossessed. Yet, they are all that protects the untouched lands that are left. They stand in the way. It's why there are so many human rights violations. On an international level we have no voice. Not a single seat in the United Nations from the western hemisphere is an Indigenous nation. Why? Think about that. What kind of racism does that boil down to?"

David's voice has gone hard. Penny stands still for a minute. She studies his face then looks toward the shaft of sunlight streaming in through the window at the end of the foyer. David's stands framed in the light, dust motes dancing around his head and shoulders.

"It's true. I've spent most of my time thinking about technology and it's effects on the natural world. I even looked at some of the mechanisms employed to keep the system in place. At class disparities and competition. I've looked at consumerism as a cultural artifact, held as sacred as any religion. I have even thought about the increase in human violence as an environmental symptom. But in all that, I obviously overlooked something right in front of me. I overlooked the communities which are still connected to land in a healthy way as an opposing force to that system. A true natural sustainability. As the only hope for protecting biodiversity!"

David watches her move her hands. Her long fingered art hands. They move with such grace as she gestures to make her points. He nods and takes one of her hands in his.

"Penny, I've waited for a partner to be with me where I stand. Oh, I don't mean the usual boy-girl thing. Although that would be the greatest with you. I mean someone who feels and knows why I have to do this. You know? Like you need to paint. I was hoping maybe you could go to Chiapas with me. It's a fact finding trip prior to the Indigenous Environmental Network meeting at Chickaloon Village. That's a huge gathering of Indigenous people and environmentalists around this kind of work. It would be great to get you to speak on one of the Network's panels on the human effects of globalization. You've looked at those things. Would you? Stand with me?"

"David, let me think about it. Okay? I just don't want to jump too quickly into this. I can get pretty obsessive and as I mentioned earlier, I think the kids are just beginning to get grounded in their own culture back home. I think it's important to find out, though. I really don't know very much first hand."

David doesn't push any further. They finish their coffee in silence. He waits for her to talk some more but she stares out the window with a faraway look in her eyes. They stand drenched in the spring sunlight streaming onto the green tile floor.

Back inside the conference room they listen to other speakers. Each of them presents specific information with slides or video on particular current struggle areas. The stories mesh and overlap as one story. Ecuador, Bolivia, Peru, Chile, El Salvador, Columbia, Mexico. Millions of brown people, despised, abused, hungry, landless, reduced to slave-like labour. Disease and death.

Maria, a woman speaks about Guatemala. She shows slides. Images of death and torture. Images of brown people in total poverty. The earth's people. She describes Guatemala as the key to opening the door to American free trade. She finishes by addressing the audience.

"Democratization? At what price?" she asks. "When all it really means is to further dispossess the desperate."

Then David walks to the podium to offer encouragement to the Native American delegates who will speak tomorrow. After Maria's graphic images the mood is sombre.

"My talk is about standing with them."

His soft voice carries in the room, so quiet you can hear the slightest movement, as he covers all the points he has just made to Penny. He raises his voice when he makes his final points.

"If you don't stand with them you are standing with those against them. Think of the blood on the hands of those whose money in America does this."

He is looking at Penny when he makes the next points.

"People who live in the relative comforts of this country can't know, unless we make sure they know. When we know these things and we stand by, we are no less guilty. And so we must sacrifice our own comfort and complacency to bring change, or we stand with blood on our own hands. We would not tolerate these acts by government here, why should we tolerate what their trade agreements condone?"

He closes reminding everyone about the next day's agenda.

He sees Penny's cheeks flush. He sees her drop her eyes and he knows what her answer will be.

The sweet grass braids are thick that they hand to her and David after the last speaker is through, and they are thanking the participants. Later, they eat moose stew, pink atlantic salmon, fiddleheads and bannock and a sweet, sweet apple dumpling with rice and raisins. There is cornbean soup and white clam chowder. After the meal, the drumming and dancing is started by a children's group, their high chipmunk voices singing an intertribal song. Their cultural instructor, Kim, is so proud.

David and Penny stand together, between the Indigenous delegates talking in small groups and the children. That is where they stand together, as night draws a curtain across the sky framed in the long windows before them, and a thin waning crescent moon appears in the West.

POEM FROM HER DIARY

Globalization

something about breathing
in the dirty
buzz words
and missed manners
a global design
of conjure and conquer
situating the hilarity
as common text
a mastering and the master class

I imagine Coyote
standing on a marble pedestal
fifteen feet above
is he holy
as he is trying to see how far
his piss will arc into space
a golden connection
to the big mother
his features
exquisitely executed
in blue veined alabaster
an icon
in a temple constructed
for his worship
poems and prose
scattered at his feet
and songs filling the air
dedicated to him

those are the choices

the question of globe plotting
plot-izing the globe
marking into plots
person by person
as in story plots
as in house plots
as in evil plots
as in grave plots

and Coyote pissing around

At last the plane is coming in for a landing. Below the city is spread out under a brown smog. She notices the army carrier planes on the ground before she gets off the plane. There are armed soldiers walking in twos back and forth in front of the landing strip where the plane now taxies. The pilot comes on and speaks in Spanish and then in English, welcoming the travellers. David looks over at Penny.

"Well. Here we are. I hope Antonio is here. My Spanish isn't so hot. We still have to get through customs and immigration, too."

The walk through customs is actually not very difficult. The official speaks to them in Spanish and they answer in English. He calls another official over and he speaks in English. He has very dark piercing eyes. He looks stone-faced. His English is heavily accented and he speaks slowly.

"What is your business in Mexico?"

David doesn't hesitate. He answers in a clear calm voice.

"We are on holiday. My wife is an artist. She is hoping to paint some scenes of your beautiful country."

The official smiles tightly and nods curtly.

"Very good. Please present your passport whenever you are requested. Your bags will be inspected through that door. You will return this portion when you leave. *Gracias*."

The bag inspector is fat and jovial. He thumbs through their clothes and pats all the pockets. He looks in her cosmetic bag and sniffs her shampoo. He picks up David's camera case and opens it. The sketch paper and pastels he doesn't even touch. He smiles and says something in Spanish. David just nods. Finally he motions them to zip their bags and proceed through the turnstile gate out to where people are waiting for the arrivals.

As they walk away Penny looks at David and asks him in a low voice.

"What did he say?"

"I don't have a clue."

They both laugh. Once they are outside, in the busy arrivals, they begin to search for Antonio. He is nowhere around. As they stand waiting numerous cab drivers attempt to grab their bags and offer to carry them out to their waiting taxi on the curbs outside. Once David has to actually wrench his big black wheeled bag away from an extremely pushy driver.

Penny looks around nervously. Penny notices they are almost all dressed alike. White shirts, black pants, dark sunglasses and shiny black hair.

It seems like all the people here are watching us.

"I hope Antonio shows up pretty quick. What'll we do if he doesn't?"

"It's really hot in here."

Just then Antonio strides through the crowds toward them with two other young men. As they reach David, Antonio reaches out and shakes hands with him. The hoard that was gathering around them starts to disperse. Antonio speaks to them in halting Spanish.

"*Ola. Buenos dias.* How was trip? *No problemo? Si.* We go. *Vamoosa.* We have not long. Flight to Tuxtla Gutierrez."

David picks up his pack but one of the two young men smiles and takes it from him. Antonio nods at David.

"*Por favor*, allow to assist. Appreciate to work."

The other one reaches over and takes Penny's pack.

Outside, the full heat of the sun blasts them. It is so bright. Penny squints against it.

Light. It's bouncing off everything. The sun. It's so strong.

As they proceed to the small van waiting, they are intercepted several times. First by an Indian woman selling handmade pins. The pins are single coloured threads twined around wire with tiny bits of brightly coloured fabric for clothing and hats. She thrusts them at Penny with an imploring look. She has a small child in a sling around her middle.

I wish I had some pesos.

Another, is a man who is selling newspapers.

"*La Journada?*"

Antonio stops and hands him several pesos and they continue on to the van. As they load their packs in the back and climb in, two other North American Indians greet them from the back seat. David climbs in after Penny and shakes hands with them.

"Wade, this is Penny. Wade's Lakota. This is Gerald. He's Mohawk."

Penny shakes hands with them. The inside of the van is like an oven.

Antonio introduces the four other men.

"Carlos. He is Maya from near Ocasingo where we go. Marcos is from Panama. Antoline is from Ecuador. And Emilio is from San Diago. He translate. *Si? Bueno.* He explain things."

As they settle into the van, Emilio, sitting next to Penny by the window begins to speak. His voice is soothing and calm.

"The organization of this *consejo* is accomplished by our brother's from the Indigenous Organizations for Regional Autonomy along with our organization, which is a *Xicano* organization in the USA supporting the concept of regional autonomy for Indigenous Peoples and organizations. I will tell you more as we go along. However, as you know, we first catch our flight to Tuxtla. At that point we'll transfer to another vehicle and go up into the moun- tains to San Cristobal de las Cases. As you are aware, there is still a great deal of nervousness and we will likely be stopped by the Mexican army patrolling the area. If that happens, you must let me or Antonio answer all questions. Have your passports ready."

He reaches into his knitted satchel and brings out several plastic covered cards attached to heavy cord and hands them to the two Americans and to them.

"Hang these press identifications around your neck. Questions? No. Okay. Here's our terminal. Stay with me through the lineup. I have all your tickets. Antonio will keep the others together. Penny, take David's camera and hang it around your neck. Keep it there, please."

The terminal they now enter is smaller, very crowded and dirty. Cigar and cigarette smoke is thick in the air. Papers and debris litter the floor. Drink containers and empty bottles sit near over-flowing trash cans. The lineup is long. They stand in line and wait. It doesn't seem to matter to anyone that their boarding time comes and goes long before they reach the counter for their boarding passes.

They are escorted right out onto the tarmac as soon as they proceed into the waiting area. The plane is a mid-sized Air Mexico prop. They climb the stairs with their packs. Inside it is stifling hot.

There are other Americans among the thirty or so passengers. Two couples sitting several rows ahead talk and laugh loudly, obviously partly drunk. The flight attendant smiles a wide bright smile when she speaks to them. Her smile disappears when she approaches their group. She surveys them, her face distant and cool, and asks something in Spanish, nodding toward the Indians in the group. She doesn't even look at her and David or the two other North American Indians. Antonio responds in rapid Spanish and she nods curtly and moves on. She returns from behind them distributing small paper boxed juice cartons. Tiny paper cups filled with a thick dark bitter coffee follows. Beer in clear bottles are served to the American tourists with the same flash of white teeth, who pay her in American dollars. A few "business" dressed Mexican men also order beer and pay her in pesos.

Penny thumbs through the airline magazine in the pocket in front. Much of it is in Spanish, however she notices real estate ads are in English. She stops to look at one and shows David. It has a photograph of some Mayan ruin in the background, lush greenery surrounding a villa type building. The advertisement reads, "Buy Mexico. Real Estate Available in Prime Location."

Emilio sits quietly next to them reading the La Journada. He points to a photograph of three ski masked men in camouflage holding automatic weapons.

"There has been some unrest in the states of Oxaca and Guerrero. There is a short mention here of EZLN members calling for a continuing solidarity of action. The Mexican army is officially denying their involvement in the execution style killing of fifteen resistance members in that area, blaming it instead on underground drug dealers."

None of their group comments or even looks at Emilio. Finally the pilot comes on over the crackley speakers and speaks in a flow of words. Emilio nods at them.

"We'll be landing in ten minutes. Antonio will get some food to take on the bus. If you have American dollars, a good idea right now is to take any big bills out and put them in an inside pocket. Leave only small bills in your purse or wallet, in case you're asked to hand them over to army officials for inspections on the way. You only want them to see little or no American money. *Si?* We'll get some water also. Each one should get a big bottle. Okay? Stay by me, please, when we land."

The plane is now circling above a smallish city. It looks beautiful. Palm trees and white buildings sparkle in the clear sun.

When they arrive, they walk right off the plane and into the small open air terminal. Another small bus is parked with others waiting inside. As their bags are being loaded an army vehicle moves alongside them. The dark green tarp over the back holds a dozen or so men in fatigues holding rifles in the back. The truck is heavy, belching black smoke and bouncing along noisily. The men in the back look young. Many of them look Indian. As Antonio and the several other men approach with brown packages and plastic bottles of water, the army truck slows beside them. The driver's companion points toward them and the truck slows to a crawl. It finally moves on.

As they wind through the streets of Tuxtla, hoards of well dressed white tourists crowd the streets lined with open air shops selling merchandise of every description. Clothing, pottery, crafts and jewellery. The small city is clean looking and seems almost American except for the narrow streets and wild traffic. As they begin to leave the business district behind, the outskirts begin to show signs of poverty. Miles of shanty town buildings made of scrap wood and corrugated tin give way to low brown mud-block buildings with flat dirt roofs. Finally these give way to mud huts with thatched roof tops.

They pass many brightly dressed Indian men, women and children carrying bundles on their backs or herding small flocks of sheep or goats. Bicycles pulling two wheeled carts and single horse drawn wagons loaded with fruits, vegetables and other goods, outnumber the motor vehicles in these sections.

As they begin to climb up the winding roads away from the valley into the mountains, the land opens up in places to corn fields inter-spersed with small Indian mud huts huddled together here and there. Between the fields they pass several large wealthy ranch type complexes with stately buildings and wide long driveways lined with palms. Emilio points toward them, a look of anger on his face.

"Those are owned by the landlords. Families from the *conquistadora* of centuries past. A few wealthy families who control things."

Antonio hands a package to them and they unwrap it. Inside it is a cooked chicken. He passes them another package with some corn tortillas. Emilio shows them how to break pieces of the chicken and wrap it in the tortillas. They pass the packages back to others behind them. They pass around a jar of small chile peppers. Penny doesn't take one. Some fruit is passed around. Emilio takes the apple from Penny and hands her an orange.

"Please, the orange is better. The apples need to be peeled. Eat only things you can peel or is cooked. No fresh vegetables. No water from the taps anywhere, even to brush teeth. *Si?* Chilies are good too. The heat is good for you."

He smiles and hands her the jar again. She takes one out and nibbles it. It's fiery hot. She takes a mouthful of chicken and corn tortilla and chews. Her lips are burning and her tongue feels numb by the time she finishes the rolled up tortilla and the small chili pepper. She can feel it warm in her stomach. The water she sips from the plastic bottle only makes her mouth feel hotter.

How can they eat those peppers like they were pickles?

The men are all speaking Spanish around them. The bus is moving slowly along behind another vehicle letting a herd of sheep pass. As they round a corner the truck they are following slows to a stop and the driver speaks rapidly to Antonio.

"Army check point ahead. Looks like they will check for papers."

Two men in uniform walk toward them from each side, rifles pointed forward. Penny can feel her heart begin to beat faster as they approach the front widows on each side. The driver greets the one on his side in Spanish and Antonio in the front seat speaks to the other one. There is a rapid exchange and the one on Antonio's side motions with his rifle for everyone to get out. Several other uniformed men with rifles appear as they climb out and stand together by Emilio and Antonio. They are pointing their rifles at them as Antonio and Emilio take out their papers. One other man examines them and moves to them and the two Americans. He asks something in Spanish and Emilio answers and turns to them.

"He wants to see your passports."

They hand over their passports and wait as he looks at each and flips to the photographs of each of them. Finally he looks up at

Emilio and speaks again in rapid Spanish. Emilio shrugs and points to the press identification around his neck and turns back to them.

"He wants to look in your wallets. Hand them over to him one at a time."

Penny is first. The man stands squarely in front of her as she reaches inside her belt pouch for her thin wallet. He flips through it and thumbs the dollar bills she has left in there. He hands it back without speaking and takes David's wallet. He looks at David's Indian Status Card for a moment and speaks again in rapid Spanish. Emilio answers him briefly.

"He wants to know why you are here from Canada. I explained to him that you are writing an article for tourist purposes."

The other uniformed man is talking more loudly with Antonio and the South Americans. There is a flurry of conversation for some tense minutes. Finally, they hand the passports back to Antonio and motion them to the back where the bags are piled. They open the back and the bags are opened one by one by two of the uni-formed men. Penny and David stand watching as their packs are unzipped and searched. The van is also searched.

Finally after another flurry of conversation with Antonio, the bags are put back in. The man who checked their passports nods at Emilio and motions with his rifle for them to get back in. They stand with their rifles still pointed at them as the driver pulls slowly away. Nobody speaks until they are out of sight then Emilio speaks in Spanish to Antonio.

"They wanted to know why you travel with so little money. They were looking for guns, too. It should be okay from here on. We'll be in San Cristobal in about half an hour. We'll be staying there for the night at a small hotel. We'll leave for Ocasingo in the morning. We don't want to be travelling in the mountains after dark. There is curfew, he says, because of the unrest in the mountains. Did everyone get all their money back?"

Wade, the Lakota man answers.

"I had a twenty mixed in there with my dollar bills. It's gone."

Emilio smiles at him.

"Yeah. I saw that. Nothing we can do. Keep your money in an inside pocket all the time. We'll get some money changed into pesos in San Cristobal. Okay. Carry pesos. It's better."

The bus is now entering the outskirts of the small town. All around them are small shanty type buildings interspersed with red mud-block huts with small yards surrounded by mud-block fence waist high, holding chickens, sheep and goats. Indian people dressed in brilliant colours walk along the narrow dirt walks by the road pitted with holes. Bundles and packs of all sizes strapped to their backs. There are children, barefoot and thin, walking everywhere.

On the road, cars, carts, wagons and some horseback riders move slowly along, weaving around each other. As they reach the central areas, small shops of every kind line the streets. The buildings are all low adobe type buildings whitewashed or left the brown of baked earth. The streets are narrow and hundreds of people fill the streets. Indians dressed in their traditional colours far outnumber those dressed in more European style dress.

Finally the bus pulls in front of a locked iron grill gateway and the driver steps out and walks through a small iron gate set into the side of the surrounding white washed wall enclosure. After several minutes he emerges and the gate swings inward to let them pass into the inner courtyard. The courtyard of the inn is Spanish in style. A brick courtyard encircling a small garden with palms and brilliant flowering plants. The clean courtyard is surrounded by low whitewashed buildings framed with dark wooden beams and red tiled roofs.

As the group in the bus climbs out, the proprietor comes out to greet them, speaking in a flowing Spanish to Antonio and the others. He greets the North Americans with a simple nod. He and Antonio go into the small receiving area to register for the rooms. The bags are unloaded from the back of the bus and lined up along the front of the office. The driver waits until Antonio comes out with keys for everyone before he climbs into his bus and slowly backs out of the courtyard. The gate clangs shut behind him and locks. Antonio speaks momentarily with Emilio who nods and waves them over.

"We'll get everybody settled into their rooms and then we'll walk over to the meeting place. There will be food prepared there for us. These keys are for the rooms. Keep them locked even when you go to another's room. Carry passports and money with you and camera's. Do not drink the water or wash your mouth with it. The gates are locked always. Only with keys can you pass into the courtyard through the door after dark. Okay. We be back here in ten minutes. Wade and Gerald share a room. David and Penny next to you. Antonio and I share a room next to you. The others will be across the courtyard from us. Come."

Emilio walks briskly toward the rooms nearest the office picking up his backpack as he motions them to follow.

Their room is small but neat. It has a bed with a white cotton coverlet and a small wooden set of drawers. They have a tiny toilet room with a small wash sink and mirror. The walls are white and bare. The narrow window facing the courtyard has a red lace work curtain.

David stretches out on the bed and bounces, waiting while she uses the toilet.

"I don't think you should wash your hands in the water, Penny. Just put some of the bottled water on a cloth and sponge your hands and face with that."

"David, you know I grew up on the rez back home. The water we carried in buckets to use was lake run-off. I grew up drinking the water that geese and ducks swam in, and cows and horses watered at, not to mention the beavers and otters and other stuff. People in the city get beaver fever and other stuff. We don't. But, I guess you're right. Maybe they have different bugs. It's not a good place to test it out unless I had to."

"Well, we better get out there. We're going to go over to the meeting place."

As David and Penny arrive at the group waiting at the gate, Emilio joins them.

"We're going to walk over to the meeting. They're waiting over there with food and coffee for us. Let's go."

They file out through the small gate in the wall and out into the street. The scene changes abruptly. Out there the street is dirty and crowded. They walk along the street, the men speaking in Spanish. Wade and Gerald catch up to them. He looks around and turns to David.

"The country has been run by the same government for about sixty or seventy years. Even though there are elections, they're rigged. About eighty percent of the people live in extreme poverty. It's disgusting that the US and Canada are in cahoots with that kind of government. Have you been here before?"

David shakes his head.

"No, but I thought it would be good to find out about the Indian people. You never hear media coverage on them. They're probably the worst off. Why did you come?"

"Me and Gerald both work with the Indigenous working group in Geneva. There was a small delegation of Mayan people who invited us to come to see if there was some way we could help. I haven't been in Chiapas before, but I have visited some of those sweat shops that spring up along the US Mexican border. American companies that set up shady assembly operations, paying cheap wages to the desperate, mostly women and children, in the worst possible conditions you can think of. Things that wouldn't be allowed in the US They move as soon as they get found out. It makes a person sick, to think of the US profiting on the suffering of people, because that's where all the money drains out to. It doesn't stay to help the people here."

Gerald nods and points to the crowded streets filled with people.

"I'm also following up on some reports that there is a serious body parts trade going on."

David looks startled.

"What?"

Gerald looks at him steadily for awhile.

"Grown people forced by poverty to sell blood, kidneys, skin and corneas and so on. There are reports coming in from all over Central America and South America of disappeared children. In Guatemala, for instance, people are attacking Americans, because of suspicions around the kidnapping of Indian children for sale.

Where in the hell do you think they take them. To look after them? Shit they're vampires."

David looks sick.

"Fuck, what next!"

As they walk past the low mud-block dwellings, small Indian children approach them with their hands out, asking for pesos. A small girl barely up to her waist grabs Penny's arm and tugs. Penny turns to look at her. She has a huge lump on the side of her throat. It is red and swollen with pus running out. The little girl has her other hand on it. She makes small mewing sounds of pain. Penny stops just for a moment. The girls mother, holding a smaller child by the hand with another in a sling over her shoulders, speaks to the child, calls her away. Penny takes the girl's hand and walks over to the mother. She feels her chest tightening, her throat hurting. The mother, a tiny Indian woman with large sad eyes stares her straight in the eyes.

"*Por favor, Senora?*"

At that moment Emilio moves next to her. He speaks for a moment to the woman in Spanish. He turns back to Penny.

"Her daughter has an infection. She has no money for medicine or food. She has nothing to sell. She came from the mountains, her relatives are missing. She has no relatives here."

Penny feels like she can't breathe.

"How much will medicine cost? I can't walk away."

"Penny, there are thousands like her, and worse. All over this country. Displaced, sick and starving. Masses of them crowding into the cities and finding it worse."

"I can't walk away. It might be no help but I can't not give her something."

She reaches into her belt and takes out the small rolled up wad of American dollars and hands it to the woman. The woman takes her hand briefly, tears filling her eyes as she nods and speaks to Emilio before turning and walking away.

"She said to thank you, and for the Gods to smile on you. Let's go the others are waiting."

As they approach the rest, the two Mayan men walking with them nod to her. Carlos speaks in Spanish to Emilio.

"They say you will see much suffering like this. There is nothing for them. They try to take care of the ones in their villages, but many have left the villages because the men have had to leave to try to find work. There isn't enough food. No medicine. The fighting makes it worse. They have no choices."

Penny looks at David. She can see the look of helplessness on his face. Wade and Gerald look the same. Nobody says anything more to her. She walks silently along, looking at the Indian people now beginning to get thicker on the sides of the street. They have blankets spread out, selling corn, beans, tortillas and handmade goods of all kinds.

Finally they reach a long low building with a hand painted sign in front. Several Indian women with long braids wrapped in coloured yarn wearing dresses embroidered with brilliant flowers stand at the door to greet them. Inside, the room is dimly lit with one bare electric bulb. Wooden benches are arranged in rows facing a narrow wooden table with red earthen bowls of food. Several Mayan men stand up and speak briefly. Emilio nods and translates to them.

"Please, have some food. It is simple. Tortillas and beans. Also coffee if you wish. Once you are all seated the meeting will begin. Just to greet you and fill us in on the current situation."

Once they are seated and eating, one of the men stands and begins to speak. Emilio translates as he speaks.

"This is the gathering place of the Mayan cooperatives from this region. Textile and coffee co-ops. They greet you and express their gratitude for coming. The situation grows much worse since the uprising. They are experiencing a market shut-out. It has caused severe economic hardships in the last two years. The market boards do not buy their goods or their coffee. It is to squeeze them out of production and force them to sell their lands cheap. They say it is an effect of NAFTA. The constitution no longer protects lands held in common by villages. To force them to sell to outside privatization. Tomorrow, you will go to the village. You will see the sheds filled with harvested green coffee waiting to be bought. It is their hope that you will also participate in a Mayan ceremony. For tonight, that is all. The road is very rough and you will need to rest tonight. We will spend the night up there in the main village. They wish you a good night."

The rest of the meal is spent with people sitting in small groups speaking. David asks to take some photographs. He walks around taking a few photographs, of the Mayan men with their wives, in front of a large sign with the organization's name and insignia. The tortillas are made with thick hand ground corn. The beans are hot and spicy. Penny's tongue and mouth burns but she is hungry and she cleans out her thick earthen bowl with her tortilla.

Dusk is beginning to gather shadows as they head back to the inn. The streets are empty. Only a few army and police vehicles move slowly about. The streets seem eerie and ominous. Emilio translates for the Mayan men.

"There is still curfew here. Nobody allowed after dark. It's dangerous, even now, to walk around. But we stick to the main streets and we'll be okay. It's not far."

Finally, back in the inn courtyard, they gather briefly in a circle. Emilio translates for Antonio.

"We leave as soon a daylight comes. About five o'clock. Take your water bottles and a sweater or a wrap of some kind. It's colder in the mountains. Wear comfortable walking shoes and only a small bag or pack. We'll be hiking tomorrow. We'll have coffee here and some bread before we leave. Please rest now and be here ready to go in the morning. Have a good night."

Penny lies awake, long after David is snoring beside her, face toward her, arm resting across her stomach. She can hear music drifting in the air. The room smells musty and it is stuffy. The images loom in her head of the market square in San Cristobal. Images of the foreign tourists walking around, self-absorbed in bargaining for the cheapest prices. Their eyes. Filled with a distant contempt and greed. Images of spaces crowded with brightly dressed Indian people. Thin, tired looking people with dark sad eyes, backs bent under bundles. Images of crippled and blind old people, begging, and skinny children with their hands out. Over it all, the girl's pain filled face with the huge oozing swelling on the side of her throat. And the eyes of her mother. Staring straight into her soul. All of it mixed together like a collage.

What was that look? Accusing? Maybe. Defeat? Almost. Pain? Partly. Not fear. A knowing of some kind. Knowing what? Knowing the wrongness of it all? What the goddamn hell kind of a world is this anyhow? Vultures on a cheap vacation, flocking here looking for a deal. It's criminal. Is this what the American dream is about? To be able to do that? Be a tourist, peering with curiosity at the suffering?

It seems like she has barely fallen asleep and David is shaking her awake.

"Penny. It's time to get up. Let's get going. How'd you sleep? Not too good, huh. You got shadows under your eyes."

"I just couldn't get the images out of my head. You know? How do those tourists do it? Just walk around and buy stuff and then fly home? Damn. Oh damn. I keep seeing that girl. I hate it."

"Penny get yourself together. You don't fall apart. You witness it. You tell about it. You do what you can. If you can. It ain't gonna go away. Not for some time. Now get yourself in gear. Okay? That's my girl."

He puts his arms around her and pulls her to him and strokes her hair for a short time. She draws in several long breaths and nods.

Outside, the others are gathering in the early morning light around the white ironwork table set in the courtyard. She sees the Mayan men looking at her. They converse quietly in Mayan then to Emilio in Spanish. Emilio looks at her and then at David.

"They wonder if the *Senora* may want to stay. She would be comfortable and safe here. Maybe she has stomach problem? It will be a hard trip, they say."

Penny and David look at each other.

"No. She comes. Penny?"

"Tell them not to worry. I just didn't sleep too good. My stomach's okay. Nothing a little strong coffee won't fix."

He translates back to them and they smile and nod. Antonio arrives with several containers of coffee, a small pitcher of milk, brown lump sugar and some thick white cups. He also has a tray of bread. Smallish plain loaves and lightly iced, thick biscuits. They pass the bread around and drink coffee, dipping the dry bread into the strong sweetened coffee not speaking. Only when the coffee and bread are gone does Antonio speak in Spanish. Emilio nods and looks over at Wade and Gerald.

"You two and Marcos will go with another group. Antonio will go with you as well. They will take you to talk with one of the liberation organizations in another village. It is best for us all to leave together in two vehicles. Another vehicle will join us once we reach the forest cover, and your vehicle will depart. Carlos and Antoline will come with us. We will meet in the same place if all goes well and arrive together back here tomorrow before dark. Si? Okay. Lets go. Everybody got their passports? The vehicles are outside."

Outside the gate two smaller vehicles are waiting. David, Penny, Emilio, Antoline and Carlos get in with the driver. Marcos, Wade, Gerald, Antonio and the other Mayan man, whose name is never mentioned, get into the other vehicle with the driver and they begin to drive through the narrow winding streets. They begin to climb almost immediately. The road, winding away into the mountains is already steep, narrow and pitted with holes. Along the road, a steady stream of Indians walk down into the town below, backs loaded with bundles. Several times, they slow to a crawl as they pass Indian men on horses carrying huge swaying bundles of wood and other things wrapped in blankets.

Finally there are fewer and fewer people and the trees begin to thicken on all sides as they criss-cross small dips and openings, revealing small huts with thatched roofs huddled together with patches of corn around them. Each time they seem to be reaching the top, they come out to more mountains, higher and thicker with trees. The trees are all strange. Vines and strange vegetation thick at their bases. A few times Penny catches a glimpse of bright colour in the trees above them, but they disappear quickly. Emilio and Carlos speak in quiet Spanish.

"There are families hiding in the forest. Carlos mentions that the army raids, looking for rebels in this region, has frightened many of the Indian people. These hills, overlooking the Lacondon jungle on the other side, are where the strongest fighting took place. They do not fear the EZLN. And their men are always at risk, to be accused of assisting or to be taken into the army. They cannot tend to their crops. You will see some of the places where their homes were bombed and their corn crops burned out. Their goats, sheep, cattle and horses are let go, and roam the hills. It's very desperate here."

Several times they stop briefly at a fork in the road. The sun is now full up and the road is narrow with big rocks and wash outs which they move slowly over. At the third stop, at a fork in the road, the vegetation and trees are so dense around them, that when another vehicle emerges and moves in behind them, it happens so quickly Penny is amazed. Barely a minute passes and the vehicle carrying Wade and the others disappears down the road from which it emerged and they continue on with the new group behind them. Nobody speaks but she notices Carlos and the driver tilt the mir-rors on each side out toward the trees around them. She sees them glancing back and around, for several miles before they relax.

Finally, with the sun straight overhead, they reach a smallish valley which flattens out to a clearing. Small patches of corn and other crops are scattered quilt-like over the clearing between half a dozen groups of huts, four or five together. A small low building, near the centre of the clearing, has a white flag on a pole waving and a small-hand painted sign. Penny sighs with relief as they turn into the path leading to the building.

God. Talk about needing to pee.

Emilio, turns and smiles at them.

"Everybody okay? We stop here for a short rest and relief and maybe drink some water and we continue on. Carlos says this is one of the villages that is somewhat intact. This is a school. Nobody in school now, though. We'll stop for about fifteen minutes. The village is mostly empty. People up in the mountains."

The vehicle behind them pulls up next to them and a group of three Mayan men and two women climb out. They greet Carlos and the driver and glance shyly at her and David and nod. Penny nods at the women and then at Emilio. There doesn't seem to be any other people around.

"I need to use a toilet."

Emilio translates in Spanish to the women. They nod and smile at her. She follows them to the back of the low building made of poles with open holes for windows. In the back there is an enclosure made of upright poles waist high. There is nothing in there but a hole in the ground with poles laid across it. One of the women pulls up her skirt and squats over the opening between the poles and relieves herself. Penny goes next. It's hard to manage with her jeans pulled down to her knees. She almost loses her balance when she finishes and tries to stand. One of the women steadies her with a hand on her shoulder, and Penny laughs embarrassed. They both smile at her.

The group is now sitting on the steps of the school passing around a plastic bottle of water. Penny watches David snapping photographs. Penny reaches in her bag for the bag of trail mix she brought along. She takes some and passes it to the women, who watch her every move. They take some and pass it to the men who shake the nuts, raisins and pieces of dried fruit into their palms, examining each one before eating them. One of them indicates the mix and questions Carlos. Emilio explains in Spanish and then translates back.

"They say it's good. They thought it was your traditional food."

Penny closes the ziplock bag which is still half full and gives it to one of the women. She smiles shyly and tucks it into her string bag hanging from her shoulder.

"Carlos says we are about an hour from the village where we will spend the night. The co-op organization will have prepared some foods for us and we will eat and then hike for a short ways above to see one of the places where the homes were bombed out during the fighting. This co-op has textiles as well as a coffee storage building. This evening there will be a ceremony after the meeting and supper. So now we go again."

As they move away, after they are on the main road, Penny glances back at the buildings they just left. A small group of brightly dressed figures emerges from the long low building to stand on the steps and watch them leave.

The rest of the ride doesn't seem long. They climb again along a narrow road with dense forest on each side before coming into another larger clearing. This time a small valley in a kind of flattened dip between two hills. There are clearly fields growing different kinds of crops around a small village centre. There are huts scattered in small groups here and there between the fields. Penny can see goats, sheep and chickens wandering around the buildings. Indian people are walking along the narrow road leading to the village centre.

The village is a small collection of mud-block or pole buildings and huts with thatched roofs around a small plaza. It isn't really a town. There are no shops that she can see, although a few of the low rectangle buildings have hand painted signs in front. There is one large building set back behind the others. It is made of cement block and has a tin roof. It seems to loom over the other buildings. It has a huge set of doors in front, large enough for a truck to drive into.

They pull up in front of one of the buildings with a hand painted sign in front. As they climb out several Indian women come out and stand on the steps to greet them. They are dressed almost identical. Penny suddenly realizes that all the women they have passed are also dressed the same. The same bright colours and patterns of large embroidered flowers on their white blouses. The same striped short cloak pinned at the neck covering the shoulders and the same coloured woven wide sash belt and black skirt.

Carlos and the other Mayan men call out greetings to them and they lead the group into the building. Inside the walls are lined with woven textile material of all sizes and colours. There are racks of white blouses with and without embroidery. Brilliant coloured sashes, belts and bags are stacked in piles everywhere. She can see rugs, blankets and skirts and the short cloaks hanging on wooden pegs. They walk through the long room and into another in the back where there is a table set up with bowls of food and wooden benches arranged around the walls.

They eat quickly as the usual greetings and introductions are made. This time the tortillas are served with a chicken stew with boiled potatoes and beans. It's good, the first food Penny has eaten without the hot chilies. Emilio translates between mouthfuls of food.

"This textile co-op is a Mayan women's organization. They are weavers and make the wool and cotton. They sew the garments and other things by hand. All the work is for market. The wool takes much longer to spin and dye and work. The work is the highest quality. Now they have difficulty selling their work. Cheaper manufactured goods are replacing these carefully handmade items. This brings much needed income to the families of this region. It is their hope that perhaps in some way we can be of some assistance in this. They have great pride in their work."

After the meal they are escorted to the large shed holding stacked bags of green coffee. Inside, walls are stacked to the ceiling with sacks of coffee bearing the insignia of the Mayan men's co-op. Emilio talks with the Mayan men in Spanish for some time before explaining to David and Penny.

"They say that they are forced to pay for the sacks and hauling before the harvests. It takes all their money for a year in advance with the hope of selling the coffee at a price which returns their costs of harvest and so on. They sell it green, and so get the lowest prices. It is the best coffee in Mexico and sells for far greater prices once roasted and packaged. The market has shut them out by lowering the prices to such an extent that they cannot even pay costs. They have not sold any significant amounts in the past two years since the NAFTA agreement and the huge drop in the peso. They believe it is to force them out. To have to sell their lands. They say there has been oil and gas discovered in some of the areas surrounding this region. They are afraid most of the time that they will lose their way of living and be forced, as many already have been, to give up and live in total poverty, scattered and landless. They are hopeful that we might be able to assist in some way to direct market for them."

David and Emilio continue talking as they walk out of the cool dark interior into the sunlight. Penny looks around the village as they walk through it and away toward the hill above. The yards are neat and clean. A few goats, sheep, horses and chickens are in pens behind some of the huts. The mud-block huts are kept up and neat, some are decorated with various bright coloured rugs at the steps and hangings to cover windows. There are vegetable patches in every yard. They pass several old men in white short cotton pants, belted at the waist with a brilliant sash, bent over weeding or hoeing or simply sitting and smoking. Clothing hangs drying in the sun and Indian women sit outside in the shade grinding corn or spinning. They look up and smile as the group passes. Children run about, playing. They are healthy looking. It is the first time Penny sees children smiling and laughing. A few of them follow the small group.

One of them, a little girl with long black braids neatly tied together in the back by a brightly coloured yarn and an embroidered white blouse and skirt identical to the women, walks shyly by her talking in Mayan. Penny looks down at her and she smiles, chattering on without realizing Penny can't understand her. Beside her, Emilio laughs as Carlos translates to him what the girl is saying.

"She asks if perhaps you are deaf. She is asking you why you dress wrong. Did something happen to you? Will you live here? Why are you so tall?"

Penny smiles as Carlos explains to the girl.

I wonder how the future will treat her. How long before the pain of just surviving silences her? Who in the fuck thinks free trade will offer any-thing but shit to these people?

She can feel her anger somewhere deep down inside, hot and burn-ing. The girl moves away waving and smiling as they begin to climb the hills above the village.

The climb is difficult. The land is rocky and spiky sharp plants grow in clumps everywhere around other tall weeds and short spiny brush. There are pines with long thin needles that grow between other trees she has never seen before. The birds, which flit about are brilliant and small. They sing clear trilling songs. Once something rustles in the grass nearby and the men ahead all stop at once. They wait until the rustling moves away from them before they continue on.

The ground becomes so steep at one point that Penny finds herself looking directly at Emilio's heels in front above her. They climb this way for almost an hour stopping only once to rest briefly. Penny looks back down at the village. It is small in the valley below. The valley is narrow and long and in the distance she can see other small groups of dwellings. The land is green and yellow. A warm golden yellow where the corn patches are.

When they finally reach the top which slopes gently then flattens into a high valley, Penny's legs are shaking and her mouth is dry. The wind is cool though. Ahead of them are several groups of mud huts. The thatched roofs are dark and falling apart. As they approach them she can see huge holes where the earth has been exposed. Weeds grow in the holes. Several of the huts are only half standing, parts of walls, a pile of ash and rubble.

The men stand quietly for several minutes without speaking before Carlos speaks in Spanish to Emilio. Emilio walks around and picks up shell casings from the grass. David and Penny pick up a few and examine them. Most are small brass casings, but a few are large. David turns over several large pieces of shrapnel sticking out of the grass.

"Goddamn it! USA. issue. Jesus Christ! What the hell is that doing here!"

Emilio turns to him and Penny.

"Exactly! Carlos was just mentioning that helicopter raids dropped bombs on these huts. He said it happened in many villages during the worst of the fighting. They were shelled and burned out. That hole over there used to be a hut. Carlos said they used flame throwers to burn the crops and dropped fire bombs on huts suspected of hiding rebels. He said some of the helicopters were definitely American. Lots of women and children and families killed this way. Many men died here trying to fight off the army to protect their families. The Mexican Army rounded up many of them.

They are disappeared. It is the Mexican Army the people here fear. They are the terrorists. He said that even now there are reprisals and raids take place every time there is unrest but now most of it is in the jungle areas. Ocasingo was one of the towns that the rebels took during the uprising. The people in these outlying villages are choiceless. It is terrible and will become worse."

Penny feels strange. Her head feels light and she can almost hear a low buzzing sound. A familiar electricity surges through her. She looks around in panic trying to push it down or away. She closes her eyes and replays the images of the peaceful village below.

It's too much like a nightmare. I can't think of what took place here during the worst. I can't think of the beautiful women and children blown apart.

She tries to stop them but images of bleeding limbs and parts of torn bodies in brilliant cloth, visible through thick smoke and flames and dust, begin to form. The red, red blood everywhere on the torn earth. She can smell it and hear the screaming as camouflaged figures with guns move among the shadows. She's breathing hard, trying to catch her breath when she hears David.

"Penny? Was that climb up too hard? Here sit down for a minute."

He has her by the shoulders and pushes her down on a large rock. She opens her eyes and David is staring at her. She just shakes her head and breathes slowly. The other men are watching, concern on their faces.

"It's okay David. It's just hard being so visual in the head. You know? I see images. I can't help it. They just are there, alive. I'll be okay. Tell them it was the climb. Whatever. Let me sit for awhile."

Emilio is near enough to hear. He nods and turns to reassure the others. She sits while the men talk and David walks around snapping photographs. Finally, Emilio and David call her and they start the long silent walk back down to the village.

The sun is low in the sky by the time they reach the co-op building. The women are waiting with coffee and food. Penny picks at her food. She feels drained. Empty. Tired. One of the women sits next to her and then speaks quietly with Carlos. Carlos and Emilio talk for awhile and then Emilio turns to her.

"The women say to wait until morning for the meeting. They say it is not good for you to think too much. We will go, now, to the ceremony. It will be good for you. There are Mayan priests, from the old religion, here from the mountains. They will perform a blessing for the village and for us. Please, you should have a little food."

Penny eats. The soup is thick with corn and meat and other vegetables. Though she isn't hungry, the food is somehow comforting to her. The woman sits all the while watching her. Her eyes have the same knowing look.

When the meal is through they all walk to the large coffee shed. The sun is setting when they enter the building which is now lit with one light hanging from a long chain from the centre of the ceiling. People are sitting around on rugs and blankets spread around in a circle. In the centre of the circle are four small Indian men with dark wool clothes. There are rows and rows of small candles standing on the cement floor and a small fire burning on a rounded pile of dirt on the floor. They are escorted to the inside of the circle, next to the candles. Emilio sits next to her and David with Carlos beside him. As soon as they are seated one of the men begins to speak in Mayan. Carlos translates into Spanish for Emilio and Emilio in turn translates into English.

"They give greetings from the mountains. They will create the ceremony tonight to give blessings for the village. They will give blessings for the visitors. They will recount the prayers of their ancient ancestors. These will connect us all with the mystery. I will not translate the prayers, only for us to focus and listen to the sound of the words and to watch the fire in the candles once they are lit. Each is a fire within. When the candles are all complete in their burning, then our prayers are complete. We begin now."

The four men begin chanting prayers in a sing song tone while lighting the candles one at a time. The sound seems familiar to Penny. The room around seems to deepen in shadows as the chants go on and on. Sometime close to the end of the lighting of the candles, Penny hears a sound above her. She looks up at the same time David and Emilio do. The bulb on the chain is swinging back and forth in ever widening arcs. She feels the tingle on the back of her neck as her hairs rise. It moves all the way down her back.

Carlos, next to Emilio, notices them watching the chain swinging farther and farther. He shakes his head and points to the candles. Penny pulls her eyes away and focuses on the candles. They are all lit now. Each small flickering flame is dancing and casts small shadows around them. The four men stand facing outward toward the people, chanting, with their arms lifted high. Their language sounds so much like her own. Penny follows the sounds in her own language.

Fill me with the spirit of these, my relatives, as their beloved land fills them. Blessings for them in the suffering they share as a burden to become a force against what is to come. Blessings for them as the hope for us all. Bind us together so we might walk together toward the light.

As the candles burn out one by one, the chain swinging above them begins to slow. When the last candle flickers out, Penny looks up. The chain is now still.

As they line up to shake the hands and receive an individual blessing from the priests, they speak briefly to each one. When Penny reaches the last Priest in line, he speaks quietly in Mayan to her, while Carlos and Emilio translate.

"There is always light if we keep the flame in focus."

Later they walk in the dark back to the co-op building, the air is cold and the wind is blowing. Emilio translates David's question to Carlos.

"Why did the chain swing like that? Does it always do that?"

Carlos answers and Emilio translates back to them.

"Carlos asked one of the Priests about it. They said it was show-ing that the power is there. Among us. A mystical force."

Why doesn't it stop the violence toward them?

Penny doesn't ask the question. Instead she imagines it again as she looks up at the sky which is brilliant with unfamiliar stars. She plays back the image of the light swinging and swinging back and forth above the shadowy figures huddled together against the backdrop of sacks stacked to the ceiling. A small collection of Indian people, gathered around a fire against the cold around them.

Their sleeping arrangements are in the main room of the co-op building. Mats have been placed for them on rugs and there are warm colourful blankets spread out. Penny has no trouble falling asleep as soon as her and David curl up together and the single light is put out. The room feels friendly and familiar. She feels like she is back home when she was little and Tupa is there crooning to her when she is frightened.

In the morning, the meal is simple again. Sweet bread and coffee. The meeting during the meal is short. The women sit with the men. After the usual greetings and short reminders of the purpose of this visit the men request proposals from the visitors. Emilio speaks first.

"Brothers and sisters, I would like to outline a proposal. As you know, this is our second visit to this region. We have seen the conditions you have to deal with. Our members are also faced with poverty and hardships in the USA, though not as severe as yours here. If we could bring coffee and other goods up there, we could market at a better price. However, as we do not have money except what we raise, we would need to work out an understanding that will be fair. We propose to raise money to buy green coffee at your full cost. Once we recover our full costs for transport, roasting and packaging from the sales, we share equally the profit. It could provide some income to members of our organization to roast and package and market. Other goods, as well, might be good. Some of the textiles and so on. It means an association based on a spiritual work of mutual fair benefit. A unity of trust and assistance. Take this into consideration. We will meet with the other organizations back in San Cristobal tomorrow with the same proposal."

One of the men from the organization also stands and addresses the group while Emilio translates back.

"We are heartened by your proposal. We will take it into serious consideration. As you know, we are desperate to sell our coffee, even to get our costs back. We have been forced lately to sell to coyotes, who give the worst prices. They know we have no choice. These coyotes are the same bandits who wait on the roads and hijack our trucks when we try to take them out to sell in Mexico city or Vera Cruz."

David stands up next to address the group.

"I do not have a proposal, however, knowing the situation here, we will find a way to help raise money, if the proposal is acceptable. I will also undertake to meet with Indian organizations back in Canada who support the concept of regional autonomy to create an association with our brothers in the USA. Perhaps out of this we can create, together, something which can grow strong."

The men and women stand and shake hands with each of them before they begin to disperse. Penny walks around with David looking at the textiles.

"I'll get some of these blouses and some bolts of material for give-away back home. I don't have much money but it will help a little. I will wear the blouses with pride. I'm gonna try to get some environmental groups back home to buy more. I don't know how to help any other way."

Emilio translates her words to the women who wrap her purchases into a neat bundle for her to carry. They nod and smile shyly at her.

People stand out in their yards waving at them as they board their vehicle for the ride back to San Cristobal. The sun is shining and the village looks peaceful. As they pass the corn fields leading into the village Penny looks back at the village for as long as she can see it.

The year of Indigenous Peoples. Declared so by the United Nations. What a damn farce.

A deep and silent rage settles inside. A rage for all that she is somehow complicit in, simply by being.

PROSE FRAGMENT
FROM HER NOTE BOOK

IS THIS PART OF THE POEM
OR IS IT NON-FICTION?

globalization and supremacy deceit and grudging paternalism sys-
tematized racism colonial practise and government structured
racialization power enforcement might makes right the colour of
oppression and racism is money and blood

I THINK IT'S PART OF THE STORY
OR THE PLOT

A piece here and a piece there

The Alaskan sun is coming up. It is Solstice June 21. There is a sunrise ceremony at the sacred fire. The Mayan priest from Guatemala, is running it. Four candles encircled by flowers with a wax fire are in the centre. It is dusty and cold. People from all over North and South America stand huddled together encircling the middle where the fire burns. The midnight is light. No dark. The priest explains his name. Thirteen Deer. It is a date on the Mayan calendar.

The Spanish interpreter explains that the prayers and acknowledgments are to spirits of animals of each day the past year. This is a new year. The priest is explaining the Mayan calendar and his role of priest to study and predict the events astrologically into the material world. To keep track of movement into large change effects expected as predicted by calender and astrological events.

Penny stands with David, his arm around her.

Weird about Thirteen Deer. It keeps flashing in my mind. I feel so tired. It seems like the dust is just hanging in the air and I can't breathe right. This midnight sun is messing up my head and my body. David seems distant. I wish I felt a little better. Just be with him. He's such a good person.

After the ceremony, they all walk back to the big tent to eat and begin the celebration of the new day and the new year. The foods of the people from Chickaloon are the main course. Salmon, smoked and barbecued, caribou, berries of all kinds, along with bannock and fry bread. The solstice party with dancing, singing and eating lasts for a long time.

David still sits quiet and contemplative with Penny throughout the meal and the festivities. As the party begins to thin, Penny turns toward David.

"David, in the airport coming here, I was stopped by two students from Iraq, who asked me to help. To donate. To write my name. It was such a small thing. A few ink squiggles on paper. A piece of paper hardly big enough to make a fire with. They showed me pictures of men hanging. Eyes bulging out and cut off arms and legs. David I'm a visual artist. Picasso's Guernica is the state of the world. They showed me Canada's permissions to let them solicit. There were the tears in the one's eyes. The great grief I felt can never touch the pain that those mutilated bodies have felt. These are people like us. He looked at me and he knows, and I know, the same thing. It is ordinary people who suffer. Trying to survive, to live."

He studies her for some minutes and nods listening.

He's going to remind me about the reason for gatherings like this. I know, but what do I do? What?

"David, I feel this overwhelming anger somewhere deep inside. It's like all the images just begin to stack up inside. It's like being continuously battered from inside and I can't do anything. I'm having a hard time painting because of the images. But they scream at me. I feel like I'm going to break. It's like I'm sinking. I don't know what to do. I hate painting it. I hate it! I keep thinking of those Maya priests and the one here. If all we can do is watch the turmoil get worse, what's our role? What's the good of those ceremonies if they don't stop what's coming? Isn't it hopeless then?"

"I guess if I didn't have hope I wouldn't be here. Maybe neither would you. I know the feeling. I'm not an artist so I don't see the images. That must be hard. For me, it's more like a voice, inside, which never quietens. Maybe the voice of the suffering. All I know, is that to stay sane, I have to try to do something about it. It drives me, as well, and all I can do is to keep looking for what might help. It's that, or let the rage take over, let it spew out. That or give up. Either way, I might as well be dead."

"I'm not sure I feel hope. I know I feel good at these things, they are hope filled and maybe that's the way to the answer. A way to keep sane. These kinds of gatherings. Maybe the man who spoke about the concept of *Aztlan*, a place now hidden, and the path to its return, has the answer. To always look toward that place filled with warmth under the sun. Maybe it's the only thing to hold on to for now. But I want it to be true. It's like this huge darkness is looming world-wide and consuming everything good. And it's so much stronger than the small candles and flowers at the centre of these circles. I only wanted to paint the light and the flowers."

She feels the tears welling and she can't stop them. David leans over and touches a tear on her cheek.

"Your grief is where the hope resides. Without it being felt as deeply as you feel it, we are truly without hope. I was thinking of the priest's words about their knowledge. How, over eons, they perfected a science to understand and predict great cycles of change. It reminded me of that conversation you had with some of those academics on systems thinking and deep ecology. The thing about fractels. The way patterns in each minute thing is repeated in ever larger form reaching into space and the stars and into eternity. Somehow, together as human beings, we have become a force. A large movement of change. Maybe change which is now inevitable."

"If what is happening is a pattern which leads to the inevitable, as you put it, then what is our part?"

"I don't have any answers. I just know that we are human, too. Us Indigenous Peoples, we didn't do this. We are the ones who resist the insane destruction. More and more non-native people stand with us and resist, too. Together, we are millions strong, world-wide. A mystical force, if we maintain the focus. It seems to me that the most basic of instincts instructs us to yearn for peace and health. Cooperation provides a better chance. Everything in nature counts on this and learns it or perishes. I don't believe that aggression and violence is a natural human instinct. I believe that peace is survival. It is evidence of evolution. It must prevail in the end for the human, or we will not survive. And so we must continue to find ways to increase the possibility of this happening wherever we can."

"It doesn't seem probable or possible to me. This global system relies on the violence of poverty itself as a way to insure commerce continues and expands. It squashes people who are at the lowest of income levels, insuring hatred and more violence. More malevolence in an ever-increasing spiral outward towards all-out catastrophe."

Penny stops momentarily to draw a shaking breath. David listens without comment.

"It makes work-dependent have-nots out of the local peoples and cold murderers out of the have's. Corporate rights versus human rights. It's the monster whose masters sit in shining towers in cities far removed from the suffering. They can't afford to feel the searing pain of those being crushed. It's getting stronger and more vicious. And everybody gets snared in its diabolical methods. From the woman in the grocery store buying a banana to the unsuspecting voter who wants a better tax cut. We get tainted with that blood without even realizing it and without knowing its effect somewhere else. I know, I'm going on and on about stuff you already know. It's just that I feel so much. I don't know what to do with it. Anything I do seems so small and inconsequential next to what has to happen to halt the devil incarnate."

"I hope you can remember some of the stuff you just said in your talk tomorrow. I know there doesn't seem to be any hope, but maybe just saying those things is important. Breaking the illusion of western development and progress as a world order is critical to changing it. Many environmentalists just see the focus of the area they are striving to save. It seems to me that it's important to see the deeper levels of where our everyday lives stay ensnared in the whole system and what we each can change. It can add up. Maybe the hope is in the small things that each person of conscience decides not to do rather than what we actually do. I only know that you make a lot of sense to me. You do."

Penny sat there awhile in silence.

Maybe he's right. That there is hope. Maybe I just need to throw myself into the fray and rage as loud as I can. With my paintings and with my words. To scream and scream until I have no more voice and there is only silence. I see now where that print came out of.

"David, I will walk with you a ways on this path. I have to find out, I guess, where it's leading to. I feel more on solid ground with my kids. They seem to be taking root in the community and I have this big, big family surrounding them now. They won't slide away eas-ily, anymore. I'm having a hard time painting, right now, anyway. I'm tired. I feel bone weary. I'm gonna call it a night. Or as the case may be, here, a day."

A narrow trail filled with the whispers of leaves scarcely touching pulls them along rousing the chittering of sleeping birds at white night solstice. It is past midnight, now, in Chickaloon and there is no night, only a ghostly dawn. Penny looks at the deep lake beside the trail leading to their camp.

No stars here to shoot ice spines into velvet blackness. No sequins speckle the lake's still cold surface. No frogs raising a crescendo answering star songs so old the frogs and we humans disappear. Still Aztlan calls me from the depths as Coyote tries once again to climb the spines of light up to the star sisters. Yet, I know the spines of stars are there reaching down into the lake. Down to the stone paths of Aztlan. Down to its fires surrounded with flowers. I know this ghost light, hiding star shimmering, is not to be trusted, but my cell memory is strong and Coyote knows this path too.

They stop to make an offering at the flower circled fire.

NOTES IN HER SKETCH PAD

The story was always to unearth the myth makers. The demons. To subdue them. To redraw them. Toward nature's way. Now the story is about virtual life. Or non-life. Trickery. Sorcery. Now, opposition to the witchcraft culture of destruction means resisting the politics of information. How can we do this when the world-wide net is the trap. Is it possible in this reality? Oh, Coyote, stop fooling around.

The lineup at the Osoyoos crossing is long as the cars pull up one by one to the window of the US Customs.

Oh, shoot. I should have just flown into Vancouver instead of saving a few bucks and driving to Spokane. I'm gonna miss my flight to LA. I hope David remembers to meet me at the right time. Cripes, I didn't even ask him how to get out to the conference site. Shoot I feel tired already and I still have a couple of hours of driving and then the flight.

Finally she gets to the window. The Customs and Immigration man is red faced and mean looking. He studies her for a minute in silence.

"Where are going and how long will you be in the US?"

"I'm on my way to Spokane to catch a flight to Los Angeles. I'll be there until Sunday."

"What's the purpose of your trip?"

"I'm attending a conference at UCLA."

"What type of conference?"

"It's a conference of Indigenous people on the biodiversity."

"Do you have identification?"

Penny hands him her passport. He flips the pages looking at the stamps.

"What sort of work do you do?"

"I'm an artist. I teach."

"Your passport shows a lot of travel. Are you an activist?"

"I do lectures."

The Immigration man studies her passport for several more seconds.

"Are you Indian?"

"Yes. I guess by your description I am. I'm Okanagan."

"How much Indian blood do you have?"

"I don't know. Do I need to know that to visit the USA?"

"I need to know how much blood you have?"

I'm full of blood. Just cut me and see. I'll spill out onto the floor. Maybe spatter some on your smirking face! I am full of the blood that moves up from the ground you stand on. The very minerals your house sits on travels through my veins and will be in the veins of all my relatives for generations to come! I have lots of blood in me. A red line that moves like a river roaring over the falls at my grandparents home, harnessed to feed the power lighting your office. A river you will not stop no matter how many dams you build, no matter where you divert it. I have a lot of blood. Who took yours?

"I have an Indian Status Card. The Okanagan are from both sides of this border."

"It doesn't matter to me. I have to know what blood quantum. By US law you have to have at least one quarter blood quantum. Now are your grandparents Indian?"

"Yes, they are."

"You look pretty light to me. I could pull you in and make you produce evidence that they are. Now let me ask it another way. Do you have white parents or grandparents?"

"I don't think so."

"Somebody was in the woodpile. Well, we could spend all afternoon on this. You Indians think you can just waltz around anywhere you like. There are laws, you know. It don't make any nevermind to me but that stuff going on about the logging and that environmental shit don't go over in this country. We have ways to deal with it. Now move along."

Penny grits her teeth and slowly puts the car in gear and begins to move. He is still glaring at her as she pulls away.

No wonder some people go on a rampage. Freaking racist. Somebody in the woodpile! How in the hell am I supposed to know which grandmother did what? God, if they only knew the depth of insult those border crossings are to us. There are laws! My ass. It was pure lawlessness, and still is, that allows aggression and theft of our lands. This is my country and why am I the alien? Who is the real alien here? I spit on his shoes.

The rest of the drive is easy. Before long, the forested hill country of the Colville Reservation gives way to Grand Coulee Dam, harnessing the great mother river of her people. Wheat fields roll past as she finally reaches airway heights. She only has minutes to park and get her boarding card. Finally she can rest a little as she settles into her seat for the long ride to Los Angeles.

I feel like I'm on a treadmill. I don't know how David can do this constantly. It's just been one meeting after another. And things just get worse. Even those trips to Geneva. It's just a constant meatgrinder. How is a person supposed to endure it? When every turn something worse turns up. Now this conference. Patenting of living things including people! What kind of scary bullshit is that?

She falls asleep watching a sad movie about a child with cancer and the parents' fight for a rare treatment cure. She doesn't know how it ends.

At the LAX, David is waiting for her at the gate.

"Hi. How was the flight? Okay, I hope. Anyway, since you sent your bag with me and don't have one now, I came by bus and I thought we could hop a shuttle which takes us not too far from the bus terminal. We're staying with some friends out near Santa Anna. We'll drive over to the meeting tomorrow. Maybe you'll want to take a look at Disney World. It's not too far from where we're at. Everybody does."

She laughs.

"Oh, I just got a glimpse of Disney's world right at the border crossing. No, I'll pass. I would never live it down anyway if word got out to some of my activist friends."

The shuttle drops them in a dirty and shabby looking business section. The haze of the sky is an angry red, fringed with dusty tangerine, which fades into dirty sepia as the sun sinks rubber-ball red toward the oceans rusted surface.

"I can see the particles in the smog!"

It shrouds the figures against the buildings across the street in a thin veil. The humidity is unbearably heavy.

Different than the exhilarating humidity of the sudden summer thunder storms in the Okanagan. It must feel this way in hell.

David doesn't answer. He just keeps walking.

People move around them trance-like. They jostle and shuffle past. Eyes vacant with misery or crazy with pent up rage. Homeless people, some standing absently begging, others wrapped in a dirty blanket or simply sprawled against the buildings take up every space available on the sides of the street. Two blonde, stringy children walk among the homeless, aimlessly turning over every promising looking piece of litter. The stench of piss and rotting garbage is overwhelming. Cars going past blare their horns angrily in the slow crawl of choked traffic. The sharp smell of exhaust fumes overrides the faint traces of ocean salt in the air.

"This is hell! Think of that! Hell as something right here, claiming millions. Los Angeles. This City of Angels is everything but that. How can anyone live here?"

David just nods as he quickly guides her away from a hostile looking man wearing several rings in one nostril and a muscle shirt showing his densely tattooed arms. His hair is dyed pure white with two thin streaks of black from the temples to the back. Her heart is beating faster and faster. Suddenly, there is panic rising and swelling inside.

I feel like I have to run as hard as I can or scream until my throat is raw. I want to breathe. I want to see the clean blue of the sky and pure yellow of the sun on my skin. I want to reach up into the air and rip away the mantle of death hanging over every thing living. I feel as though I am stuck in a Salvador Dali painting. I can't shake the surrealness of this insanity surrounding me.

"How many children have to grow up and die here without having seen the clear blue of a spring sky? How many have never taken in a lung full of clean air or eaten clean fresh food from the earth? What kind of human sacrificing takes place here every year? How many daily are laid before the altar of the almighty dollar?"

Oh, my beautiful human brothers and sisters, when should the abuse to the children stop? And when should the human right to breathe be returned?

Penny's clothes are damp and clinging to her. Her skin feels gritty and unclean.

How can I walk past these destitute people? I feel like stopping to offer something to each person. I feel guilty walking by knowing their despair. That's what it is. Utter despair. America, land of the free. Free? What a joke!

"David. I can't stand this. My eyes and throat sting and burn. And deep inside I feel this fear. I didn't know it was like this, right here in America. It's a living death. These poor people. It's no different than what we seen in Mexico. How can they live like this? It's not even living. How can the rich and the powerful not do something about this? How? That's the scariest part. They must feel something. Why do they just look away and throw a little money here and there, to sooth their guilt? They could do something collectively. They could. Why don't they? Why?"

David hesitates a moment as though he is about to answer. Instead he shrugs and keeps walking. Penny can't shrug off the images forming inside her. She continues talking trying to make some sense of it.

"You know what I think. I think they must believe these people deserve what they're born into. They despise them. They think it's right for them to suffer. They believe they're superior and have more of a right! They see it as normal. They'll collectively kill to keep it the same. It's some kind of fear! Like the deranged acts of a tyrant father knowing he's losing control. He doesn't dare even think of the abuse he causes. He has to believe it's right! It's a massive social dysfunction. A mass insanity that just escalates with more inequity! People have to believe in the rightness of it!"

She stops right there. Her voice has risen and she's almost shouting. An old man sitting on the street directs a string of obscenities toward her and it suddenly seems like those seemingly oblivious people, around her and David, are gravitating toward them, Silently, without any indication of communication with each other, without directly looking at each other. They stare at her and David and move in tighter toward them. Their eyes, on her have the same knowing look as the Mayan woman. He turns toward her taking her arm and moving her along.

"We can't stop. We have to keep walking. It's not far from here to the bus station. We could have taken a cab. But that's a lot of money to use up sailing past these people throwing more fumes on them. We can give money to people, you know. I do when I can. It doesn't help though. It's just one more meal or one more fix. This isn't even anywhere near the worst parts of LA either. You don't even want to be in those parts for any reason. It's worse than a nightmare. Penny, get yourself together. This is what it's all about, the new world order. There are cities like this and worse all over the world."

"Do people even think of death from this as a sacrifice to the wealthy? Sacrifice as surely as though each child, woman and man is being lead to a bloody altar. Yet probably each who dies from living and breathing this was born to walk these streets believing in the right for this to be. It's so obscene. So absolutely wrong. This is progress? This is civilization in the most powerful country in the world?"

They are getting nearer to the all-points terminal. Drug dealers and muggers are beginning to move about more freely. Two mean looking skin head types are watching them openly. David puts one hand under his loose shirt near his belt. They turn away.

"Stay right by me. Don't for any reason look at anyone. Keep your fanny pack in front with your hand on it. The bus will be just as bad. If we have to stand, lean right against me as close as you can. It'll be full. It'll be fine. It's daytime. We'll get to Gustavo's before dark."

He's scared, too! There is something menacing in this whole scene.

"David, I was just thinking it feels pretty tense, or something. Is that just me?"

"No. Earlier at Gustavo's place, I heard that in another area closer to the inner city, a lot of Black people are gathering and it's almost getting to be a riot. It's about them cops getting off that beat and killed that Black guy. It's just so damn hot. This heat wave won't help matters either."

As they speed through the streets, Penny can see the thick yellow-brown smog settling even heavier to the pavement. There are six lanes of traffic going each way on the Santa Anna Freeway. Before long, a knot of police cars blocking part of the freeway, is slowing all traffic and allowing cars to pass through two lanes. The bus driver turns his radio on. They all hear the staticky report of the sporadic freeway drive-by shootings. They hear the report that the rioting has turned uglier in the city. Nobody comments. Cars crawl slowly for over an hour as the traffic thickens in the late afternoon rush. They pass several accidents, one with a vehicle on fire. In the west, the sky is slowly turning a deep angry red as the sun drops behind the buildings silhouette black and menacing against a thickening shroud.

NOTE FOUND IN
HER SKETCH BOOK

You have one day to be ready. Maria said this. She has seen it. The world will go into a struggle. It must. There is no turning around. Reformers are everywhere. And I think, Oh Margaret, your *Handmaiden's Tale* may not be a fantasy. It comes, the long deep shadow just before dawn's first light.

The paintings are lined up against the wall as the curator surveys them. His hair is sticking straight up in hard little spikes on top. He has on a silk hand printed shirt open to the third button. His sandals are soft brown leather with crepe soles. He has on an a wide silver bracelet inlaid with turquoise, jet, coral and mother of pearl worked in a Zuni sungod pattern. The ring on his right hand matches the bracelet.

I wonder how much he paid for that set. Did the artist who made it get anywhere near what he paid?

"These are lovely, my dear. I love the violence of the colours. So often, the images and the colours don't work together. I particularly am drawn to those violent images in the series on *Mud Huts, Bombs, Java and Trinket Time.* Such boldness. And your thematic use of what appears to be cracks opening up in all the pieces is so effective to tie them all together. What I'm concerned about, though, is the extreme graphic quality in some of them. Bloody limbs and coffee cans? Camouflaged figures and bloodied bodies in corn patches? Bombed mud huts and trinket shops? So much violence and blood. I know they're great for shock value, but really, my dear, will they sell?"

"Sell? I'm not worried about that. I want to show them. To talk about them."

"Unfortunately we do have to worry about such things. The costs to maintain this lovely gallery are outrageous. I would be taking a risk, here, even with that series on *Home, Home on the Range of the Homeless.* They work as a political statement, I suppose. But they're so very negative. The eyes in every piece, so haunting, so filled with despair. I think the *Dying City Scapes and Goats* series may work best. A little on the macabre side but not without some humour. They're a little more conventional in approach, as far as subject matter goes. I want to show you in your best light."

His voice is syrupy and suddenly Penny can feel the heat rise.

I feel like pushing his goat head through one of the paintings.

"Show me in my best light? It's not about me. Shock value? Damn right! I want to shock some sense into people. I want them to see it for what it is. There's a fucking outrage happening out there, in case you haven't noticed."

He looks at her with wide eyes. A nervous little laugh, almost a giggle escapes, before he sighs and answers.

"Oh! Please! Calm down, sweetheart. Such passion. You artists. I love it. Don't misunderstand me. I utterly love your work. But my dear, have you thought at all about the collectors? They want something that can hang well. Just a teensy titillating and thought provoking. These are difficult, but your works do seem to sell very well. Your sense of colour and composition is so extraordinary, we just may get away with it. Let's try it. Let's just leap in and see, why don't we? I will want to discuss your prices and our terms with you, though."

"What exactly do you mean? My prices are set. What about your terms? Aren't they always the same?"

He scratches his head and rubs his chin, nodding just slightly.

"Well, yes, they usually are. But when we take this kind of risk, which may well be the case with this show, we do have to try to recoup something of our investment from what does sell. Look, to be honest with you, I know what sells. It's what I do know. At the bottom line, this is about the business of selling, no matter how you look at it. Who buys the works? People with lots of money. In this business, social consciousness is secondary. Art sells, not politics. You do have something of a unique balance between the two and so you might get away with it. But it is a risk. I would want to take several of the really harsh ones right out of the show. It would tone it all down and be much more palatable. I want to propose a higher percentage on each work, just as insurance."

Art! What the hell would any of them know of the hours of agony I spent trying to pull the images out of my head and getting them to work exactly right on the canvas. What the cost is, for those I paint about? What the cost is, for me in having to know about it and not be able to do anything but paint it? It's about business? Fuck the whole stinking shit.

She can feel her blood begin to boil. Her voice is shaking and she feels like smashing something.

"So you want something safe? Safe so it will sell? You want to jack up your cut because my work might not hang well on the fucking walls of the ass-holes who are the major cause of this shit? Fuck that."

He stiffens. His face going red.

"Please! You don't have to swear. That's right. It's reality. Art is something only the wealthy can afford. They set the parameters of what is defined as art, by what they are willing to pay a good price for. You can't be so naive as to think otherwise. Art is a class state-ment. If it fetches a handsome price, it's art. If it doesn't, it may as well be graffiti. Those 'ass-holes,' whether they are the major cause or not, are the ones with the bucks, sweetie. Their money pays my bills and yours. It's how it works. Their walls are where these works will hang if they sell. So let's understand each other. Galleries in this country exist only because of that, not for any other reason, and whether you like it or not, paintings and art exists in this reality only for that reason. So, unless you want to give your paintings away, we have to work out something we both can benefit from."

She feels like someone has punched her in the stomach.

He's right! What the hell am I doing anyway? Riding on the backs of the suffering? With some kind of lame bullshit idea that it might get somebody thinking. What the fucking kind of stupid insane jerk am I anyway?

She can feel a buzzing in her head. She can feel a tightness in her throat and chest, like she's being squeezed. She shakes her head to try to clear it but the feeling is welling up so strongly it's almost choking her. The eyes, staring out from every painting, all seem to be looking at her. They look accusing. They stare and stare right through to her soul. It's like the cracks are all widening to suck her into them. She feels like puking.

What have I done to myself? What have I bought into?

She feels like she is looking from somewhere above at the whole scene around her. She can see the paintings and she moves woodenly toward them. She kicks at the one with bloody hands reaching for smiling plastic Indian doll figures. She kicks and kicks until her foot punches through. She can hear the curator yelling something but she can't stop. She moves from one painting to the next punching holes, ripping and smashing them. She can hear someone sobbing and swearing. It's her. The curator is trying to stop her, trying to grab hold of her, shouting.

"No, No, don't. Oh, God please don't! Stop! Oh stop! I'll get your husband. Oh God, don't, don't do this."

She just pushes him away with all her strength. He is shouting and begging and finally he runs from the room. Almost all of the paintings have gaping holes and rips in them and lie twisted in piles around the floor, before she hears David's calm voice. His arms surrounding her. He is murmuring words she can't make out. All she can do is sob and laugh hysterically at the same time. As she slumps against him, she can feel a sound come from somewhere deep inside and something shifts inside her. She wails, her voice high and girlish. Something inside breaks. Something which can never be whole again. She lets David pick her up and carry her out to the car. She feels like someone she cannot let go of, has just died.

Inside the car, David cries with her, crooning and rocking her. He whispers to her, about not letting her go, about not letting anything happen, but the gathering shadows of twilight in the street surrounding them whisper, too. The leaves which are falling in the crisp wind are scudding along the pavement, whispering. The shadows close in around them long before she stops crying and David starts the car for home.

*T*hey were points of madness—pointed—
or pointing, she never could differen-
tiate. Not like the petals of the wild
sunflower pointed outward in every direction surrounding the
brown centre with bright yellow. But the same green bough being
turned to point toward her again and again.

The long corridor stretches out in front of her. The lights along it are dim, they are screen covered bulbs from the forties. There is a sweetish mouldy smell hanging in the air stronger than the faint disinfectant and boiled cabbage smell. The brown and yellow tiles are worn smooth in some places. Strange sounds come from behind closed doors. Along the hall several elderly women and one man sit in wheel chairs, staring vacantly ahead, thin cloth slippers dangling from pale bony feet. One is talking in a monotone to no one in particular. No one answers. Further down the hall, a man strapped into his chair is cussing in an unbroken string of words. He directs the words toward them, watching them pass with obvious rage. David glances sideways at her.

"It's always pretty depressing. That's why I like to come as much as I can. It's awful for her. I know. You don't have to come if you really don't want to. You could go and have coffee in the lounge. She doesn't seem to really know anybody. Even so it's hard for me not to come. I think it's mostly for me."

He said that at this exact point last time and I backed out. I'll make it this time to see her. She'll probably call me Sophie again. I hate that and David knows it. Shit. It has to be okay. This ain't about me.

She continues walking, looking straight ahead. David glances again at her and takes her and squeezes it gently.

"Thanks."

At the door, he stops to look at her momentarily.

"She doesn't remember the real me, either. Most times, she's talking to the me from twenty years ago."

"But she remembers Sophie all the time."

He looks miserable.

"It's not really her, either, I think it's just an association or something. Sorry I'll try to..."

"No, I'm sorry. Let her be. Let's just have a good visit with her on her terms, okay?"

David's mother is sitting up in bed. Her white hair framing her face like a soft bright halo. She has a fading flowered shawl wrapped around her shoulders.

It's something about that shawl and the thinness of her shoulders. I wish she wasn't the way she is. I'd really like to be able to talk with her.

As David walks to her side and hugs her tightly for a minute, she smiles past him at Penny.

"Mom, you look nice today. You have your shawl on. How are you feeling? How's that hip? Is it hurting quite a bit still?"

She nods, looking a little confused.

"I was waiting and waiting to go to the store, David. I thought your dad would have been back to get me by now."

David's sigh is barely perceptible.

"Mom, you can't go anywhere right now. You broke your hip and it has to get better before you can go outside. I brought you some fry bread and Saskatoon jam that Penny made. Do you want some?"

David opens the plastic bag and takes out a tupperware container with six pieces of fry bread visible through the clear plastic, and a small jar of jam.

"Penny? Do I know her?"

"Mom, this is Penny right here. She picked the Saskatoons for you."

She looks curiously not saying anything.

"Hi, Sadie. I thought I'd make you some good black tea with canned Pacific milk to go with the bread and jam. How does that sound?"

Sadie glances back at David. He nods reassuringly at her.

"I guess that would be fine. David, you know what? I thought I heard somebody singing a little while ago. Was that Sophie? She has such a nice voice. Only she sings western songs. I like Indian songs. Maybe it was her."

"No, it wasn't Sophie. We haven't been together for a long time. You keep asking about her and I keep telling you."

"I thought it was her singing. She sings like my girl used to. Your sister Rose had the best voice."

"No. Anyway, Penny is going to make that tea and we'll have some with you. I brought along a video of the gathering out at Old Howard's place. They played some stick games there. There's some songs on it. Do you want to watch it?"

"Okay. Who's Howard?"

"An old boyfriend of yours."

Sadie looks worried for a moment.

"I'm just kidding, Mom. He's a neighbour, and it's branding time. So, people went to help."

"Oh, okay."

Penny serves the tea in styro cups and the bread in a paper plate. She pours milk from a little can of condensed Pacific milk and adds sugar from a baggie. David watches her butter and spread jam on the still warm pieces of fry bread.

The video player is on loud. Sadie watches intently. On the video, people are walking around in the corral shouting and talking to each other. Cows bawling for their calves drown out the voices of people. Suddenly the scene shifts to a group sitting in the grass playing stick game. The bones pass over to the opposing team. They begin to sing, the drums all in time. Automatically, Penny begins to sing along.

Wewa's song. It's nice, whoever is singing it.

"David. That's a good song. A winning song. Your girl can sing it pretty good. Hey, girl, come over here. Sit down and let me hear you sing."

As Sadie patted the chair next to the bed, Penny set the tea and bread down on the tray table.

I feel silly.

David is looking at her.

"I'll serve the tea, Penny. Go ahead, sit down and sing."

As Penny sinks down into the chair, Sadie Walker leaned over and smoothed her hair just lightly.

Oh! Why am I thinking of Tupa? She doesn't even look anything like her. Oh, Tupa. Tupa, my Tupa.

From somewhere tears well up and slide down Penny's face. But she continues singing, her voice growing stronger. At that moment Sadie put her flower-shawled arm around Penny and hugged her.

"Here, share my shawl Girl. It's a little chilly right now. Let's sing together. Okay Girl?"

They sing together. Wewa's song. David joins in. Sadie claps her hands and pretends she is pointing a game. They laugh together.

"That's my Girl."

Penny closes her eyes and sings.

Tupa, Tupa. It's your voice too.

It is a winning song.

NOTE FROM HER DIARY

*I*t seems to me it is always what you do, not what you say that reveals, that compels the change. I am struck by the awesome responsibility of that, yet in this diary I seem to capture more than all I have ever done to stop the insanity.

The noise level is phenomenal. Someone is laughing and laughing almost diabolically over the other voices. Bits and pieces of conversation in male and female tones. Here and there the chirping voices of children all mix together. Rolling waves of sound wash over her as she stands looking around her. Killing time.

Cripes, look at the people. Like ants or earwigs, scurrying in bunches. Maybe it's just me. I haven't been feeling like myself lately. I just feel so drained with all the past weeks workshop on that awful shit. DNA. Commodification of lifeforms. What next! Wow, there it is! It's eyes look like they're alive.

The totem Karen had told her about stands serenely watching the hordes moving by. The buttery soft-looking cedar seems to glow.

"Pretty amazing, isn't it? I always get goose bumps looking at the eyes."

The friendly looking man in casual khaki pants and a white short sleeved shirt smiles at her, a floral beaded bolo hangs loosely around his collar. His hair is sandy, a little grey at the temples. His eyes are an amazing hazel. Tiny flecks of gold and patches of green float in the deep amber iris.

An unfamiliar accent. Probably Métis from back east somewhere.

"Yeah, it's the first time I've seen it. It seems to be floating off the marble."

"I think it's the way the artist saw the world. Do you know who the artist is?"

Oh, oh this seems to be getting a little friendly. What if he's some lunatic or something. I'm alone and it's night. Maybe David's plane can't land. It's starting to fog up out there.

214

"No."

Turning away without making eye contact again is difficult without looking at the eyes one more time and the tiny laugh wrinkles at their corners. The half-question, half-smile expression changes. Disappointment is instant. The second her gaze slides past and toward the throng crowding past.

Shit. Stop now. David's on his way. It's been too long. Three months! It's his pheremones drifting by, dearie. Move. Walk away. Yeah that's it. Don't look back now.

The crowd pushes her away toward the fast food counters. She lets herself be carried along. The posters, pasted billboard style across a wide expanse of wall, catch her eye. One is of a field of Okanagan sunflowers in full bloom.

David, David. We're getting so far apart. One night and then you're gone again. I should go down now to arrivals. It's about twenty minutes now. Shoot, I really wanted to look at that totem for awhile.

Turning quickly against the tide churning around her, like rough waters, she glimpses Mr. Hazel Eyes again. He is standing looking at headlines on a newspaper.

What the hell happens when total strangers click? Is it just pheromones? I feel like I've met him somewhere before. The familiarity of his eyes. His expression. Like I could run my fingers along his cheekbone and down his chin and would know every curve, every line, even the texture of his skin. Jesus, I'm staring! Oh no! He's looking right at me! Oh what do I do now? Walk away! Walk away!

Mr. Hazel Eyes smiles a great bright happy smile-to-see-you smile. He walks over to where she is stuck to the floor.

I'm waiting for David. What am I doing?

"Do you have any idea why in the world I shouldn't tell you that you look so familiar? Have I met you somewhere?"

His eyes are sparkling. His smile is infectious.

I'm so sad right now. David, David. Ten minutes to David and then this.

"I don't think so. Maybe. You look familiar, too. I'm sorry I'm meeting someone. David. He's going to come in, downstairs, about ten minutes from now. Are you from around here?"

"I used to be. I've got a three hour wait until I'm on my way back to London. Ontario that is. I'm Gard Danials, by the way. How about you, are you from here?"

"Penny Jackson. No. Well . . . actually from the interior. Oh, too bad. About the wait that is. Well . . . I'm going to check the screens. There's a fog moving in pretty fast."

"Penny."

Speaking to her back.

She turns and makes eye contact. Her breath catches.

"If the plane is delayed or . . . would you consider keeping company for awhile? Oh, maybe not. Sorry, I'm not trying to pick you up. It's just . . . "

He looks bewildered, flustered and nervous all at the same time.

"No. It's fine. Yes, I mean. I'll check the screens. Walk with me?"

Now what? What did I do? David's plane'll be here in five minutes. Oh God! His shoulder touched me! Oh damn! Oh David, David, David.

"I kinda hope it is delayed. Not that I wish inconvenience to you or. . . ?"

"David."

"David. Your husband?"

"Something like that. My significant other most times. He lives with his work. Mostly it's away now. Well, to be fair, I live mine too, but I don't travel that much."

"Uh huh. Watch your step there."

As they step onto the escalator, his hand catches her under the elbow. Electric shocks run up her arm. He's standing close enough for her to smell his cologne or aftershave. It smells clean and sweet at the same time. His hazel eyes are on hers and she can't pull her eyes away.

I feel such an absolute fool. What if he is a pervert or a criminal, a rapist or a killer? Is this the way it happens? So powerful an attraction. Like a magnet . . . you're powerless to stop. You follow him to his car willingly.

"I don't think it's foggy enough for delays. Why London?"

He smiles again, the corners of his eyes definitely crinkling.

Around forty-two I'd say. Maybe forty-five at the most.

"I lived here for awhile. I left a few years ago. Actually, after my divorce. I was out here seeing my son. You have children?"

"Ah, here's the screen. Lets see, ummmm 311 Canadian . . . Yes, three. Two girls and a boy. Not David's. A bad early marriage. Three. They're almost all grown. Oh! It says delayed! I better check at the counter . . . "

"Well, maybe we'll have a chance for coffee. I'd like that."

Her heart is beating faster as she turns to look into his eyes again.

And then what? On the plane in a couple of hours? What?

"Well, maybe."

At the desk the attendant taps on the keys as she looks quickly up at Penny.

"I'm sorry, I don't have a confirmed time of arrival. The fog seems to be settling in. It could be rerouted to Calgary tonight. Stay close for an advisory. We should be able to tell you within half an hour."

Gard smiles at her.

"Shall we?"

"Yes. I think I need one. Thanks."

Now what? What? What? Half an hour!

He suddenly touches her hand.

"Penny. Penny. I don't want David to come. Am I out of line? What if his plane is cancelled? Mine probably will be too. Penny . . . "

She stops dead still.

This is moving too fast again. I should have kept walking the first time. I gotta get things casual again.

"Let's get that coffee. If his plane is cancelled, I go. My friend Karen was going to join us for dinner. I'll just get her to meet me here. She lives five minutes from here. Your plane won't be cancelled anyway. The fog usually lifts around eight."

His expression changes almost imperceptibly.

"Oh! I don't mean . . . "

His face reddens and he looks away momentarily.

"I meant, it would be nice to get acquainted. But just that. I know. I know. I'm a total stranger. Let's have that coffee. Okay?"

He suddenly smiles again. The green in his eyes going deeper. He's careful to make direct eye contact only for a moment. It's enough.

That's not true. It's not "just that." It's exactly more. That's the point of coffee, isn't it? From the very first minute.

"Okay. Let's go. Those stools over there facing this way should be fine."

For the first time she looks directly into the depths of his eyes and smiles. She hears his breath catch.

He's no stranger. I'm getting ready to play this out.

"Penny. I just want to say, I don't do this. I'll show you my son's picture. My ID. Call Karen if you feel safer. I don't know what's happening. Even if my plane isn't cancelled or David's, I would want to ask if I can see you again."

He looks miserable for a moment when she doesn't answer.

What can I possibly say to that? No. Maybe. Don't talk about tomorrow. Let's just be in this moment. David. David. This is totally unexpected. Only half an hour ago every piece of the puzzle seemed to fit, and now, suddenly, nothing fits. I need something real right now. Life is so precious and short as it is and I just want to taste the richness of it while it lasts.

But sadness is already there, looming toward her. For her, for David, for the long gaps between. It's that moment-to-moment she is already moving toward the pain she knows surely awaits ahead on this road. But for this instant, for this and for as many as can be possible her blood sings. And breathing is sweet.

The announcer suddenly blares out.

"For those awaiting Canadian flight 311 from Seattle, that plane has been routed into Calgary. Please check with Canadian for arrivals in the morning from Calgary. This is an advisory. All further incoming flights will be cancelled until further notice."

She walks with him toward the payphone.

"I'm going to call Karen. Maybe we could meet her later. Let's just go get something to eat. I'll figure something out. I have my car here. I can drop you wherever you want after. Do you have any bags to pick up?"

"They're already checked in. I'll leave them. I have an overnight bag. I'll just go and check in for a ticket change for tomorrow. I'll be right back."

Rerouted to Calgary. David will go from there on to Toronto. And from there to New York for the Indigenous Fair Trade Summit and the preparatory working group. Oh well, Penny, he isn't an angel when he's not around. He's normal. Just relax. If things don't feel right, just eat with him and drop him. Enjoy it. You'll be seventy and you'll be wishing you didn't throw away such moments.

She watches him walk back toward her, tall, lithe sure of himself. The way the light glints off his hair. She feels his rhythm. She catches her breath.

"Let's go."

It is foggy and damp outside. He stops to put a light jacket on. At the car he drops his bag into the back seat.

"Let's go over to this restaurant I know not far from here. It's really nice. Over by the waterfront."

He smiles at her.

"Sounds good to me."

The drive is short. She doesn't talk at first. She listens to him talking small talk about the weather telling her bits about himself.

"I feel like I'm in somebody's story. I'm a writer. I'm just in the middle of writing my first novel. Sometimes it's lonely. The life I lead. It's a solitary sort of preoccupation. You never told me if you were an artist or not. They way you studied that carving tells me you probably are or should be."

"I am. I was. I'm not doing it now. I seem to be writing quite a bit lately. Mostly articles. I don't have any training, though. I just read a lot. I'm a closet poet."

He laughs.

"A closet poet! It sounds like being gay or something. You should take a workshop course and come out of the closet. I write mostly because it's the only thing I can do. It's kind of an obsession. Oh, I work at a job. You can't live on your writing in this country. Anyway here we are. Penny. I'm glad just to talk with you. I'm a writer. I like meeting people and talking . . . "

He leaves it open. She glances over at him. For a moment their eyes lock. Somehow his eyes are darker, the gold flecks warmer.

"I feel alone in my world at times. This is one of them. It's good to connect with other artists. I suppose it's the creative mind. The monumental aloneness we seem to have around others. It gets to you. Yeah, let's talk and talk. About everything."

The dining room has gas candles and brass reflecting warmth. Peach napkins and soft brown wood panels. The waiter comes to light a candle on the table and recommends tonight's dinner. They order without bothering to look at the menu. Penny feels light-headed and overly warm.

I wonder why I feel tired so much of the time. I should be feeling great right now. I should get that check up I guess. Been putting it off for way too long. Oh well, food'll fix it. I just wish I had more energy. Maybe I would be out there with David. Instead of sitting here with this strange sweet looking man. Talking. Maybe that's enough. Maybe I don't need to feel someone holding me. Touching me. Making me feel alive. The world is so screwed up, I need respite. I need sweetness.

"My brother is an artist. You might of heard of him. Ron Danials. He paints rock forms from out our way. New Brunswick. He's not a big name or anything but his works are starting to get around. That comment you made in the car about monumental aloneness. What is that? I have lived with it and felt it all my life. I sometimes feel resentment having to talk the trivialities of everyday living. It's what caused the problems in my relationships. It goes down to such a serious depth sometimes. I know my brother feels it. He loses himself for long periods sometimes. It's dangerous ground."

"It's what I've felt most of the time. More so when I was painting. Now, I spend a lot of time in activist circles. Environment and Indigenous Peoples rights. I set up talks on protecting local Indigenous economies. I organize groups to buy handmade clothing and stuff. What I call direct sustainable support. I do information talks on biodiversity and its connection to humans and healthy land living. I even do information around talks on this new thing. Biopiracy. Collecting gene samples from unsuspecting Indigenous people. What makes me so mad is that they want to collect from tribes going extinct. To research in medical applications. A contribution to humanity. Bullshit! It's because there's big money to be made by whoever makes some kind of discovery for use on the diseases caused by all the shit they've created. I notice there's no sexy research money thrown at cleaning that up. We've made contributions enough to last a millennium. That's why some tribes are going extinct. They now want our genes. Most of it just makes you feel so hopeless."

Gard stops eating his salad for a minute. Fork balanced halfway to his mouth. He has a look of open concern.

Oh cripes. How did I get on that topic? I just want to talk about other stuff and get it off my brain for awhile.

"I don't mean to sound so harsh. It's just that I was here attending a workshop on that topic and it's made some kind of deep soul impact. It's like I feel violated at some depth that I can't even describe. Anyway let's not go further on it. I just want to get it off my mind for a bit. I want to talk about something real. Tell me a little about yourself."

"Yeah, I grew up in New Brunswick. My mom's people are from around Big Cove. But we're non-status. My dad is Métis from Ontario. Nothing extraordinary. I guess. Lots of brothers and sisters. We were poor. My dad and mom always worked and they gave us a good childhood, though. Lots of singing, good food and family. Mostly good memories there. I guess I was lucky. They encouraged us and supported us. I started writing early. Maybe writing was a way to get heard. There were so many of us that you never could get a chance to say anything. I have stories and things published in different anthologies. A collection of short stories and some poetry in a collaboration with four other writers. What else. I can dance a mean jig and right now I'm in a depression. Like you. I'm a poet. People are my palette. The poetry dries up when the aloneness moves in."

He looks at her for a long moment then continues.

"I don't try to control it. You know, when I slide into the full taste of things around, I drown in it. I write then. I taste and taste. And suddenly I feel a flattening out. The colour seems to fade from all the things around me. The world goes dull. Black and white and grey, without sparkle. Until someone touches it in some magic way. I feel it could die easily when the world is flat. I feel thin and wispy. Like a shadow. Insubstantial. Like the real world is somewhere else."

"Yeah. Exactly."

She doesn't say anymore.

I want to reach out and touch him. I feel like he's talking about me. I feel naked. I want to touch his face just lightly with the tips of my fingers. My fingers. My art. He know this place of shadows. He goes there. I can't get any nearer. I have to be careful with this. Let it be clean. We have to be friends. Oh, but it would be so sweet. I could lose myself. Lose me.

When it comes, the pepper steak is good, hot, juicy and tender.

"What about you. Relationships? I mean. I'm not prying. It's just that I . . . Oh, I don't know . . . Maybe the question is how has it worked for you? As an artist. Maybe it's just being a poet. It just doesn't work. So I live with the aloneness."

"It hasn't really. For me it's like a clear line drawn at my feet. I never cross that line. Sometimes I think it makes me cold. Unable to give totally of myself to another person. I haven't had the best of records in relationships either."

"Do you always keep the line so clear because of your art or is it something else?"

"I'm not sure, but on the other side of that line it's slippery and dangerous. I have no control on the other side of it. I create a facade which keeps the line there. I allow only a glimpse of me. I'm an artist but I'm not sure that's what it's about. Maybe it's what fuels my art. What makes me an artist. Keeping it locked in."

He looks at her a long moment.

"I dive into it. Totally. Then I feel alive and fully in reality. The experience. It's about poetry. The poetry of it. I want to keep that but it gets interpreted into something else. Sex maybe. Although that's part of it, it isn't about the poetry though. Love? I don't know. Obligation? Usually. I keep looking at maple trees for instance. The red and gold against green. Its poetry speaks to me. That isn't about colour but that is part of it. The poetry that is a certain person speaks to me that way. But no one has ever shared that poetry with me. So it never works out."

The warm apple crisp with walnut ice cream arrives. It melts on her tongue.

"Have you ever fallen in love with another poet?"

"I think I have. The poetry of her was the sound of her voice at first. And when I heard her poetry it became the person. Usually, the poetry is something about the physical being. With her it was also her mind. The two together. The poetry from the body and the poetry from the mind. Perhaps it was conditioning that made me have to separate the two. The Madonna woman of the mind and the Eve woman of the body. I couldn't experience them as the same person. I found that I needed to preserve the Madonna. We never became lovers. Tell me about the artist in you."

"It was a perilous thing. Being a woman and an artist. The artist that was in me. It was a glowing inside. Like fire heated lava. It made life hard because it burned all the time. It's immense and owns all of you. The artist in me risked too much if anyone got too near the woman. You draw a line beyond which the path is treacherous and shadowy. And so the monumental aloneness. It's tragic that a man can never touch the artist across that line. It's tragic that the woman who is a poet dies if her body crosses into the poets terrain. How tragic for the writer and the artist that they stand outside life's fullness. Or perhaps it is everyone else who lives outside arts fullness. With David, I have stood with him on that line, though I am alone much of the time, still."

"Maybe it's because opening up and experiencing that way depletes the art. You fall absolutely into it. It takes you away from your soul and that is not living. It is simply enduring. It is death."

"But still, there is the undeniable aloneness."

"Yes. There is."

226

His eyes have gone sad. He looks deep into her eyes. She doesn't look away. She finally looks toward the candle burning in between them. It has burnt low and the flame is sputtering.

It's like someone dear just left. I'm going to cry if I say anything else. Madonna? The pure one wins again.

"I'll drop you wherever you want to stay for the night, Gard. I'm very tired. It would be good to see you again. Let me give you my card."

"I will cherish every moment of this night. And every moment in the future. I'll just get a room at the hotel you're at if it's near. I'll get an early flight if the fog lifts."

In silence they walk out into the greyness. Into the fog soaked night. They drive through the quiet streets of Richmond, a heavy grey mist swirling around them. The street lamps cast dim glowing circles with darkness looming between. She can hear the ocean's crash somewhere in the distance beyond as they walk toward the hotel she is staying at. A ship's fog horn sounds forlornly as it passes on its way out to sea. She holds him for a moment too long in the small hotel lobby before she leaves him to check into his room. The night is already long.

LETTER TO ENVIRONMENTALIST FRIEND

Dear Tannis:

I was thinking of you and I thought I would write this note. I'm sorry I haven't had much time to be a friend lately. I seem to be caught up in this pile of work around food security. It just gets worse as every day passes. I recently attended a conference that scared the shit right out of me (Good thing too). Did you realize the things they are doing to food these days? Well it can hardly be called food anymore, is the upshot of the whole issue. Nutrition is not the objective, anymore, of agriculture. In fact it may be the biggest source of malnutrition in North America now. I'm feeling defeated and overwhelmed. I just wanted to touch base with someone out there who speaks the same language as me. Am I an extremist or is everybody around us anesthetized by the treadmill, either trying to stay on it, or running it? I'm feeling tired, tired,

tired. How I long for the time I was twenty three and knew I could change the world.

Tannis, I should have chosen to douse this fire inside of me. I should have piled up tasks enough to last until I was seventy-five. I should have tried to love Calvin Klein and antique furniture. At least I should have run for council in my home town or gotten hired in the social department. I could have found things to eat away at my time, ad nauseam. Instead, I listened to something inside that kept telling me something is wrong, wrong, wrong and we are all paying for it, and I can't even get what it is untangled from everything else. I have looked for it in all kinds of places. Although I seem to have seen more things in my life than anybody I know around me, I still can't get a clear view because so much is happening so fast.

I just recently had a thought about why I wasn't looking for what is right. I'm thankful at least for having blindly let my biological process lead me to a right place, in having my three kids, though I am guilty of not being the best of mothers. I didn't wish for them to catch my obsession, but I should have enlisted them! I owe it to them. That's all I can give them, really. The truth. Think of that, to slay the tooth fairy, Easter bunnies, Santa, Halloween and Valentines, all in one fell swoop. What kind of culture masks the gluttonous monsters sucking hardearned paychecks from unsuspecting parents with such cuteness, pastel and brightness? That institutionalizes it?

It would be good to spend a few days with you and others just to talk about this. I really need to re-energize. Do you think a person could get ill feeling like I do right now? In any case, I do know you are running flat out most of the time on the spent uranium issue. And thank God for those people out there who are working to try to conserve what's left. Call me sometime even if you don't have time to drop a note.

Luvs, Pen

It's a new day! A new day.

Penny was standing at the door looking in. She could feel the sleepy cobwebs in her eyes as she looked into the room. She was looking at the green, green boughs under the long pine box.

Tupa!

She could feel the great hard lump again inside her chest.

My arms are so heavy. I've got to turn around, I don't wanna see.

The long pine box was there and she couldn't move.

Tupa! My Tupa. Where did you go? Why can't you get better now? Get up! Get up! The sun is coming up! It's a new day! I'm scared! Why do you have to go away? I'm scared, Tupa!

"Penny, come here little girl."

Momma motioned to her and patted the seat beside her. But Penny couldn't move. Her chest and her arms got heavier.

My breath hurts. Gramma! Where is Gramma! Why isn't she right here?

"Gramma! Where are you? I don't want her to go away too! Grammaaaaaaa?"

"Shhhh, shhhh little girl. Your gramma went to sleep for awhile. Don't cry now. She isn't going to leave. It's just Tupa is gone. She told you why. She's too old to be here. She told you that. Shhh now. Shhhh."

"I don't want Tupa to go without me. I always go with her wher-ever she goes. She lets me. Let me go with her. Let me go, Momma.

Let me go!"

Penny struggled to run toward the long pine box. Her mother held her in her arms tightly.

"No! No! Penny! Don't say that! Dad come here! Penny here's Granpa."

Penny could see her Granpa cross the floor around the chairs of the other old people, who were now all standing facing her. The hum of their prayers got louder and louder and then began to fade.

"Somebody get some water. Oh, help me. Penny! Drink! Put it on her face! Penny, stop now!"

I wonder who that is screaming and screaming? Why do I feel so light? Like I could float up into the air?

The shadows rose up from the feet of the Elders facing her. They loomed toward her. The lights grew dimmer and she could see the shadows begin to dance. The humming was a song. A song Tupa sang to her.

Who is that talking and talking to me? I only want to hear the singing.

"Penny! Stay awake! Breathe! Breathe! She's having some kind of spell! Wake her up! Pour that water right over her head! Don't let her faint! Penny, look at me! Your gramma is here!"

Penny could hear her gramma's voice from far away. Her sweet, sweet voice talking calmly in their language.

"Penny. You don't be scared. I'm not going away. Your Tupa told you to let her go. You come with me now. We can go pick some wild rose to put with her. You let me wash the shadows away.

Come to me. Come to me."

Her gramma stroked her wet hair and she could feel the warmth come from her and the terrible hard tightness in her chest broke apart into little slivers. Like ice under the sun. She could feel the tiny pieces spread through her body as they melted away.

It's cold here.

She suddenly heard the rain outside. It was pounding against the windows behind Tupa's long pine box. She heard her mother sobbing as she turned to walk with her grandmother toward the rain and wild roses.

The ground is covered in hard snow. It catches the sunlight here and there. Its crunch is brittle. The wind is blowing dryly lifting tumble weeds and sending them spinning over the white field stretched out on into the horizon. The pall bearers are black dots bundled against the freezing cold. The long line of people following the them are bent against the cold wind. The sun looks pale, low in the western horizon stretched flat into grey.

David takes her arm. The snow comes up to the top of her boots. It's hard walking. She feels the bitter cold seep into her. It seems to take her breath away.

I'm never going to make it. I feel so weak. It's the cold. One step at a time. This woman who goes home now in this cold. I wonder if all her work for the Indigenous people will have been worth her giving of her life. It just doesn't seem fair. It's wrong. She was noble. A shining light in the dark.

This friend of David's. So like him. Her work. Her energy. It's hit him hard. And I need to do this with him. To stand with him at that grave and what it represents.

"David, I'm so cold. I don't feel good. Maybe I have the flu or some' thing. I can't seem to catch my breath. Maybe I should get back in the car. Maybe we could just stop for a minute here."

He turns to steady her letting her stand leaning on his arm.

"Penny, you've been complaining so much about being tired lately. You don't look well. And you've lost so much weight. You've been pushing yourself too hard again. We don't have to go to the grave site. I spent time with the family. I just wanted to honour her. She must have suffered so much at the end there. Nobody can really say how bad it might have been, but she died for her work. She stood on ground many will never have the courage to stand on. Her murder is a violation to all of us. All of us who struggle with our brothers and sisters in the south. It's true she somehow got caught in the struggles crossfire, but her death was for all of us. She was such a strong good person."

"I know. I grieve for us all. I didn't know her that well. I've only heard her speak a few times. But those times she filled me with hope. Like it could be done. The thing we stand for. It leaves a big hole. I feel it somewhere inside. A gaping hole filled with black rage. I felt that same thing at Gustafasen. How can we allow this to be without becoming violent. David, it took something from me. I can't go on."

"I'm having some trouble with that, too. Let's head back to the car. Her spirit is everywhere. Her family and her relatives honour her return to the earth for us all. I've been here with them since it hap' pened. They know I'm going back with you today. I don't like goodbyes anyway. When we get back to the Okanagan, you're going to get checked up. You've just been too stubborn."

The walk back to the car is just as hard. David walks with his arm around her. When she finally sinks into the still warm interior. She closes her eyes and sinks slowly into sleep. She hears the motor start as she drifts into the silence. The warm, warm silence of sleep. She wakes briefly as they stop to gas up and he asks if she wants some coffee. She doesn't even answer. It seems for a long, long time she drifts in and out of sleep, the only sounds are cars moving past and she dreams.

Lena is standing next to her. Lena looking like she did at sixteen just before she left with that first guy. Lena is talking but she can't hear her. Her voice is muffled. Penny turns and it's Julie. Julie smiles and points toward a group of people standing in a circle. They walk toward the circle. There are white people and Indians standing looking at something. A man with a long braided ponytail turns toward them. She thinks it's George. The man they met at the gathering. He tells them that it's somebody's grandparents. They are encased in ice. But she can see them through the ice. Frozen in perfect beauty. The long grey hair of the woman is fanned out into the ice. Its strands look like they are moving. She is wearing a flowered blue silk shawl. The man is wrapped in a Hudson's Bay blanket. The long brown butt of a rifle is nestled against his cheek. What are they doing? Penny asks George. George tells her that the people are raising them up. The people standing in the circle raise their hands palms toward the block of ice. The grandmother begins to stir, her hair moves as she turns to stare out at the people. At her. No! No! This is wrong! Penny shouts and shouts. But nobody listens to her. Beside her Julie takes her arm. We have to stop them Julie! Tannis is sud-denly there too looking on in horror. And Delila, too, from Arizona. Her long black hair is loose from its braids. Delila, shouts too. Leave our grand-parents alone! You already took everything from them! She is crying and she throws a handful of papers she is carrying. The wind picks up the sheets and sweeps them up into the air. George shouts. Look out! He turns to grab Delila and Penny. Julie and Tannis are already running. The grandfather is sitting up, the rifle in his hands. Shots ring out. People are screaming and falling. Indians and white people alike. Penny runs as hard as she can. Lena stands in the distance waving frantically at her to come.

David is shaking her.

"Penny! Penny, what's wrong. Are you okay? You're making funny sounds. You're crying! Bad dreams? We're gonna get a room here. It's way past midnight and the storm is turning into a blizzard. We can rest and eat. There's a truck stop restaurant next to the motel. Do you wanna talk about it now or later?"

"God. I just had the worst nightmare of all time. I'll tell you later. Holeee. I must have slept for ten hours! The drive out must've done it. I shoulda got Dustin to help me. I'm feeling shaky but quite a bit better. The rest did me good. Maybe we should go eat. I think I'm hungry."

"Yeah. Me too. I didn't want to stop and wake you. I got coffee and chips back there a few times. I already checked in and took our bags in. Do you want to go to the toilet or anything?"

"Yeah I guess I better. I'll scare the shit out of all the truckers with my hair all over the place."

In the motel's small bathroom she uses the toilet and washes her face. As she brushes her long hair and clips the barrettes back into place, her dark circled eyes stare back at her. She notices the white strands picking up the harsh florescent light making them glow against her dark hair. Her hand stops for a moment in mid-air.

White strands of hair. I'm a grandmother, too. I wonder how Shanna is making out with her little ones. Jeyd and Raella. What a sweet, sweet boy. And that girl so chirpy and bright! My grandchildren. Who is this woman who looks so sad? Why is she so sad? I don't even know her. She has everything. A family, grandchildren, and a good partner. Yet she looks so utterly sad. What's wrong with me? How did it get to be this way? Why the despair?

They walk to the restaurant. It is filled with truckers. Smoke and stale grease hangs in the air. An old time juke box is playing a scratchy old Presley tune. Elvis croons to the waitress carrying plates of hamburger and fries. She's in her fifties. Her body is soft and puffy from eating too much fried foods and starch. Her hair showing an inch of grey, dyed a brass yellow, is tucked into a hair-net. Her crepe soled shoes squeak on the tiled floor as she turns toward them.

"Evening, Kids. Pretty nasty out there. Specials chicken fried steak. Beef noodle soup. Not too bad. The cook throws in extra beef and vegetables. Coffee? I'll be right over honey. I didn't forget your gravy Ernie."

She speaks to the beefy man sitting in the booth across from them. She looks tired. She's sweating and wisps of hair are loose around her face.

"I'll have hot tea. And the soup with some toast."

The waitress looks over at David.

"I'll have the special. Coffee. The soup, too."

Penny watches her practised hand make quick marks on the order pad. "I ain't nothing but a hound dog crying all the time." She croons along with Elvis as she turns toward the kitchen.

I wonder how long she's waited tables here. Probably all her adult life. For peanuts too, I bet. I bet she doesn't even dream of a mansion and swimming pools now. I bet all she wants is little time to get off her feet once in awhile. And one day she'll have a heart attack or something. Or get old and try to make ends meet until finally she gives in and goes into a nursing home to stare out the window.

Penny looks at David. He looks bleary eyed and tired. He's watching her.

"You should eat something with more nutrition. That soup isn't much."

"Nutrition! I hate to think what's in the beef. I don't feel like eating much. The soup will be enough. Do you know that there are a bunch of studies being done on the growth hormones, antibiotics and the preservatives in the beef causing all kinds of problems in people especially kids? I don't mean to spoil your meal or anything. I wish I had some saskatoon berry soup and good chunk of roast deer meat with home grown potatoes on the side."

"Mmmm. Me too. We'll have some when we get home. I'm hungry enough right now to eat anything. You won't spoil my appetite. But you're right about the beef. That latest stuff on the mad cow disease. Now that's scary. I'm glad we're not in England. Jesus, what the hell are the people supposed to do? They should stuff it down the throats of whosoever bright idea it was to grind up sick sheep and beef guts and brains into their feed."

He grins at her and sighs. Soup arrives with their coffee and tea.

"Now what was that dream about?"

"I don't know for sure. It was awful. George, that guy who told us a similar dream was there. It was about two old Indian people encased in ice and a bunch of Indians and white people doing something with their hands to raise them up. I was trying to stop them. Julie, an old friend, and Tannis were there. Delila, you know her, the one who does all that work against gene hunting. She was there too trying to stop them. Anyway, they started waking up and the old man had a rifle and he started shooting. People were screaming and falling down. I ran and Lena was there too waving at me to get out of there. I was more scared than anything I've ever felt before. Not because of the shooting. But because they woke up. The grandmother stared right at me. I kept saying. No! It's wrong! I woke up feeling like something really awful is going to happen. Like doomsday or something."

"You been working too hard on that shit. That stuff you were telling me about. The things they're doing. I mean it's like the new frontier. Putting human genes into pigs and tobacco plants and God knows what else now. Doing all kinds of different things to plants to make them pest and disease resistant. To make them last on the shelf. Like that tomato. Even making new bacteria and killer viruses for weapons. Maybe not here but somewhere. And grow-ing human tissue to sell. They're starting to grow body parts from unborn baby cells."

His chicken fried steak covered in gravy arrives, french fried pota-toes stacked high on his plate. He puts salt, pepper and A1 on his steak.

"And cloning. Maybe it's about that. They need certain blood types and I heard pureblood Indians had it. That's why they died from whiteman's diseases. Something's gonna backfire. I mean, now they're finding that bacteria mutates and penicillin and sulfa drugs don't kill them anymore. Superbugs. What do they think's gonna happen in a few years when the bugs mutate because of all this? It's like science fiction. You been on the front line with it too long. Maybe it will be Doomsday. But I don't think we can stop it now. There's too much money in it. That ancestor grandpa with the gun, maybe their spirits are mad. That whole thing about collecting DNA from our long dead ancestors. Now that's creepy. They're probably secretly cloning them or some damn thing. Anyway, it's too big. People want quick fixes for disease so they can go on doing the things that cause them in the first place."

He cuts into his steak. Penny has stopped eating. Her soup bowl is still half full.

"Except that most people can't afford the quick fixes. The biggest part of the world can't even get the medicines that are available. That's just it. All that. I can't get it out of my mind. It's like the world is gone crazy. That dream, maybe it's just what you said, because I work on telling people about it. It just makes me want to explode sometimes. And now I feel like giving up. I guess you're right. I'm tired. Empty. But what'll my grandkids grow up in? Right now sex, the most natural instinct, is a risk. Where did that virus come from? It hits right at the centre of human existence. David, I feel defeated. We're putting together a good fight. But I feel an urgency. It's like that dream, maybe. It's too late. And all there is to do is run like hell but to where and to what? It's all around us."

She watches David eat. Her stomach feels queasy and the tea is now cold. She drinks it anyway and takes a few more bites of toast.

"The spirits. They don't believe in them. I'm not even sure I do anymore. I know I used to. Why don't they do something if they're there, watching? All the Indian people and the ceremonies they do, should count for something."

David finishes eating. He slowly put his fork down and picks up his napkin to wipe his mouth and hands.

"It's not for us to know. The world has to transform itself. It never stops doing that. Whatever is going on has the human at its centre. We are spirit, too. We have a hand in which direction it goes. We can't throw the towel in because it looks impossible. The odds are stacked against us but I believe the spirits of the earth can tip the scales. Things could change in one day. We just have to live in the best way doing right in what we were each given to do. Even if it doesn't happen in our lifetime, the generations after us have to have a chance. Life is precious. We know the spirits are there in all the things that live. Those ceremonies, where they come to our medicine people, are real. Not hocus pocus. You know that. It's what strengthens me when I'm down."

"I know. It's just that sometimes I feel like we've been abandoned. Forsaken. In the absence of the sacred, like that guy, Jerry, who writes about deep ecology, said. It's not healthy to feel this way, I know. But I do."

"Penny. Let's go get some sleep. We have a long drive tomorrow. It'll be good to get home for the winter. I'm planning on sticking around for a good two or three months before I get on the road again. We'll have lots of time to talk and talk. Right now I just want to hold my lady's tired bones and make her smile."

Penny nods. He looks weary and sad but his eyes shine when they meet her's. As they walk out together into the freezing cold, the juke box is playing an old Jimmy Rogers song. *Walking down the railroad donno what to do. I'm walking down the railroad feeling kinda blue.* The fine drifting snow stings their faces as they walk toward the room to rest awhile before the long road home.

Fox walked up to the pile. It was just a pile of shit. Suddenly the pile of shit moved around and started laughing. Fox looked around and they were all over the place, coming to life. Fox took off running. Coyote stopped Fox. "What're you running for?" Coyote asked. "There's a bunch of stinking turds all over the place. They're alive," Fox said. "Damn." Coyote said and scratched his head, "I just nap for a few minutes and they start stirring up shit again. This time I'm gonna make them eat it." Fox looked at Coyote for awhile and nodded. "That I have to see." Coyote just grinned and grinned.

Penny kneels in the sand, her knees making pockets in the cold sand. Slowly her body bends forward like playdough melting under the sun until her head touches the grains. Her forehead pushes into dry heat. Hard tiny grains push against her skin. Her head makes a pocket and she feels the tears roll toward her scalp and down into the sand. She can hear the tiny whispers of sand as they *plop, plop, plop* down onto it. She imagines the grey sand marbles forming near her hairline. She can hear her breathing. Her ragged breath pushing puffs of sand up. The sound is rhythmical, in time with the waves crashing against the rocks rising out of the sand all around her. The worn-smooth bedrock hulking against the waves. The simple movement of water changing rock to sand.

I can't let this happen. It can't be happening. I should've listened to David and got a checkup sooner. Cancer! Cancer! What did I do wrong? What didn't I do? It's something I never thought could happen to me. Oh God, I don't want to die. I can't. I haven't done enough. I should have done more. How am I going to tell David? No! No! Oh No!

She beats the sand with the sides of her closed fists, puffs of sand rising and settling quickly with each hammer of her fists. She can feel the sand grating and peeling the skin on her hands but she doesn't stop. She beats until her hands are raw and the pain is unbearable. Finally she lifts her head and screams outward to the sound of the waves roar. Her voice joins the screaming of gulls and the whine of sand grating against rock. The sound is raw and terrible. As raw as her bleeding hands.

Finally she straightens up as her throat grows raw and all she can do is whimper. She stands that way facing the blue green of waves stretching out to the horizon. Finally she turns to face the world. Around her the city line of Vancouver glitters in the early spring sun.

Wreck Beach. Oh God. What now? Wreck Beach. A wreck. I had a wreck. I'm wrecked. What to do? What to do? I got to get a grip on this.

I can't just give in. Why me? Why? I don't deserve this. I don't want it. I don't need it. Take it away. Take it away. Oh God, how many people have had to go through this? Why? Nobody deserves this? What the hell is it? Oh God I have to get a grip. I gotta think this through. I gotta do every-thing I can to stop it. Oh God, all those people who already have died. All the people who have died. All the ones who are dying, right now all over that city. All over this country. All over this world. I'm just one. I didn't do anything wrong. It wasn't me. It's the price of all that progress. I'm a human price.

She looks back at the car parked in the lot. Tannis is waiting there. She is standing outside the car leaned against it watching her. She walks back toward the car slowly. When she reaches it, Tannis walks up to meet her. All Tannis does is reach out and take Penny in her arms. She holds Penny like that for a long time. Finally, it is Penny who moves back.

"Thanks. Let's sit for awhile. I need to talk."

"Sure. There's a bench over there. I'm here. I'm glad you asked me to come with you to get the results. It's bad huh? By the way you looked when you came out. Oh, you don't need to talk about that if you don't want to. It's why I didn't pry when you said to just drive you somewhere. Anywhere. I figured you needed to just be, for a bit. I'm just here, Penny. What ever you need to talk about? Okay?"

Tannis walks with her to the bench and pats the stone seat as she sits down. Her smooth face is etched with tiny wrinkles at the cor-ners of her eyes. Her curly brown hair blowing around her face has streaks of grey. She has a wrap loosely covering her sweater and khaki pants. Penny hugs her warm jacket close.

"I feel so cold. I'm cold all the time. I get so cold and tired all the time."

Tannis takes her wrap and covers Penny with it.

"Here, put this on. It's warm. It's wool. One of the weavers over on the Island did it. Do you really want to sit out here. Maybe we should go over to my place. I'll make some hot tea."

"No. We'll go later, maybe. I want to be out here. Yeah, it's bad. I have cancer. Some kind of weird, rare kind. I don't know anything about it. I'll find out more later. All those of tests at the clinic. I kept hoping it was just some kind of bug or something. Chronic fatigue or whatever. I'm not even sure where it is exactly. I don't know what can be done. I have to go back tomorrow to begin all that. I don't even know how to talk about it. I mean, what do I say to David when he calls? What do I say to my family. I feel like I should reassure them. Tell them I'm okay. It's just a little cancer. Oh God, I'm scared. I feel like running and running or something. I don't know how I feel. I can't really believe it. Cancer!"

Suddenly she starts crying again. The tears silently slipping down her face. She can't stop for a long time. Tannis just sits with her arm around her. She doesn't say anything, just pats her on the back. When she looks up Tannis has tears in her eyes as well.

"Penny, you have to fight it. Fight it with everything you got. People do beat it. You can't give it the upper hand. It's just another thing you have to do. Oh Penny, I'm so sorry. It's so unfair. Dammit. It's so Goddamn unfair. All this shit in the environment. In the food, in the air, in the water. Stuff we don't even know about. It makes you feel like blowing things up. And you. You. I wish I could do something. I feel helpless. It just doesn't make sense."

"I know. I was thinking stuff all the way here. Crazy stuff. Angry stuff. I guess I thought about God, too. If there is a God, why do this? Why let this happen? Why does it have to be like this? Why me? I don't know. One minute I think I'll just wish it away. I'll just get better. The next minute it crashes down on me. I have cancer. My body has cancer. Why? What is cancer? I mean, I know it's the cells gone wild or something like that. Out of control. But what is it really? You know I'm Indian. I don't think of God as some big person who controls everything. I'm not really sure of how I think of God. God's always been just sort of connected to life. The environment or something like that and we're just a part of it all. So are we doing this? Are we the cancer? I'm sounding crazy even to myself."

Tannis sits there thinking and nods.

"No. It's not crazy. We did all this. I mean, we the humans. We're out of control. We are to blame. Not the animals, or the trees or the water. Us. But it's like we are powerless to stop it. To change it. Each of us is just part of something so huge, as individuals, we have no choice but get swept along with the tide. You know, as well as I do, that it doesn't have to be the way it is. There are better alternatives to the way we do things. That's what this whole environmental consciousness is about."

Penny doesn't answer, she just stares out at the water and listens. She turns nodding as Tannis continues.

"But it would take some kind of total revolution to stop it. People don't do that kind of thing unless they're pushed against the wall. Unless they're forced to. Unless they feel and know their very survival is at stake. It's still not clear to people that it's almost at that point, right now. How many people do you know that have died of cancer? That have it?"

Penny suddenly feels the anger again. She answers Tannis this time.

"How many do I know about? Too many. Everybody in North America and other parts of the world knows somebody right in each of their families or immediate circle of friends or co-workers that has died or has it. It's like there is this massive denial around it all. We just hope we somehow escape it. We just try to fix the person that gets it. And we grieve for the person when they suc-cumb. If somebody were lining up all the people who have died from cancer, and were shooting them one by one, we would go to war to stop it. Well death is death. From cancer or from guns. We should have the basic right and freedom to live without that kind of threat hovering over us. People have to stand up and fight it like a war. We are at war."

Tannis turns toward her. She's nodding, an intense furrow on her brow. Penny goes on. Her voice is steady now.

"The trouble is we don't recognize the enemy. We buy the stuff that causes it. And we're content. We're dependent on it. We never get to see what kind of shit commercial food growing does, what making things like shoes, cars and buildings does and so on. We just use them. And then there's the things you talk about, the past nuclear testing, the leaking plutonium and the accidents. Sure we're getting more sticky about environmental controls. Pushing for minimum standards and stuff, but it's cumulative. It stacks up. Against us. And we get cancer. And we fight valiantly, a lonely personal battle of life and death. We fight it alone. There won't be any hue and cry to avenge my death. No uprising against the causes. When is enough? When every single person gets it instead of the probability of every third person getting it?"

"It's true. Everything you said. Penny, I promise you, I will take it up. It might take time to build the forces but we have to. No, we wouldn't stand by and let people get shot down, one by one. It's the same. It needs to be said exactly like that. Enough is enough. I hear you. You were mentioning about your beliefs. What do your people say about cancer? What do they say it is?"

Penny sat looking out at the city scape surrounding them, silent for awhile before answering.

"I don't think they have a word for it. At least not any I have ever heard, and I speak the language. One thing though, I was thinking coming over here. I was thinking about our Coyote stories about the flesh-eating monsters during the transformation of the world into this one. That's what came to mind. I'm being eaten by something which I can't see. It was the image I saw when that doctor described the kind of cancer I have. What it's doing. My own system attacking itself. No foreign bugs or virus. Not my blood but certain tissues or something like that. Those stories tell of how the world had to be rid of the flesh-eaters so we could survive. How they conjured themselves and how they shape-shift and change their form continuously. They were banished but only if we kept the balance which was established. The balance is the natural order in this world. Now everything is out of balance. We are causing another transformation. Our old people say they're back. In all kinds of different forms. Not just cancer, but aids, mad cow disease, superbacteria, mutant viruses and so on. It makes sense to me, literally and metaphorically."

Cancer to Indians

"What do they say can be done?"

"They don't. Only that we have to try to restore balance in the natural world. That it's our duty even if it means suffering or death. Because we face death anyway. Not everybody believes that. But I guess I do, now. God didn't do this. The natural world did. Unless you think of the natural world as God. It's only doing what it has to. It will restore balance. We put the things out there which was not meant for our bodies to have to deal with. Our own bodies are part of the natural world. It's part of what we have conjured on the earth."

Tannis shook her head.

"But you, as an individual, and as a Native person didn't do these things. It's the corporation's, the money mongers. They are responsible."

"Oh, I'm not individually responsible but my body is working as it should. It's trying to find a way to transform, to cope with things confronting it. If we don't restore balance, eventually all living things will mutate to a new balance. We're all locked into it, whether we are rich or poor, whether we are plant or animal. Humans may be spared or not. Probably not. We have removed ourselves so far from the rest of nature, that we are the most vulnerable. We think we can escape by making newer better drugs and so on, but all we do is set ourselves up to be weaker. We are like the dinosaur. We can no longer cope with the earth natural transformation. Anyway, enough of this. I'm freezing. I needed to talk about it. To try to make some kind of sense, for myself, of it. A way I can see it and not let it crush me. I'm sorry I sound so malevolent and foreboding. It's how I'm feeling right now, though. I have a better insight, now. I can talk with David and my family. Thank you so much Tannis. For being here with me through this part."

"Penny, it's you I want to thank. You put some things in perspective for me. I know what I gotta do, now. I won't stop the fight no matter what. I'll get others talking about it too. It's what I can do. I won't give up either. I'll take on NAFTA, the W.T.O. Whatever, wherever. It is a war. Let's get you back to your hotel now. Penny, fight it. Okay? Do everything you can."

As they drive away from the beach the sun is setting over the waters and the tide is moving in. The water rushes in great foamy breakers over the dark rocks at the water's edge. It is transforming the rock, particle by particle into sand.

NOTE IN HER DIARY

G ard
the next night I walked alone to the
water's edge
there was suddenly a feeling
as though a shadow had reared up
from the ground and was looming over me
the dark water roiled sleek black liquid glass
stillness
I am afraid

Lena walks up the steep hill toward her mothers's house. She can see the bright blue door. It stands out against the stark white of the house. It is the only house with a door like that on the hill. All the houses on that part of the reserve look a lot alike, the colours ranging from mostly white to off-white to grey, and a few with light pastel colours. All the doors match the houses.

Thinking of it now, Lena realizes that it is funny how she has always thought of it as her mother's house rather than her father's house, although it had been his idea to paint the door a bright blue. He had said that the houses up there on the hill all looked too much alike, and their home would be easy to see because of the door. She had known he was right, but there was a question that had always been silent, "Who would have a problem?" She had known that all the Indians in a thousand mile radius knew each other and that they didn't find their way to each other by the description of their houses.

As she walks toward the house she realizes that she had kept that door in her mind all the years she had been away. It was there as always, a bright blue against the white. A blue barrier against the cold north wind. A cool blue shield against the summer heat. She remembered having hated the door and having wished it would just be white like the rest of the house. But while she was away, it had been the part of the house that had been a constant clear image. Behind that door, warm smells and laughter mixed into a distinct impression of the way it was back home. Her mother, long braids tied together in the back, smiled at her from behind that door.

Now, she walks up the hill toward the house carrying the one bag that holds her things. She feels light, weightless and somehow insubstantial like the last fluffseeds still clinging shakily to the milkweeds that line the narrow dirt road gutted with deep dry ruts. In this country the summer rains leave cracked mud tracks which freeze in the fall and stay hidden under the snow and ice in winter.

At this moment she feels she can easily be lifted to float up and away from those deep earth gashes, to move across the land with the dry fall drifting of seeds and leaves. She had this dirt road and the mud in the spring and the dust in the summer, the ruts in the fall and the ungraded snow in the winter. She mostly hated the dry milkweeds crowding together everywhere. As always, the lumps of soil are uneven and slow to travel over on this road. She feels like turning and bolting back to the bus to catch it before it can leave her here, but running is hard on this broken ground.

The door seems to loom ahead of her, although the house is no taller than the rest. She hates the way all the cheap government houses on the row facing the road are so close together and have paint peeling and dry weedy yards with several mangy dogs. She turns to look back at the road winding steeply down to the cross-road where the bus stops momentarily to drop-off or pick-up people from the reserve. The freeway stretches away into a hazy purple distance where night is beginning to shadow the land. Only the white line dividing those coming from those going is visible after a certain point. The red tail lights of the bus are fading straight into that shadow line between sky, asphalt and the dark-ened earth.

Turning she faces the rest of the climb. A single black crow is sil-houetted against the deepening blue of the sky higher up on the hill. It caws at her from its perch on the steeple cross of the village church, raising a raucous in the quiet. The crow screeches and flaps its wings, dives over her mother's house, and then flies lazily over-head, looking down at her as it passes, flying over the dirt road toward the crossroad in the direction of the twilight.

She watches as the crow disappears into dark blue. She knows his name from the old stories. She wants to laugh and say it. She knows he hangs around only in the summer months and then flies away when the shadows in the fall grow long and the days short.

She wants to say, "You, old pretender, you don't fool me. You're not going to preach to me, too, are you? You're no smarter than me!" Instead she finds tears wetting her cheeks.

Her tears bring the memory of a dream from the week before when she had started the long bus ride home. In her dream she had been in a large building with many bright lights and shiny reflections. Although there was a lot of noise, she couldn't see anyone. She felt totally alone as she walked down a long white hallway. She remembered looking, one by one, at the doors she passed, feeling like the only thing behind each one was a patch of sky. In the dream she remembered feeling something like dizziness as she saw how many doors there were and how they seemed to stretch on and on without end into darkness. She recalled running and stumbling past the doors and calling out. When she awoke she had been crying.

She is almost at the top of the hill now. She stops and puts down her bag. A couple of reserve dogs bark at her and then wag their tails, trotting toward her, making dog-greeting noises in their throats. She looks down at the one, that was obviously a lady dog with her sagging dry milk sacs, and strokes her ear. She thinks about dogs like her, in the city she has left and says, " Mamma dogs don't just walk around free, there, you know. You're pretty lucky to be here.". The lady dog sits down and thumps her tail knocking over some of the weeds, sending puffs of seed floating with each excited wave of tail.

From behind the houses, farther up into the dark hills, she hears the high far away yipping of a coyote. She sees the dogs ears perk up. She sees the way their eyes glow a deeper orange as they forget her and point their noses toward the hills above them. A low crooning echo rumbling deep in their throats. She, too, looks up there and whispers, "How are you brothers?" in the language. She knows them, too.

She thinks of that one coyote in the papers, in some city, that had got trapped in a hallway after coming in from an alley door. How somebody mistaking it for a dog had opened an elevator for it and how it had ridden to the roof of an apartment building and ran around crazily and then jumped to its death, rather than run back through the elevator door and riding back down into the hallway to run out the alley door. She had known that it hadn't been a matter of animal stupidity, because a coyote always remembered where it had just come from. She had secretly known that it had more to do with the quick elevator door and the long lonely ride up to the top. She thinks of the coyotes hanging around in the cities these days. Nobody wanted them there, so nobody made friends with them but once in a while they made the papers when they did something wrong or showed up, trotting along Broadway, cool as can be.

Lena thinks about all the time she has spent away from this place of hard cracked earth, seedpods and clean coyote prints in the new snow up in the hills. She looks up at the bright blue surface directly in front of her waiting to open and feels the bone-aching, deep tiredness of long journeys over the hard even surface of freeways into alleys and white hallways. As she reaches for the door knob she looks down and realizes that the freeway's white line and the mud ruts end here, right at her mother's door. The door that her dad had painted bright blue so that it stood out clearly against the white.

LETTER TO DELILA

Dear Delila:

I'm not gonna come out to that coalition and strategy meeting of church, environment and Indian organizations against commodification of the sacred. It sounds hopeful. Maybe once the bigger churches get into the act there will be some better legal work at the international level done. I have to stay put for awhile. I just had a bombshell dropped on me. I had some tests done and I found out I have a rare form of cancer. I've never even heard of it. I don't even know where it is exactly. It's sort of like leukaemia but it's not the blood. More like the nerves or something that makes them work. It's been showing up in people exposed to strong pesticides and some gulf war veterans. It makes me tired. It's in a stage where I could beat it. I'm trying some kind of megadrug therapy in Vancouver at the clinic there.

David's coming out instead. I wanted him to get out for awhile.

He's been hovering too much. I hope you don't mind too much. I've been keeping him up on everything. He's a good speaker too.

You don't get your worry wart all inflamed now. I'm gonna do everything right. I know enough about vitamins and Indian medicine to know I have better than a fighting chance. I decided, too, that I have to change my lifestyle. So I'm not gonna be doing any activist stuff. My sister Lena is going to move home. You know I told you about her. She's been living in Vancouver for awhile and she had a son. Well it's lucky I came here. Toby, her little boy got taken away by welfare, here, and I'm working things out to get him back. Even if I have to quit this therapy to do it. I want to spend as much time with my family as I can. When I get home, I want to make things right for her. There are a lot of other things I need to do there. I want to make sure everybody changes their bad eating habits. I even got David to lay off fried foods. Anyway let's keep in touch.

A sister, Penny

This wreckage, now it seemed at this moment, even more than that which Tupa had known, was to be her legacy. This brown dirt swiftly flowing away with the torrent, falling and falling.

"Penny? Awake? It's time for meds again. Here dear, just move this up a little. That's it honey. Pretty bad, huh? You have visitors. You want a few minutes? Here let me brush your hair for you. You'll be feeling a bit better in a minute."

I can't go on! It just makes me so sick and weak. I just want to go back to when . . . whenever . . . just not now . . . with this. I gotta look okay for them. It's just for a little while. Oh pleasssssse go away now, for a little while.

"Okay, get my bed up. Thanks."

Shanna, face drawn and tired, walks briskly toward her, hesitating, stopping a few feet away, checking. Her dark hair is oily looking and her sweater has an old mustard stain.

Hotdogs. Jesus, I wish she wouldn't feed them that shit! All those chemicals and who knows what.

"Hi my girl. How'er you? You look good."

"Hi Mom. Didn't wake you, did I? I hope you weren't waiting for me. The drive down was pretty bad. Flooding and road closures. I thought I could've got here yesterday, but my boy Jeyd is sick again. I think it's because it's spring. His asthma, you know. It gets worse. I don't like to leave too much when he's like that. Paul is back from up north. I'm sure glad. He works hard. You shoulda seen him wolf down my special hotdogs and beans. You know the way I put some extra cheese right in the pork and beans, and instead of hotdog buns, I split open the hotdogs and lay them on toasted kaiser rolls and pour the pork and beans over it. I put some canned green giant beans on the side. That's his favourite now, you know. I told him what you said about eating healthier. So he's eating'em. Jeyddie still don't like vegetables or stuff like that. I don't know how I'm going to get him to eat them. I had to bribe him and let him have some pop if he ate'em."

She stops a moment and smooths her mother's hair and goes right on chattering.

"It worked but I can't afford pop everyday. It's hard enough now that I had to quit my job over at the Kentucky Fried Chicken, to stay with him 'till he gets better. I used to be able to bring some of the stuff home that didn't sell. You know they only keep stuff that's cooked that day. Course the salads and stuff lasts forever, so I never got to take healthy stuff home. Just fries and chicken. But it helped. I don't know what we'll do if Paul doesn't get on with that new crew up there that's burying stuff coming from them oil refineries. They get almost three times what he gets right now. He said you get used to the smell. Crunching up the trees and spray-ing that stuff that kills everything except grass, to clear for the oil and gas exploration, doesn't pay too good. Lots of guys are avail-able to do that."

"Shanna, that sounds bad. I hope he doesn't get on there."

Shanna decides to ignore what her mother just said.

"And you know, I think my cousin Bitsi is get'n too big for her britches. Even though we took her in she don't even have respect anymore for Paul or me. I told her to come with me to see you but she's got a new guy. I sure don't like him. I get worried. She runs with some rough crowd now. She'll come and see you though. I know you was always her favourite. Well I guess I should go. Mom, is there anything you want? I know it's pretty rough for you. But you got all of us. Mom, all of us feel the same, we love you."

"Shan, listen for a minute. I want to tell you something. I don't know what the doctors have been saying to you. But I know, you're worried. So I want to tell you this. I see things. You've known that. This is something I don't understand. I think it's like a roulette game. When the wheel spins around, the ball falls. Somebody gets struck with cancer. Somebody gets sacrificed for the what the human has done. This time it happened to be me. Each person hopes it will be somebody else. Nobody ever thinks it will be them. When it finally hits home that it affects each one of us, then maybe something will get done. It's not right for just one person to escape. We all share in the crime. It isn't about me, or the next person or the person before me. It's bigger than that. It's the whole world. It's out of control. I just got to do my best to fight it."

Oh, damn, she's looking at me that way again, like I'm talking gibberish.

"Mom, we know that. Anyway you'll get okay. Don't talk that way. You just gotta be positive. That's what the doctors say. I know you were travelling before you got sick and getting into all that spiritual stuff, and that's good especially now. But it ain't all that bad. There's lots of good medicine those doctors are researching and they'll cure you, like they will Jeyd. The world is getting a lot better with more and more new medicines, pretty soon there won't be any more sickness."

What happened here? How could I have spent so much time speaking out to people and not have been able to get my own daughter to see it. Damn it! I was given responsibility for her and her sister and brother! I'm so stupid. I should have spent all my time making sure they did things different. What's the difference if I die, it's them that's got to at least have a fighting chance. God, I can't be too late.

"I'm gonna get out of here pretty soon. I'm really sick right now from the drugs they're using to help get my body to fight the cancer. Once my system starts to stabilize I can go home and only come here once a month. I just let myself get too outa whack. Not eating and sleeping and stuff. So don't you worry. Okay?"

Shanna nods and hugs her mother.

"I wanted to ask how Auntie Lena is making out now that Toby is back there with her. Is she doing alright. Tell me the truth."

"Yeah, I guess. They moved into that old house next to Auntie Jo. Toby spends a lot of time with her. Lena's not doing that bitching stuff if that's what you're asking. She's having a hard time of it, though. That guy she was with in Vancouver caught up with her. He's just an ass-hole. Drinking and farting around with other women. I wish she'd dump him. Why do you think she has to have guys like that all the time?"

"Oh that Lena! How's everybody else? It's only been two months but it already feels like years."

"Everybody else is okay. Merrilee woulda come but she had this gig. She sure is playing some good stuff. Her own work. Did she play for you when she was here a couple of weeks ago for that music festival? Yeah of course she did. That guy Marty, the one she talks about all the time from up Vernon. Too bad he wasn't with her when she was here. He's really got a really good voice. Knows all the old Indian songs. They sound pretty cool together. I think he's gonna take little sister from us. Or maybe we'll take him from up there. He's been hanging around helping out at uncle Andrew's. He knows about farming. He calls himself a seed saver. He's even got Dustin going on a new scheme. He's got this friend back east who plants to save seeds from old Indian crops. Indian corn and beans and stuff. He says the best food is from the old crops. They're gonna talk uncle Andrew and Charlie into trying out a few plots. You know Dustin. He just lives for planting. He can make anything grow."

"That's good to hear. I can't wait to get home to see that. And baby girl, Rae? She still having ear infections? It's got to be that cows milk. Did you take her off it?"

"Yeah. She's been fine. We give her that soya milk like you said. It's kinda expensive but she's worth it. Jeyd is getting used to it in his mush too. Grandma got some new glasses and she's gonna try beading again. I was kinda worried about her. She always worries about you. She was staying over at Charlie's for awhile when she was sick but she's home again. Lena goes over there a lot to help her out. David was there before he came out here again. He must be still in Seattle or he'd be here right now. She sure was glad to see Lena move home."

Here it comes again. I feel like my eyes are gonna fall shut. I get so tired so fast.

"I'm glad you came to visit, my girl. It's been pretty lonely here, with David gone. I'm sorta getting tired. Are you gonna stay the night here in the residence? Lets breakfast here with me before you head back. Okay? I'm going to rest again."

"Okay Mom. I love you. Night, night."

As Shanna hugs her she feels her eyes shut and already the drowsy half sleep begins moving her away into greyness. She thinks of the green soft grass starting to show in the fields. And the yellow bells sticking their heads up on the hillsides above her mom's house. A longing deep inside, for the smell of new sage, carries her into the nights dreamless drug sleep.

She stood on the porch one night and called and called because no one was in the dark house with her and she was too little to light a lamp. She called her sisters, and a high thin voice answered from the darkness outside from the spring where they went to get buckets of water. She went down to the dark, dark spring to answer the call and later when she walked back she found everyone sleeping in their beds. The fear and the springs gurgling are still clear. But there, sandwiched between one memory and the next, a black silent moment.

The lines at the corners of Aunt Josalie's mouth make her look like she is smiling even when she isn't. Even when she is crying. But today she is smiling. There is always a clean even smell coming from her. Toby watches her climb the stairs slowly, her wide brown shoes scraping their toes against the narrow steps, dress flapping around her jiggling behind. It isn't polite to say "butt" about aunties' behinds even though they are the same thing.

"Hey Auntie, d'you want me to carry your stuff?"

"Nah. I ain't got much. I jus' bin thrift shopping around. You wanna come up fer some juice?"

"Yeah I guess so. What'er you smiling for. Did j'you find some good junk?"

"Sorta. I found a new sweater fer you. It ain't even got any buttons missing. But this is the happy thing. Your best Auntie Penny's coming tonight. I saw your mom last night and she said to clean up and git some stew made up. You know your Aunt'll want some with mostly carrots and squash. She likes that healthy stuff."

In the warm kitchen smelling something like bacon, Toby sits swirling the grape punch watching the little purple powder grains at the bottom make a moving circle.

"She problee'l have some presents fer us. I wish she'd jus' live here with us all. I always can't wait te see her. She's sick, I know, n' has te stay over there in Vancouver to see the doctors, but how long'll that be, forever?"

"Don't say that! It's jus fer now. Where's your Mom and them? Are they out again? You by yourself again?"

Toby sees that she isn't smiling anymore. It is hard to make her smile much now.

"She's sleeping'n that guy, Harry, he's there sleeping too. They got back while I was sleeping I guess. Anyway, I don't wanna make noise too much. Mom's always grumpy an' anyway I like it here. You don't git grumpy. I did'n eat. Can I have a bread?"

"Oh that Lena! She just never changes even she's home now. Oh well, go ahead, I'll put some peanut butter on it, okay. Your cousins'll be back later too. I knew I shoulda just sent you along with them to help out with the first cut haying, even though they're all older than you. You could've at least helped a little. You're kinda puny though. I guess it's the big city pollution stunted you. But you could've eaten the sandwiches and the apples and cookies I sent with them instead of starving all day."

Toby thinks about Vancouver. What he remembers most is the sounds of the sirens at night. Every night. And the piss stink on Hastings where they stayed before he got taken. He doesn't want to think of the rest.

"I sure hope Auntie Penny's not staying on Hastings. It's too dirty there and some guys get knifed, you know. She should just run away from them doctors for good."

"You never mind about that. She ain't anywhere near there. She was at the clinic. That Lena! She shoulda never stayed there after she had you. She's got no brains. But we sure are glad she did finally have a little nephew for us, even though you're quite a lot younger than all your cousins and she's older than me an auntie Penny. And we sure are glad she came back here after they took you. Good thing we got you back. Nobody's ever gonna take you away from us, no matter what your mamma does. You're home now with us!"

Toby bites slowly into the thick peanut butter sandwich Aunt Josalie set in front of him. It is all like a bad dream now. Being taken. That's what it was. Taken. He would never be taken again. He would die first. No matter how. He would.

"You're Auntie Penny's gonna be home now, instead of just visiting for a week at a time. She only has to go to Vancouver once a month. She's gonna get better. Thing's are gonna get better here too. She'll straighten up your mom. Auntie Penny's real smart. She's the one got you back from the welfare. She's the smartest of us all. She got educated. Nobody here ever done the things she did. She's a big artist too. Only now she don't paint pictures like she used to. Maybe now she'll get back to it. Maybe that's why she got sick. She never shoulda stopped. A person's got to do what they were given to do. They can't jump over it. You remember that, Toby."

Toby finishes his sandwich and sits listening. He likes Auntie Josalie because she always talked to him. She always has time to talk and talk. She had a nice voice. It sounds like she is hugging him when she talks. His mom is okay. But she is grouchy a lot. She doesn't have time. She always said so. But Aunt Josalie would talk as long he listened.

"Like your mom. She was meant to do something but she took off to the city and never stuck around long enough to get it. Everybody's got a gift they have to work with. Otherwise things don't work out for them. Me, I knew I was given the gift to look after the things in the family. To show them to whoever wants to know how to do the old Indian stuff. You know, cut meat and dry it and can berries and fish. Sew moccasins and ribbon shirts and make quilts, like Grandma. All that. You just remember that. You always like to make things. I see you do it. Build little things outa pieces of wood and cardboard and colour them up. They look nice. I picked some more stuff up for you at the dollar store. Glue and some glittery paint. Here take a look in the bag."

He takes the bag and looks in it. Sure enough there is a big white plastic glue bottle with a pointy top. And little bottles of glittery paints. Silver and green and red and blue and others at the bottom of the bag.

"Wow. Thank you Auntie. Wait'll you see what I'm making. This glue is just what I was wishing for. I gonna finish it right now. Okay! Get me when Auntie Penny gets here."

He can hardly wait to try the paints. His heart is beating fast as he grabs his new sweater and picks up his cap. He holds the bag held tightly in his hands. Auntie Josalie is already busy chopping a huge green squash by the time he opens the door into the bright sunshine.

She stood facing the dark bitter rain which slanted down to seep into all the cracks to run brown and finally to wash away rich soil leaving only pebbles and rocks. The window framed her with light. She stood there long, letting the rain speak to her of this moment between. Of her, sandwiched between the rain, beating the dry thin earth away, and the light behind.

Behind her, Raella's little girl voice chirped.

"Gramma, come on we're waiting for you! What are you looking for? It's dark'n scary out there. Come on, we need you to play too!"

"I'm coming, Rae, but don't wait for me. I'm looking at the down-pour coming down."

And she stood before the shadows curtaining the world and spoke the words which held her.

"I need some time."

The window is open and the soft summer breeze blows the curtain slightly. The field next to the house where the corn grows is green gold in this light. The rustling of the corn stalks make a soft whispering harmony. Crickets are trilling in droves among the corn. Near the window, a bumble bee is noisily buzzing around the waist high sweet clover.

Penny can see Dustin and Marty hoeing between the rows, their shirtless brown backs bent over the hoes. She can hear their laughter drifting on the wind to her. Behind her, she hears her mother's familiar footsteps.

"Penny, Lena just phoned. Toby's gone. Her and Harry had a big fight. He's been drinking again, you know. He straightened up there for awhile after you first came back. He was trying to beat up Toby and Lena took a licking from him, trying to protect Toby. Then Toby ran away. She's pretty worried. Josalie's on her way over there. Toby usually goes over to her place but Harry said he was going to send him back to welfare 'cause he don't listen. Harry was trying to make him drink beer with him. He was drunk. He don't like Toby even when he's sober."

"Oh damn. Did she call the cops on him this time? If she didn't I'm sure as hell going to. He can't get away with shit like that. Where do you think Toby went? He couldn't get too far. He's probably hiding somewhere. He's a street kid. He'll be okay."

"Yeah. They came and got him after he passed out and Lena called them. She's okay. A few bruises and stuff. Good thing he's so fat and lazy he can't do too much damage. She said she whacked him a few good ones over the head with a ladle. She better just quit with the guys. She's almost fifty now. I hope she goes through the change soon. That'll put a stop to that tail spin."

"Oh, Mom, but you're right. She's got to smarten up about men. I'll get David. He's out in the horse shed working on the mare's feet. He can drive to the village and ask around if anybody's seen Toby. I'm gonna go over and talk to that Lena. You just stay put here. Maybe he'll come over here. You can call in Dustin and Marty and send them around the neighbourhood to check on the other cousin's. Maybe Toby's at Mat's. Have Merrilee go up to the lake at the old cabin. He goes there with Mat when they're fishing. He knows how to get there. Don't get too riled up, Mom. We'll find him."

As Penny gets up to go to the horseshed the phone rings. She runs to pick it up, her heart beating.

"Hello. Auntie Penny? It's me Toby. I ran away cause Harry's gonna make me go back to welfare. He was fighting with my mom and me. I don't wanna go back to welfare. I'm scared. Don't let him make me. If he tries I'm gonna jump off the bridge. He's not gonna ever get me to go to Welfare. I hate it there. They hurt me there. And I don't wanna ever go back to Hastings in Vancouver with my Mom either if she leaves Harry an she said she was gonna leave him. Where is she gonna leave to? Could you come get me, and hide me from her and Harry? Auntie Penny, you got me back from welfare an' you're real smart. You can make them not take me again. Please, Auntie Penny."

"Toby, nobody's gonna ever take you from us. Nobody. Don't be scared Auntie'll come right away. Harry's in jail and your mom's not gonna go anywhere. I'm not gonna let her. Where are you? I'll get David to bring me there right now."

"I'm at Shane's house. He said I better call you. Cause I told him you got me back from welfare. His mom don't know I'm here. Shane promised not to tell anybody. He's hiding me."

"Okay. Just stay put ëtil I get there Sweetheart."

David walks in just as she hangs the phone up.

"Your mom told me what happened. Who was that?"

"It was Toby. He's over at Millie and Ted's with his cousin Shane. Shane told him to call me. Let's go get him. He thinks the welfare is going to get him. We'll go over and have a talk with Lena. I'm not gonna leave Toby there if she doesn't plan on changing her ways. Poor little Toby. He said he was gonna jump off the bridge if anybody tried to make him go back to welfare or Vancouver. That's not good. That Lena better smarten up and get her act together."

The drive doesn't take long. Shane is standing out in the front yard watching for them. As they pull in he whistles and Toby comes running over to the car and jumps in. He starts crying right away. And Penny holds him and strokes his hair, murmuring to him.

"It's alright, Sweetheart, Auntie's got you. It's alright don't cry."

On the drive over to Lena's, she lets him stay nestled under her arm.

"We're gonna go over to talk to your mom. She's never going to have that Harry ever come around again. I promise you. She's not going anywhere either. You and her are gonna stay here. Right here where me and Aunt Josalie can keep an eye on you. Aunt Josalie's over at your Mom's. They're pretty worried. I didn't phone her or anything."

"Okay Auntie. I'm glad you're so smart. I hope you never got to go to Vancouver anymore either. I'll miss you too much."

Lena is standing on the steps when they pull between her and Josalie's house. She runs down the steps two at a time and pulls the door open. She kneels on the ground and puts her arms around Toby sobbing.

"Toby, my little Toby. You scared me. Harry's gone to jail. He's never gonna come back here again. I promise you. Nobody's ever gonna be mean to you like that ever again. You don't have to be scared, I'm not gonna go anywhere from here, either. Here, let me hug you proper. That's my boy. Son, son, I love you."

Toby puts his arm around her and his cheek next to hers at the same time he looks past his mother to his Aunt Josalie waiting to hug him.

"Auntie Josalie. I didn't mean to worry you. I was gonna call you next if Auntie Penny wasn't home."

He wiggles free and runs to her. She sweeps him up into her strong arms and kisses him all over his face. He giggles.

"Lena, leave him with Jo for now. I'll come in. David, I'll call you to come get me later. I want to talk with Lena for awhile."

Lena nods and they climb the steps together to her kitchen. The kitchen is littered with beer bottles. A stale smell of cigarettes and something else gone sour permeates the kitchen. Penny opens the windows and empties the ashtrays. Lena stands there silently.

"Sit down, Lena. Are you hurt?"

"No. That shit. He just bruised my cheek. I got a few bruises on my arm too, where he grabbed me."

"Lena, I'm not gonna lecture on Harry. I assume he's history. But you better charge him or I will. You know, I never did know why you went and got yourself stuck in the life you did. It took a big chunk out of you. Maybe I shoulda asked this a long time ago. I just never knew how. Now I want the story. You grew up in the same house I did. With the same family. What happened?"

Lena sits for awhile not saying anything.

"I don't really know. I fell in love with Garry. I was just sixteen and he seemed so grown up, with his car and talk about the big city. It was like I was star struck or something. I always dreamed of going places when I was a kid. Seeing things. The world seemed so exciting and big. I used to read the magazines we picked up from the junkyard for the john. The pictures in them always showed places and things we never had. And then when we got into Vancouver, he worked awhile for the first few years and then lost his job. He started doing dope and for awhile I stayed away from it. I don't know why I never got pregnant. I just never did. Anyway, after awhile I started doing it. It took me to those places, in a way. There's nothing like it that I know of. Nothing. I don't know why I'm not dead. Eventually, I hit the streets for it. I did things I never want to remember. By then Garry was out of the picture. I kicked it a few times. Once for over three years. I always went back to it, though. It's like everything is grey compared to it."

Penny watches her. Her eyes are dreamy and faraway.

"Seven years ago, after I almost ODed, I decided to quit. I went through narcotics treatment. It's hard. I've slipped a few times. But then Toby, the miracle came. I was too ashamed of myself to come home. I thought I could do it on my own. That all I needed was Toby and the support group. But I got this need. I don't quite know what it is. It's like I can't live alone. I don't know how. Like I'm not a full person. Like my arms and legs are missing. Like I needed somebody to be there, even if he's a shit. And all of them were. Now I don't know. I haven't felt that so much here. I've been trying to kick Harry out, but he was hard to get rid of. It was family that I was really missing, I guess. The warmth of it. Like arms holding you. Being part of it. I didn't know ëtil I came home. You don't know what it is except that something isn't there. I was still just a kid when I left. I missed it so much. Oh Penny. How could I have been so stupid?"

She covers her face with her hands and starts crying. Her shoulders shaking.

"You don't know how many times I relive those years before I left. There's nothing out there, as bright and shiny as what we had then. It was like a rainbow. Those lights in the city don't compare. They're dull and dingy with what's behind them. I always looked for your letters. You never stopped writing even when I didn't know night from day and didn't answer. General Delivery, Hastings Street, Vancouver. I have every one of them. I would take them out and read them. I think it kept me alive, actually. When I heard you were sick and I had lost Toby to welfare it just abut killed me. I got pretty close to riding the horse again. Then I had a dream. It was the door on Mom's house. Anyway I came. It was my last resort. But everything was right here. Has always been. Now I want to do what I can to make things right. Help me. Show me the way. I want the rainbow back. I want Toby to trust me. I'm so tired of being unhappy."

She has her head down, and leans over on her arms, almost touch-ing the table.

Penny reaches over and smooths her hair lightly.

"Lena. You know It seems like we almost did the same thing. Sure art was my thing, but I mean leaving home. It took my kids to smarten me up, too. I haven't painted for some time, now, but there was still something pushing me. Now I have this sickness and sud-denly everything's shifted around. I came home to heal too."

Penny can see Toby and Josalie out at the garden picking raspber-ries in an ice cream bucket. Toby is laughing at something his aun-tie is telling him.

"I was thinking about what you said about not feeling like a full person. I feel that. I didn't always. I know that. I don't know when it started to feel like that for me. Maybe when I went totally inward with the art. Maybe when I left the family. Maybe it's more than family. Maybe it's our community together in a certain way on the land which makes us a full person. A thing deeper and more enduring than any one of us, which we need and makes us whole. Something which gives deep comfort and security. Which gives us grace. Maybe it's the natural state we are blueprinted for."

Something about the way Lena does not move, but sits still and listening makes her go on.

"I think it could be a longing felt by more people than you and me. It might have more to do with what's wrong with the world than we think. Maybe it's such an old and deep yearning now that it's become the norm. Only we've had something to recognize it by. People are separated into little pieces of family because of they way they have to make a living now. It's been that way in Europe for a long time. Community has come to mean a collection of people, unrelated strangers, living side by side. A town, a city. An uncaring and dangerous place."

Lena sits up and looks at her. Something is in her eyes. A sadness which is deeper than anything Penny has ever seen.

"It's funny. All the time I was away, the things which I went back to for comfort was always about us. I would lay in the dark and imagine the times we were together up in the hills with Tupa and everybody. And the big gatherings where everybody ate together and sang. And even working in the fields or making quilts with our aunties. Even our big noisy arguments about the dishes. I always remembered the sunflowers and saskatoons in full bloom and the swimming in the creek in the summer. I would fill my mind with it and cry. But it would give me comfort. Like somebody holding me. What if we didn't have that? Where would a person turn?"

"I'm not sure. Money, power, work, sex, drugs, religion? Something to focus the need on. To try to fill the hole. It's like a cult, to want. To be unfulfilled. People think those things are what they need but if you dig down, you find what they really wish for in those things is to feel fulfilled. To find that place in the sun to share with loved ones. I think it's separation from real community connected to land that is at the bottom of that yearning. Oh, people probably wouldn't agree with me because they haven't experienced it the way we did. They couldn't know. There is just the deep and constant knowing that something has got to be better than what they have. It's what keeps the machine running. A deepseated, brooding and destructive disquiet. A culture of discontent. It's what's sucking up everything clean and healthy."

"Penny, you're getting into stuff that's too up there. I know, it's stuff you were working on. But for me, it comes down to how to get past this shit. I go to group, even here, all the time just to stay clean. I don't want to just stay clean. You know? I'm beginning to feel like the group's the addiction. Like it somehow gives me the group's reality of me. A still clean addicted Lena. Nothing more. Where's the real me? I don't know where to look."

"I was thinking something of the same thing about me. Lena, I was thinking it would be good for you and me and whoever wanted to, to go up into the hills together. Like a long time ago. To camp and pick berries and dry deer meat and fish. To tell stories at the camp fire and squeeze together with all the girls in the tent. Mostly to see the sun come up over the mountains. And to see the stars and listen to the frogs at night. To just hear nothing but the wind and the birds and smell the pine trees and the wild roses. Remember how Tupa used to tell us that the berries were just waiting for us."

Lena's eyes are shining with tears. But she nods smiling.

"Everything seemed to be happy that we were there to be with them. She used to say that they were lonely for us. I remember feeling like a whole person. She used to say to wrap the light from the rising sun around you because the shadows from the dream world followed you everywhere. And she always prayed and talked to all the things. The sun, the water, the bluejays, the berries. Everything. Like mom and Josalie, she was happy for everything we had. She never asked for more than what we had. Somewhere along the line, the shadows took over. I forgot how to wrap the light of each new day around me. I need to go there to do those things."

"Yeah. But you gotta get some pounds on you. You're skinnier than a stick. Sis. I want to try to live better. You know. It's not going to be easy but there's things I can do with you and mom and Jo. You know it's like I never really learned a lot after I left home. I don't know about climbing hills right now, but I want to help in the garden and can fruit and fish. I want to spend time with you. I want to go fishing with Toby. I can help put stuff away for winter. If we have a good crop from them gardens we'll have enough food. When there's something to work at with the others, it'll help. I promise you, I'm gonna throw away the old me. I feel like I can do it."

Lena sits there, tears streaking her makeup, her arms marked with the long trails she has travelled before finding her way back home. Penny, her little sister, sits with her, pale and tired from the long days of discontent, carrying the shadows of the new world inside her body. Outside, the corn is rustling softly in the new fields planted by their boys. Above them, the hills wait listening for their footfalls on the path up.

In those long days that followed, days caught like bits of silk thread on blackberry branches, in those brief and momentary flashes of brightness lost among greenness, she could sometimes find herself.

Penny watches the trail ahead. It's steep and it curves around some rocks. The rocks are tall rounded, standing like sentinels. Grey, covered with orange lichen. The sun is hot and the heat shimmers off the rocks in waves. A slight breeze ruffles the few short poplars shading the trail. Tall firs and pines rise up on each side of the trail. From up ahead, the voices drift back toward her and Lena. Lena is sitting down catching her breath.

Man, it's hot. I'm feeling pretty weak. It's just the climb and the heat.

"Penny, maybe we should have camped down there. It's seems to be getting steeper. I don't remember it being this steep and far. It seemed like it was a lot easier to get to the berry patch."

"No. Dustin and Marty were up here a few days ago, to check the berries. You can't get to it in the truck. It just seems long. We're both outa shape. But it'll be nice. Remember that small spring? I think it'll be good to camp up there. We could see for a long ways down into the valley from up there."

"Well, it's a good thing we've been really eating good food and vitamins and taking those long walks every day. Those boys really are getting the knack of making that Indian corn and beans grow. And all them tomatoes and squash! I thought we were gonna be canning forever, last fall. I feel better than I've felt in a long time. You know, I was wondering about you. All this year you never talked too much about your health. Are you okay?"

I guess I better get a blood test done when we get down. It's time for it anyway. But I've been feeling so good.

"I feel really good. I wouldn't be up here if I didn't. That's thing about being in remission. It could last forever. Anyway, I don't dwell on it too much. I'm just glad I could do all the things I wanted to this past year. That whole thing about getting the whole family involved in the planting and harvesting. It's about the best thing we ever did. The little kids just love it. I was laughing at Raella checking on the carrots every day. She planted them in such big bunches, they look like rows of weeds. We'll have to thin them out for days, when we get back."

"How come David didn't come up? I thought he was back for the week. That load of corn he took over to the market musta sold alright. I notice he didn't bring any back."

"David's really getting that Indigenous fair trade thing going. He's setting up a new thing with that group up in the Shuswap. They're putting an organic heritage-food processing thing together. You know him. He's got all kinds of ideas for how it could make a difference. He's been pretty busy setting up the same thing in other communities, too. It's big and it's working. Anyway, Andrew and Mabel are coming up tomorrow. They're gonna truck the old mare to the lower camp by the lake, for mom to ride and the hay team, buster and brownie, for them to ride up here. Josalie's gathering up her troop to follow them. They want to get a couple of deer and dry them up right up here and pack them down on the horses. We'll have a regular old time Indian camp out. I wouldn't be surprised if some of the others in the village show up. People were pretty interested in our campout."

"I guess we better catch up to the rest, before we get too far behind."

I remember this place. We used to stop here to pray before we got to the top. This is the place I'm sure. That tall rock, the one that looks like a lady. That's the one.

"Yeah. Here, let me give you a hand. You shoulda wore them hiking boots, I got for you at the Sally Ann, instead of those old runners. I don't think it's that far now. I remember these rocks. I used to watch for them when we came up. Tupa used to say they were the guards of the blackberries. She put some copper there under that one. She said we had to pay respect to them and ask for good weather. Let's put some pennies there, Lena. I brought some."

"Pennies. Maybe that's where your name came from. Doesn't your Indian name mean something like copper? The copper woman who shone so bright people thought she was like the sun? And when she died they loved her so much she became a mountain that people went to for a vision."

"Oh, Lena, you're always so dramatic. I asked mom and she said that I was named after Tupa's mother. I think it does mean woman of copper, though."

"I'm gonna put this copper here to ask for good weather. I haven't done anything like this for so long I feel almost silly. But I was thinking, I want to see the sun come up in the morning. I'm gonna sit up on the ridge where Tupa used to sit all night, tonight. I want to put things right in my mind, I guess. I still have lots of mixed up feelings I'm packing around and I want lift some of that. I've been lucky. I've had a chance to see things go right in my family. I want to make my thanks for allowing me stick around for this."

How do I do this? Tupa always did it as far as I can remember. She always did the prayers. Tupa I wish you were here. I feel like you're here.

"Let me, put my two cents in, too then, since I'm the oldest ëtill Mom gets here. I gotta do this in the language though."

Penny watches her sister take two pennies from her pocket and kneel down by the tallest of the rocks. Its smooth surface towers above them. Near the top a slight oval overhang curves upward, creating shadows. A face with chin lifted pointing upward.

"I put these pennies here under your feet to honour you, who guard this mountain. I am the oldest of my sisters and I come here in respect to pick the sweet berries of this place. My sister, Penny, who also gives pennies, honours you of this place, where we have known so much happiness in the past. We have not been here for many years and ask that you recognize us, poor humans. We bring our children and grandchildren to you. To be filled with your spirit. We bring our sons and their uncles to hunt and fish. Watch over all of us during the days and nights we are here. We are people of this land, and pray it will always be so."

The moment seems to stretch outward from them on and on forward. Tears are silently dropping from Lena's tightly closed eyes. She sits hunched over, shoulders shaking ever so slightly. Penny reaches over and lightly brushed her hair.

She sounded just like Tupa. I'm so thankful too that she's here. Everything is right now with her finally home, and doing all the things in the old way like she's been doing. She was meant to get old and take her place as the eldest in the future. She suits it. She's really found herself. I give thanks for that. I wish her a long life with the light wrapped around her so she can be there for everybody. She's so precious to us. Thank you, for letting me see this day. Thank for the wealth of my family wrapped around me. I am full inside with family on this good day. Give us your protection while we move in these mountains, with our wild relatives out here in our true home. Accept these small gifts that it be so.

"Thank you, big sister. You know, It's seems so simple. This, and yet it's so powerful. I think now of all the time I spent chasing other things to get in touch with such power. It's all right here. I finally feel like I've came home from a long, long journey."

As they get up, Penny hugs Lena for a moment. They smile at each other before beginning the rest of the trail up.

"Well, we got a ways to go uphill yet. Let's get these rickety bones moving. It'll be near sundown when we finish setting up camp up there."

"Oh, the boys have things all set up by the time we get up there. They're in such a hurry. They've been planning for a whole month just how they'll set the tents and everything up. I'm sure glad Shanna and Merrilee decided to come after all, they'll be a big help."

"They wouldn't miss out on something like this. That Merrilee, she brought her flute. You'd think she'd get tired playing all the time."

"Her and Marty have plans to make up some new songs. Songs of the mountain's in the summer. That new tape they made, *Songs of the Corn Harvest*, it's doing really well. I heard it on the radio! They got invited to the folk music festival to play later this year."

When they reach the top, they can see the tents are already up and a fire with the black field tea pot is already steaming. Raella runs over to them.

"Hi Grama, hi Gramma Two. We thought you was gonna take forever. I saw some big blue birds hopping around. Look, there they are. They sound like they're talking."

The blue jays are hopping from branch to branch watching everything going on and squawking to each other. Penny stands still, her face tilted up toward them, not saying anything.

You, who are always here to greet us, we greet you again, brothers of this land. I've missed your voices. Let the other relatives know that the humans are here once again. We will join you for a short time in your world. Fly between the worlds to let the great keeper know that we too celebrate this fine world where there is beauty still. And we will not spoil anything. We leave it as though we were wind passing over the grasses.

"Gramma, what are they?"

"They're bluejays. Their Indian name means Travellers Between. They travel between the worlds. They can speak any language. They talk to all the other things that live here. They know things."

"Oh. Can you teach me to say their name? I like Indian words. This is an Indian camp, isn't it Gramma. We should talk Indian."

"I'll teach you more names of things here. And when you grow up you can teach them to your granddaughter. You're getting to speak pretty good Indian. Maybe these mountains will be where you live and you'll know all their real names. It's important."

"I think that would be the very best of all. Could we live here now?"

"For this week we will. And for as many times as we can. Help me get the food we packed ready for your mom. Everybody must be starving."

"Okay Gramma. Can I sleep with you in the tent instead of with Momma?"

"Tomorrow night, okay? Tonight I'm not gonna sleep. I'm gonna watch the stars all night."

Jeyd and Toby come running up to her from the direction of the little ridge.

"Gramma, come see. We found some bones and a skull. It's over there. Marty said it was the bones of a bear or something. It has big claws. Come look."

Penny walks with the boys to the little hump overlooking the steep side of the mountain. Dustin and Marty are standing looking at the skull. The bones are white. The backbone lying straight, the arms and leg bones are stretched out on both sides. The skull is lying facing the direction of the blue mountains in the east.

The place where the sun will come up in the morning.

The bones of the bear is stretched out in the exact spot an old pine tree.

This is the spot where Tupa sat, right under this tree. What'll I do. I can't move them. I'm gonna have to sit with these bones all night. What did I get myself into? What does it mean?

"It looks like it went to sleep here and died. It must have been an old bear."

Marty pokes it slightly with a stick.

"Don't. Let it be. It was probably wounded and died here. Bears usually die in their dens when they get old. Poor thing. It must have been trying to get down the hill back to its den. I wonder if it had cubs. I hope not. It looks like it's been here for a year or so. Just leave it. It'll keep me company tonight. I'm gonna sit here with my blanket all night ëtill morning."

Dustin looks at his mother with a startled look.

"Mom, is it safe? Maybe there'll be other bears around. You won't be that close to the fire."

"Oh, if there are other bears around they'll be gone. We made so much noise they'll be still running down the hill. Anyway they're not hungry this time of year. They have plenty of berries way up there in the patch on the next ridge. They won't bother me. Anyway I'll tell Old Tupa Bear there to look after me."

Penny stands there looking at the skull staring straight ahead, its black shadow holes for eyes pointed toward the east. Its white claws buried in the earth. The boys wait for her but she continues looking and they finally leave and walk back to the camp. She stands there for a long time until Raella calls out for her come and eat.

The meal of corn bread, wind dried salmon and cooked squash is brought out on the tarp spread before the fire. Hot mountain tea in tin cups are served to everyone. Jeyd and Toby hop up and down every little while to throw pieces of bread crumbs to the squirrel sitting on a rock chattering at them. The bluejays hop as close as they can before flying up into the branch above. All around them the pines are whispering in the slight breeze. Shadows are gathering under them as the camp things are put away for night, and the men decide who will stay up first for the night watch.

As Penny settles down next to the bears head, she wraps the blanket around her. Already the sky to east is black. She watches the last light leave the sky and the first bright star begin to sparkle. The bear's skull is inches away from her side.

Tupa Bear. I came here to sit tonight to think and I find you here. Lying in the place my own Tupa sat to tell me about the taking the sun of each new day and wrapping it around because the shadows of the night follow our footsteps even in the bright of the sun. I come here with shadows following close behind. When Tupa left, the shadows moved inside. It was Tupa who made the world right. She left a hole inside of me that I could find no way to fill. I let the shadows in. They whispered to me about all the things which shadows bring and I listened. I spent my time searching for light in the colours of the rainbow and tried to pull it toward me when they spoke to me. Too many shadows walk the earth and they took me away. Away from the light of each day's rising. I come here tonight to wait for the sun in the morning. I will wrap it around me and carry it home to warm me in the days to come. Tupa Bear, you must know, lying here instead of in your den, to greet death with old age. You must know how things have changed in the world. I grieve for you as I grieve for all the ones who die before their time. So many now. From the things which are not right. I have tried in my way to come to the light. Help me to lift this shadow from inside me. Fill my spirit with the wisdom I need to be at peace with each new day.

Penny's face is turned up at the stars bristling silver spines down-ward from the deepest of navy. She sways almost falling backward. The wind is picking up.

I feel the ponderous burden of the darkening sky as I begin this first song.

Her eyes are drawn to one glaring star. Down in the valley the frog voices rise to a frenzy and above her she can hear the pines whip-ping and brushing at the air in pointed green movement, whisper-ing rapidly the same invocation.

This night will be long, filled with morose shadows gathering around.

Finally, weak and tired after singing all the songs she knows, she sinks down to rest for a few moments before sitting up to sing again. Her eyes are heavy and can't keep them open. She dreams.

The bear is moving. It stands up on its fours. It turns to face her. Snuffling at her. Then it slowly lifts its great paws and stands on its hind legs. Slowly it begins to sway, dancing. At first it is dark, like the night, then it begins to turn a silvery colour like the stars. The stars spines are shooting down into the bear and the bear is glowing like starlight. Its eyes are stars. The bear has long silvery hair swaying in the wind and she looks like Tupa now. It dances, making motions with its hands, to come. She stands too and feels as light as air. She can hear the man from Mexico talking. The bear is now the Aztec man from Mexico, and he is talking to her. "We came from the stars." He said. "The gateway is just ahead. Already many people come from all directions to it. See this candle in the middle. It shines a light touching everyone who comes to its fire. Shining Woman of Copper, your light is the silvery tears even now catching the starlight. Your love of life. All your friends and your children gather close to its light. When the wind takes the candle's light, its fire is only moved to another. The Great Bear walks across the sky at night. In dreams and shadows. Without the night, no stars would sing their songs. You can dance in the star's light, too." Suddenly she sees the world from high up in the sky. The sky is dark with clouds and she feels like she is a cloud too, but she can see the world below. It is dark and shadowy but she can see tiny pinpoints of light scattered across the land. At first she thinks they are cities, but she moves close and sees they are circles of people sitting around campfires. Indians and non-Indians. People from all over the earth. Laughing and talking, as coyotes shrill their songs around them. "Oh Coyote," she says "you can't reach the stars. Don't you know, by now, that they'll cut the strings?" Coyote sits down and laughs looking up at her. He points his nose up toward her and howls. "Shining Woman of Copper. You know it's in the story. Every story. It's just the same old monsters again. I'll take care of them bastards, though. Piss on them. It's gotta be. Just keep on shining 'till the sun sets. You're free to ride the clouds. I am the greatest chief down around here and I give you that."

Penny wakes up with a start. A coyote is shrilling a song close by. She shivers thinking of her dream and laughs out loud. It is cold and dark but she feels rested and deep inside there is a feeling bubbling upward.

The night will reach its darkest soon and it will be long. But it is always darkest just before first dawn's light. And then the bright shafts of light will break over the crisp blue edges of the mountains towering to the east, and the world will be new.

PROSE POEM FROM HER DIARY

White Night in Chickaloon

The surface of the lake lies still between the hidden sisters and the sun baked stones caressing my feet in this path I follow at white night and this is the time in our history of the Americas as we walk from all directions to encircle this sacred fire creating the network of grandmother spider and we know that this fire burning at the centre around which we hold hands is the reason we come as the grandchildren of all these lands and we are bound together by old blood mixed and remixed over time as we feel its memory stir in the flickering embers surrounded by flowers and we shall move this fire from land to land and all the flowers from the South and the North will surround it moving to retrace the paths our sisters and brothers walk as words pass between the North and the South between the eagle and the condor on this old movement through eons to warm lands which our blood together

claims that which our cell memories celebrate each time we dance
to this rhythm we all know so well and the gateway to the new
world is ahead as our relatives walk on leading a path started years
ago when they remember shimmering light reflections on glassy
surfaces existing as place in the past and even now our blood mixes
and blurs the hard lines and all lands become ours the ancestors
joined by blood related through our mixing as our spirit relatives
are joined and now all our footprints move toward the sun rising
as we rise to hold hands a flower encircled fire burning bright
golden at our centre

As the day passes, the sky moves closer and heavier. It brings an obscure though ominous feeling that something is about to happen. As though, electricity, unseen, is accumulating until it can crackle and flash. As visible as the colours she saw once in awhile attached to some people. Colours she saw a few times on some animals. They always came as quick slivers of sparkle, visible only for an instant before flickering out, leaving a momentary faint haze. She was always left wondering whether she had really seen them or not.

Today she can see a similar incandescence briefly flicker through the air when she moves. There is a vague presence. A tangible something which seems to hum with a quiet insistent voice at the edge of her consciousness.

No matter how she strains to hear, it escapes.

She opens her eyes as someone enters the room. Her eyes follow the white clad figure. For a moment wondering. Then, the weight crashes against her chest again. The weight of the sky. Heavy with cloud, with darkness, with thunder. With smoke, dust and fumes. Heavy, heavy with vaporized chemicals, carbons, poisons. Particles pressing down into her pores, pressing into her breathing.

She waits, her eyes closed, letting the weight of the sky wrap around her. She inhales its breath and lets her muscles soften, feeling the tingling as her skin becomes aware of its damp greyness. She can hear her pulse pumping, slowing to match the rhythm of her deep breathing. She feels tiny, pores open, meshing with sky at the top of a mountain.

The sky.

The word. The presence felt. Enveloping her. The sky that is there in her mind. The sky seen from within. Her sky, like all skies, there

only in how the mind agrees to see it. Conjured by how words capture it. How others before her saw it. Now hers.

Sky and breath.

One and the same in her language. Once said as word, she feels the
sky images form.

Dressing. Putting its dress on.

She sees it that way. A billowing garment covering the female
form, moving with the body. In seeing sky, seeing also the warm
earth-female it covered. Finding herself in that. Finding peace.
Knowing its meaning as her own breath, her own body. She feels
light now. Able to dissipate. To move into that vaster rhythm.
The song of wings brushing wind.

She listens now and feels the sound thrumming through her. The
sky is changing. A silver brightness is spreading across the sky.
The Great Bear is walking across the night filled with stars.

LETTER NEVER SENT

Gard:

I *'ve been wanting to write to you. The last time I
saw you, we had such a good visit. I'm glad that
things are going well for you. It's good to have a
friend like you have been. I wanted to tell you how much I have appreci-
ated your words. Your mind. Your integrity. It's good to know that you
have decided to make a big leap into the abyss, after all, with such a good
person. I've had a good life with David. I don't regret, but I sometimes
dream of dancing with you. The music is always the blues.*

*Anyway I was really writing to let you know that I'm back in the hos-
pital again. I've had a great three years. Things are so good with my family.*

*I wanted to tell you something I think you alone can understand. I
should have painted what I saw. I should have let the images come out
which shouted at me. I could've gotten it to a better place. I knew that
putting images out there changes the world, yet I feared the shadows. I
know now that one should not fear them. The story must be told to be
understood and changed. One should leap into the void and let the wind*

carry you. And then things new come. I never knew how to cross that line. I should have shown you that saints and sinners are alike, too, in everything under the sun. It's all in the story and how it unfolds.

Anyway, I decided against a new gene therapy treatment that was being tested. I guess it's sort of a last ditch kinda thing. But I can't do that. Not when the source might be dead fetus marrow or brain stem cells or some such thing. I will just continue to live in the moment like I should have been all along. The sun comes up every morning and each day is new. I think of you on this warm day as the sun is rising. I think of all the poets and artists who stand and record the story. I honour you and all of us. I'm going to rest awhile, now. Thank you for being my friend.

Penny Jackson.

Copper is what the mountain was named. It was a woman. She was radiant when she took on the colour of the sun and she was pursued for her beauty but she had more to offer. She had a vast love for humans. The ones who dreamed. People climbed to quest at her peaks. Some traded pieces rubbed smooth carefully wrapped in buckskin. In other places, copper was a sign of prosperity for the family and copper crests were displayed to show how much one can give to community and to strangers of other tribes. Copper is what Tupa always left buried beneath the ground when she wanted medicine.

"Penny! Come on. We're waiting for you!"

Momma called, her voice coming from far away.

Penny sat in the willows by the creek watching tiny spotted fishes darting around, shimmering flecks of gold as they turned. The water gurgled and chuckled over the rocks. A fat blue dragonfly, wings clacking, circled slowly over her and over the fishes and the little blades of grass sticking out of the waters edge.

"Wait, I want to stay just a little longer."

But Momma never heard her. The wind took her voice away.

earth love

I said that I would
give my flesh back
but instead my flesh
will offer me up
and feed the earth
and she will
love me